The Cost of Courage

Clare vowed that never would she bow to the dictates of a guardian who treated her like a childish puppet rather than the spirited young woman she truly was.

Before she did that, she would rather risk a loveless alliance with the impeccably titled and impossibly dreary Sir Alexander Ferguson.

She would rather risk society's censure and her own virtue in the company of the notorious libertine, Harry Rowse.

She would rather risk the diabolical intrigues of her guardian's ravishing fiancée, Marianna Morton, a ruthless hussy if ever there was one.

Clare was determined to take her stand against this insufferable male power and male pride—even if she had to take it standing on the brink of disaster. . . .

The Wicked Guardian

Big Bestsellers from SIGNET

The Wicked Guardian

by Vanessa Gray

A SIGNET BOOK

NEW AMERICAN LIBRARY

TIMES MIRROR

NAL BOOKS ARE ALSO AVAILABLE AT DISCOUNTS IN BULK
QUANTITY FOR INDUSTRIAL OR SALES-PROMOTIONAL USE.
FOR DETAILS, WRITE TO PREMIUM MARKETING DIVISION,
NEW AMERICAN LIBRARY, INC., 1301 AVENUE OF THE
AMERICAS, NEW YORK, NEW YORK 10019.

COPYRIGHT © 1978 BY VANESSA GRAY

SIGNET TRADEMARK REG. U.S. PAT. OFF. AND FOREIGN COUNTRIES
REGISTERED TRADEMARK—MARCA REGISTRADA
HECHO EN CHICAGO, U.S.A.

SIGNET, SIGNET CLASSICS, MENTOR, PLUME AND MERIDIAN BOOKS
are published by The New American Library, Inc.,
1301 Avenue of the Americas, New York, New York 10019

FIRST SIGNET PRINTING, DECEMBER, 1978

1 2 3 4 5 6 7 8 9

PRINTED IN THE UNITED STATES OF AMERICA

1.

An old-fashioned traveling coach, well-kept but evoking memories of an earlier day, trundled majestically along the King's Highway approaching London.

An expert might puzzle his brains to recognize the armorial bearings on the coach panel. Ostrich feathers quartered improbably with a rare leopard rampant and three wyverns—the Penryck arms had not been seen in London for ten years or more.

The arms on the door of the coach belonged to an old and onetime wealthy Dorset family of high courage and resolution coupled with an unfounded but invincible belief in the favor of the goddess of gaming. At this time, in 1811, the Penryck family was left with its ancient seat, a somewhat Gothic abbey near Blandford, surrounded by fields productive enough to assure a comfortable life for tenants and the family itself, but without means to indulge in the excessively expensive world of fashion.

It was clear that the coach had gone a long way. Coachman all but slumped on his box, and there was even a light coating of dust on the maroon coachwork. But it would take more than these visible signs of slackening of discipline to be sure that the occupants were right rustics.

There were two occupants of the coach, maid and mistress. The mistress, sitting bolt upright and wearing an air of tiptoe expectancy, disdained the support of the maroon squabs, pounded free of accumulated dust no more than three days ago. She was a very comely girl of perhaps fifteen years. Her curls, gold as florins, hung prettily alongside a charming face with an assortment of features that, while not of classic beauty, yet exerted a beguiling charm, which, unaware, she bestowed on any living being within range. Her traveling dress was of sober hue, and cut not quite in the crack of fashion, but of excellent material, and new. An onlooker might be puzzled to note that the young miss was dressed unexceptionably as a lady no longer in the first flush of youth, and then to regard the dimples, the frank, open countenance of a girl who ought still to be in the schoolroom.

1

This puzzling young lady was the Honorable Clare Penryck, sole descendant of the Penryck family. Sadly orphaned ten years before, when her father and mother had trusted, mistakenly, in her father's ability to hold his spirited pair around a sharp corner, Clare was brought after their deaths to live with the Dowager Countess of Penryck, in Penryck Abbey.

The Tresillians of Devon, the wayward family to which Clare's mother had belonged, could not be trusted, so the dowager said, to rear a Penryck, and communications between the two families lapsed.

As a matter of fact, Lady Penryck, an austere person who had lived through the tragic death of her only son and his wife, and the less tragic loss of her bibulous husband, and had constructed a shell of some hardness around her in order to survive, dared not let her heart be hostage to any family ties in the future.

The Penrycks, of course, presented no problem, since there were so few of them that they had to some extent been absorbed into other families, and only cousins at least twice removed remained.

But Lady Penryck's own surviving family consisted solely of a vastly ancient man, her half-brother, Lord Horsham of Wiltshire, and that was all. He was of feeble health, and while he was expected to become Clare's guardian in due course, supposing Lady Penryck to die before he did, yet the last letter he had written to her caused his sister slight misgivings.

But Horsham had been hale when Clare first came to live at Penryck Abbey, when she was five. Lady Penryck, although an invalid, had fulfilled her obligations, provided Clare with an unexceptionable governess from Bath, whose name, Peek, seemed appropriate for such a mild, almost furtive person. She had guided Clare's first steps through the maze of Penryck Abbey and the loneliness of a suddenly orphaned child, and even had done a creditable job of educating the child, with the help of Miss Mangnall's *Historical and Miscellaneous Questions for the Use of Young People*, which had fortunately been published just long enough to be current in Dorset.

Miss Peek had found her charge quick to learn, with an intelligence above average, and she was hard put to keep the girl busy. But as Lady Penryck declined in health, Clare was forced more and more to take over the management of the household, Miss Peek declining in a flustered flurry of half-sentences.

So it was that when Miss Peek left Penryck Abbey to remove to Bath, to share lodgings with her sister in Milsom Street above a milliner's shop, Clare was an odd mixture of lonely child and precocious adult. Miss Peek left with mixed feelings, which she often shared with her sister, Sara, over a cup of tea, looking down into the street from their cozy living room over the shop.

"Mark my words," she said, not for the first time, "that young miss is going to make her mark in the world. I wonder how she will do, for you must know that her grandmother is failing." Miss Peek shook her head mournfully. "Yes, failing every day."

"She sounds like a spoiled child to me," said Sara with reproof. She was, if truth were told, a bit jealous of her sister's absorbing interest in the Honorable Clare Penryck. She was completely bored with the iteration of the young lady's virtues, and even the glossed-over faults, of which there were astonishingly few.

"She sounds like a rash young lady," commented Sara. "Does she never think first before she does something?"

"Oh, yes. She is a thoughtful child, much too thoughtful for her years," said Miss Peek approvingly. "I've known her to spend hours in the long gallery, looking at the portraits of the family, you know. I often wonder what she thought about them."

"Why didn't you ask her?" asked Sara dryly.

"I did. And she said something nonsensical about 'imagine having to live up to the appearance of those fierce eyebrows'! Such a child!"

Sara fell into a reminiscent mood. "When I used to see Lord Penryck—the grandfather, that is—here to take the waters for his gout, he had just such eyebrows. And a wicked disposition to match, I recall! That was the only thing I recall—and I was glad to see the end of him. Such a man! You remember him, don't you?"

Miss Peek shut her eyes in shuddering recollection. "Yes," she said flatly. "And I thank my stars that young Clare never had a chance to fall afoul of her grandfather. For she must have suffered, don't you know!"

Dismissing the Penryck eyebrows and the Penryck disposition into limbo, Sara moved on to the far more important subject of what they would have for their tea, and Clare was forgotten.

Clare herself was not thinking about Miss Peek, to tell the truth, nor even about her grandmother, of whom she had been dutifully fond, but no more. It would have been strange had she been more than affectionate to a woman who appeared to need no one to love, and seemed only to have the desire to be left alone.

Clare had no way of knowing that the pain that walked constantly with Lady Penryck—both the discomfort of her illness and the gnawing pain of her son's loss—made the dowager keep even her grandchild at a distance, and soon Clare was thrown back on her own resources, which she found, over the years, more than adequate.

Clare and her maid had spent the previous night at the Anchor in Ripley, on the Exeter Road, a rather large establishment that had at first made a quelling impression on her, until her quality had been established by the impressive, if old-fashioned traveling coach, with coachman, footman, and two armed outriders.

Now, as she leaned from the window, she could discern the smoke of the capital in the far distance, a mere smudge on the horizon. "Budge, just think! In a few hours I shall be in London! That is, *we* shall, for I cannot conceive of going anywhere without you, dear Budge."

"Like enough we'll be slaughtered together in the streets, miss," said Budge, a mahogany-faced Dorset girl, daughter of a Penryck tenant, pressed into service as a personal maid when young Clare Penryck first came to the abbey.

"Oh, Budge, you gloomy thing! My godmother, Lady Thane, will keep us safe. As though we'd be in any danger!"

Budge, whose natural gloom had been accentuated over the years by her mistress's bright and often misplaced optimism, forbore to prophesy further. The journey had been a trial to one of her ample proportions, and she had thought the beds at one inn had not been sufficiently aired.

And she positively knew she was not going to like London!

"I have been trying to imagine just how Lady Thane will look," Clare continued. "It will seem strange to have an *almost*-relative to talk to, after all this time. Grandmama's relatives are all gone, except for her brother, who will someday be my guardian. So Grandmama always said. She said there wasn't anybody on the Penryck side who could serve. Just a boy, a third cousin. I've never seen him."

"A boy?" echoed Budge. "I don't mind any boy. Never saw one."

Rightly paying no heed to her maid, Clare prattled on. She would not have admitted that the nearer London came, the more sinking she felt. How would she go on? She was, after all, much too young to come out into society. But Grandmama counseled a determined avoidance of birthdays, and had told her as forcefully as she could: "You must marry if you can. Now, child, I don't mean that you should take the first offer that comes your way. Lady Thane will see to that. But don't shy off for some missish reason."

"But what, dear Grandmama, if no one offers?"

Old Lady Penryck surveyed her granddaughter with a pride she had never allowed to show. The girl fortunately had escaped the fierce Penryck eyebrows—taking more after the Tresillians—and her tip-tilted nose and her engaging ways would be winsome indeed, if . . . Always that if. Lady Penryck wished fiercely she could give her granddaughter another two years of tutelage. But certain unmistakable signs had told her that those two years would not be allotted to her.

She was careful to make no complaint of her ailment to Clare. Instead, she simply said, "I should like to see you settled in life, my dear. And every young lady is entitled, they say, to one London season."

"But won't it be difficult for you to travel so far, Grandmama? You say that Bath is too far, but I should think the waters would help you greatly. Even the doctor says so."

Lady Penryck dismissed the doctor's opinion with a wave of her hand. She had no trust in doctors, based on her experience with them. They had not even helped her late, unlamented husband's gout. "I am not going. I am sending you to your godmother, Lady Thane. She has a house in London, and I have written to her to ask her to take you in."

Clare's heart quailed. She had mixed feelings, suddenly, longing to cling to the known security of Penryck Abbey, where, to all intents, she reigned over the household. But

London was a magnet of great potency, and the sudden glimpse of a wider horizon could not fail to stimulate her vivid imagination.

"She was a great friend of my mother's, wasn't she?" ventured Clare. She had not had any word from her godmother except for a succession of dolls at Christmastime, and even that series had ceased in the last few years. To Clare's own recollection, she had never seen her. She told her grandmother so, but, adding fairly, "Of course I would not remember if I had been a child then, would I?"

Lady Penryck said abruptly, to cover her feelings, "You are hardly more than that now. And I should not send you so young. But—"

"Then please let me stay until you think it is time," begged Clare, the part of her that was reluctant to leave uppermost.

Lady Penryck steeled herself. "I think it is time now. I have decided, and I shall not wish to hear any more about it. I have put aside sufficient money for this excursion. Lady Melvin is to see that you are properly dressed, and although I regret the necessity for depending upon a lady whose taste I do not quite like, yet I must believe that she is more aware of the fashions than I."

Lady Penryck leaned back on her pillows and closed her eyes for a moment. The interview was taking too long, and her strength was ebbing. "Now, run along. Lady Melvin expects you this afternoon, and she will know how to go on."

Clare tiptoed to the door, and turned. "Thank you, ma'am," she said softly. Lady Penryck was already asleep.

That had been a month ago. And Clare had been caught up in the swirl of dressmaking, and the constant advice and warnings of Lady Melvin, until by the time she had left Penryck Abbey two days ago she was in such a state of excitement that she could have flown to London by herself.

But then, she thought with mischievous amusement, how could she have managed to convey her dear Budge, weighing probably eleven stone, along with the trunks that were strapped to the back of the coach?

Now the outskirts of London came into view. Clare fell silent as she stared from the window of the coach. Heedless of anything except the great size of the prospect, the narrow roads where carts jostled coaches, riders pressed against pedestrians who, more often than not, retorted with flying cabbages and hurled insults.

And while, like Dick Whittington, she should have seen opportunity spread out before her, she must take her lower lip between her teeth to keep from giving vent to the strong desire to be back at home at Penryck Abbey that very instant.

The feeling did not leave her until the coach, following directions obtained along the way, turned with a rumbling clatter into Grosvenor Square.

2.

At the time that Clare was about to learn from her grandmother's lips of her great good fortune, a certain house looking out on Grosvenor Square was beginning to face a new day, a day that was destined to rock the household to its foundations.

Lady Thane's house in Grosvenor Square caught the midmorning light. The house was astir with its usual activities, more particularly in the kitchens, where Mrs. Darrin waited serenely for the bell to ring and the indicator for Lady Thane's bedroom to drop, signifying that Lady Thane had roused from sleep and was, if not ready, at least willing to face the day.

"Not like the old days, is it?" grumbled Darrin, the butler, to his wife. "Not like when there was entertaining, twenty to dinner more often than not, and such a stir of carriages in the square outside as would make a cat smile."

"And sorry enough you were at the time, Darrin," retorted his wife smartly. "Too much to do, you always said. Although you had footmen enough, and maids, too, to do it all."

The discussion was not a new one, and uncovered no new ground, and at length died of its own inertia. Hobbs, an angular, tart-faced woman who had tended Lady Thane since her marriage more than twenty years before, and therefore held a position of unquestioned superiority over the Darrins, hurried in, her handful of letters attesting that the post had just come.

"And not much in it, either," said Hobbs. "A letter from Miss Harriet, I should say Lady Cromford, and we can guess that something has gone awry down at the Hall. But . . ." She stopped short to frown down at a letter that puzzled her. "I can't make this out," she muttered, and then, the bell ringing sharply, the letter was dropped on the morning tray, Mrs. Darrin made tea from the kettle already on the boil, and with practiced efficiency the breakfast tray for Lady Thane was borne up the service stairs to the floor above.

8

Lady Thane was an indulgent mistress, relying more on the affection her servants had for her than to her management, and she was well-served. In fact, as Lady Thane's daughter, Harriet, sometimes told her, "They have little else to do than to wait on you hand and foot."

Lady Thane replied, "I do think we get along comfortably together. I am sure I want for nothing."

Just now, on this April morning, she was propped up in her bed upon freshly fluffed pillows, the breakfast tray upon her lap, and Hobbs moving quietly around the room. The draperies were opened, and the sunshine poured in.

The stack of envelopes on the breakfast tray did not receive Lady Thane's attention until after her second cup of tea. Truly, she thought, it takes longer and longer to wake up in the morning. The tea is too weak—she must speak to Mrs. Darrin about it.

Languidly turning over the envelopes, she indulged herself in her usual habit, trying to divine the contents from the outer appearance.

"This is surely a card to the duchess's ball at Syon House. But Syon House is so removed, Hobbs, it quite oversets me to think of traveling that far. Especially at night." She sighed. "I fear I must turn it down. And yet, if one continually turns down these invitations, one soon finds oneself out of the swim altogether. I don't know what to do."

Hobbs gave her no encouragement, correctly surmising that her mistress was communing entirely with herself. Hobbs placed the screen before the fire that struggled in the grate. Green wood—Hobbs scowled—and she would have a thing or two to say belowstairs about that!

An exclamation behind her made her turn inquiringly to Lady Thane. She was peering in a decidedly puzzled manner at the same heavy square envelope that had aroused Hobbs's curiosity. The butterfly patch she wore to discourage lines between her eyebrows bent with her effort to decipher the writing on the envelope.

"Hobbs, what do you think of this?"

Hobbs chose discretion. "I really could not say, my lady."

"No, of course not. But I wonder . . . I haven't seen this handwriting for years. More years than I intend to remember," said Lady Thane with spirit. She went on to remember the years.

"This certainly takes me back," she said presently. "This is from old Lady Penryck. The dowager, you know."

"Yes, my lady."

"Elizabeth Tresillian's mother-in-law. You must know, Hobbs, that Elizabeth and I grew up near neighbors and closest of friends in Devon. I was a Launceville, you know, and although there was a connection between our families, it was such a long time ago that it was of no account. But growing up together made the difference."

She leaned back against her lace-covered pillows, her breakfast forgotten. "We came out together, presented at the same ball in London, you know. Elizabeth was the prettiest belle of the season. She had at least five offers in the first six weeks!"

Lost in her reveries, she was once again a girl, dancing at four different parties every night, after a round of afternoon outings, and riding in the park in the morning. Elizabeth had married Robert Penryck and gone to live in Dorset. And Helen Launceville, not quite so pretty but much more fortunate, married a pleasant, kind man of substantial wealth—not exciting, but, thought Lady Thane, much more durable, after all.

"Elizabeth and Robert were killed in an accident on the road to Exeter. Horses ran away and the carriage overturned." Lady Thane shook her head. "Robert Penryck always thought he was a notable whip, you know, but in fact he was lamentably slow-witted. But one thing he did have—the Penryck *resolution.*

"I daresay it led to his demise—a frosty night, so they said, and the road not at all trustworthy. But they both died in the accident. I was godmother to their daughter, you know. But my own affairs were troublesome, and I let things go. When the girl was first sent to old Lady Penryck, I heard from time to time how she was getting on. But since then . . ."

She frowned once again at the letter. Had she been a woman of some sensitivity, one might have thought she was seized by a feeling of impending trouble, even disaster. But she was not, and Hobbs thought she was simply prolonging the delicious feeling of anticipation.

"What do you think, Hobbs?"

"I think, begging your pardon, my lady, that the letter might tell you what is going forward. *If* you opened it."

"How commonsensical you are, Hobbs." She broke the wafer and began to read.

"What dreadful handwriting!" she exclaimed. But the letter explained the handwriting, too.

"My dear Helen," it began. "A long time has elapsed since I have had the pleasure of hearing from you, although I have kept myself informed of your circumstances as well as I have been able, living in the confines of Penryck Abbey, itself isolated to a degree from the world of society. I have heard of Thane's death, for which I offer condolence, and, two years ago, of your daughter Harriet's marriage. You have done well for your daughter, marrying her to such an unexceptional gentleman as Braintree Cromford. I confess it is partly your daughter's felicity that prompts me to turn to you in what must be a dilemma that I cannot resolve alone."

Lady Thane turned over the letter. There was much more—and already she felt a foreboding of more than trouble. With a sigh she turned back, found her place again in the crabbed hand, and set herself resolutely to make her way through the labyrinth.

"My dear granddaughter, Clare, is my deepest concern. I myself have been far from well for these ten years, and now I find that I cannot do even the smallest things that I once was able to manage with ease. I do not these days leave my bed."

Poor thing! thought Lady Thane. Even though she herself lay comfortably in bed just now, she could leave it at will. And even such a complacent woman as herself could see that pain racked the invalid whose handwriting was so bad.

"I have made my will, and named a guardian for Clare. The will is in the hands of my man of affairs, Herbert Austin. But there is not much longer for me. And I do wish to see my dear granddaughter settled in life as soon as possible. I want her to have a season in London, and a chance to make a satisfactory marriage, before she must go into mourning, which I am sorry to say will be inevitable, and quite soon. Although, for myself, I shall welcome whatever release is to come from my discomfort, I shall rest more easily knowing that my dear Clare has enjoyed herself a little."

Lady Thane was a compassionate woman, even if her

intellect was not powerful, and the words of the letter swam before her eyes.

Lady Thane dropped the letter on the counterpane. "Hobbs," she directed, "I wish to get up at once."

Hobbs stared at her, alarmed at Lady Thane's abrupt departure from custom. "It lacks a quarter-hour of ten o'clock, my lady," Hobbs pointed out.

"I do not wish, after all, Hobbs, to spend my entire *life* in bed. I think I shall wear the light blue tunic with the gold trim, Hobbs. It always makes me feel more cheerful."

She read, presently, the rest of the letter. The child Clare was old for her age—sixteen in June—for she had been in her grandmother's company for some years, and had taken over much of the running of the establishment. She was much like her mother, Elizabeth. Thank goodness for that! thought Lady Thane. Elizabeth had been a beauty, and of a sweetness of disposition that was remarkable.

She could have taken after her father, mused Lady Thane. A man of mild enough character, but possessed of an unexpected stubbornness when it came to gambling away his fortune. The well-known Penryck resolution, while all very well on the battlefields of Europe, was sadly inappropriate at the gaming tables of the Dandy Club, combined as it was with a strong, if unmerited optimism.

If Lady Penryck wanted Clare's godmother to launch her into society, the apprehension of a decided change in her way of living was daunting to Lady Thane. But no one had ever said that Helen Launceville did not do her duty, and no one ever should.

Referring once again to the letter, she deciphered the last paragraph. "I shall pray that you will take this charge upon yourself, and will be ever grateful. Clare would travel with her maid, two grooms, a footman, and the coachman, and I trust that you will allow Budge to remain with Clare. I would not have you put to the trouble . . ." There was more, but a cursory glance indicated that the rest of the letter was taken up with civilities, and not to the point.

Hobbs dropped the light blue sarcenet over her mistress's head. From the folds Lady Thane's voice came muffled. "I must write at once. Poor child. It will be pleasant to have a young girl around the house again. I must answer all those invitations that came this morning, begging the courtesy of bringing my goddaughter. And the bedrooms, Hobbs"—her voice was clear again as the maid straightened the folds of the skirt—"I think the Blue Room will be the best. There is a smaller room next for the maid. What's her name? Budge? And there will be all manner of arrangements needed—I vow I don't know what to do first."

"Perhaps Mr. Darrin would know?" said Hobbs with a straight face.

"I should say not! I believe I know what is best in my own house. I shall tell Darrin what I wish done."

The conference with Darrin settled Lady Thane's mind, and she could rest assured that her goddaughter's comfort would be uppermost in the minds of her household. Lady Thane could then turn her thought to confiding in a few of her very *closest* friends, perhaps an even dozen of them, that her goddaughter—Elizabeth Tresillian's daughter, you know—was on her way to London. Armed with promises of cards to balls, invitations to routs, and a general certitude that she had done what she could and all must wait now upon the arrival of the girl, Lady Thane declared to herself with unquenchable optimism that the girl must of necessity be biddable, very pretty, and sweet-natured. Lady Thane looked forward to an excessively successful season.

Casting her cares comfortably away, Lady Thane ordered her barouche and ordered her coachman, John Potter, to drive to the park. As usual, the pleasant motion of the carriage, the balmy May air upon her powdered cheeks, soothed her mind as she greeted her many acquaintances. Her matchmaking thoughts, stimulated by the faces she saw, came to the fore.

Ned Fenton, for example, bowing to her now. A splendid figure on horseback, and wealthy enough to overlook the lack of a dowry in a bride, if he could be attracted.

His great friend, Benedict Choate, riding there on a magnificent black—now, *there* had been the greatest catch in London, until last fall, when his engagement to Miss Marianna Morton had been announced in the *Gazette*. Fabulously wealthy, yet he was noted for a sardonic turn of mind and a daunting curl of lip, and Lady Thane, eminently practical, told herself that he would no doubt quell, with one word, a chit of a girl up from the country. No matter! She decided she would take good care to keep Clare away from Lord Benedict Choate!

Then there was Sir Alexander Ferguson, and Mr. Marriott—wealthy, but there was a whisper that his grandfather had been in trade.

She really must get to thinking about various schemes. All in all, she must wait, she decided, until the girl got here. And then, for the first time, foreboding struck her. If the girl was not yet sixteen, then . . .

Ominous whisperings came to her mind, a reflection of her long experience in the world of society. A girl, who had no polish at all, probably reared by an old-fashioned governess, living in her grandmother's sphere with none of the amenities of modern-day living—what dreadful things might the girl do, or say? The possibilities went beyond description.

But in spite of herself, she grew conscious of a stirring of excitement as the time for Clare's arrival drew near.

It would be fun to take a young girl again to all the *ton* parties, to Almack's—where she hoped the girl wouldn't disgrace her. She could get vouchers. Lady Thane was adroit in her planning. There were several ladies who owed her favors, and she herself might give a ball. . . .

And this time, Lady Thane thought with a flash of realism, it would be more fun than dragging that serious Harriet around, a sour-faced girl like her paternal grandmother. Lady Thane had blessed the fate that had kept her from meeting her husband's mother often—but Harriet was as like her as two peas.

She must get home quickly, and accept the invitations that had come in, and get word to other prospective hostesses that her goddaughter was coming into town. . . .

Lady Thane's optimism bubbled once more to the surface as, with a lilt in her voice, she directed Potter to turn the horses and return to Grosvenor Square to await Clare's arrival.

The carriage drawn up in front of the house facing the square looked horrifyingly familiar to Lady Thane. It could not be Clare's carriage. But even though she allowed herself to hope for a moment that she was mistaken and that the carriage stood before another door, she knew with a sinking feeling that her first impression was right.

The coach had just arrived, clearly, for Darrin sailed

down the steps of Lady Thane's house, dispatching footmen in all directions, and Lady Thane's daughter, Harriet Cromford, descended to the pavement.

"Now, what on earth is she doing here?" said Lady Thane under her breath. "She'll spoil everything!"

But when Lady Thane in her turn descended from her carriage, and both vehicles were rattling away to find shelter in the mews at the back, she greeted her daughter as blandly as ever. "Do you come alone?" she asked dutifully. "How is Cromford? And the darling baby? You surely did not leave him alone in Buckinghamshire?"

"Yes," said Harriet grimly. "I left him alone, for I had heard rumors that made me, I do not hesitate to tell you, very uneasy."

"Rumors?" said Lady Thane, dismissing Darrin with a request for a dish of strong tea. "What rumors?"

"Do not pretend not to know what I am talking about, dear Mama. It's all over town. That you are taking on some total stranger to foist her upon society."

"Stranger? My own goddaughter? That is not the case at all!" protested Lady Thane. "Where did you get such a ridiculous notion? I am sure you cannot have had it from me."

"No," said Harriet grudgingly. "I heard nothing from you, so when Lady Cromford . . ."

Harriet stopped short. She had not intended to make her mother privy to the source of her information, for Lady Thane had little use for old Lady Cromford, considering her a great prattler with feathers for brains. She had pointed this out to Harriet many times before her marriage, mentioning, with deep feeling, that sometimes the grandchildren took after the grandparents—"and always just the qualities that one wishes they wouldn't, you know!"

Harriet (the picture of the departed Lady Thane, her grandmother) had characteristically overridden all objections in favor of twenty-five thousand a year and a title. Nor, to give her credit, had she ever complained about living in the wilds of Buckinghamshire, her mother-in-law in the dower house, built distressingly close to the main house. But Harriet had sufficient sense not to mention her mother-in-law unless it was necessary.

Or unless it slipped out, as it had just done.

Lady Thane's eyes kindled. "So you came to town at

that woman's behest to check up on me? I tell you, Harriet, I will not tolerate this!"

Harriet set herself to soothe her mother, with the same determination that had led her to hasten to London to protect her easygoing mother from the darkling designs of some rustic female who was so much a stranger to the family that Harriet had never heard her name.

At length, after two cups of very strong tea, Lady Thane's indignation dissipated; and once more she felt in charity with her only child.

"But you know she has led a sadly restricted life," said Lady Thane sometime later. "I wonder how she will go on. Although, as I remember Lady Penryck, she was a high stickler. But with her illness, I just don't know what to expect."

Harriet had been watching her mother closely, and now came to a conclusion. She was at heart extremely fond of her mother, and bethought herself of a way to ease her mother's tribulation.

"I shall send word at once," she said briskly, setting down her teacup and reaching for the last of the tiny cakes that Mrs. Darrin made so well. Answering her mother's uplifted eyebrow, she explained, "I shall tell Cromford that I wish to stay here with you, at least until the girl arrives."

"There's no need," said Lady Thane, knowing her protest was futile.

"You may be glad of my presence," said Harriet, conscious of a glow of pleasure at her own self-sacrifice. "She may be totally unsuited to company—if, as you say, Lady Penryck has been ill for years."

Lady Thane had no time to repent of her incautious letter to Harriet, nor to wonder which of the carefully selected hostesses in London to whom she had confided the news of her goddaughter's arrival had spread the news as far as Buckinghamshire so quickly.

Harriet said, "I shall write at once to Cromford." She left the room at once on her errand, so Lady Thane was alone when the Penryck coach drew up in the square.

Lady Thane's emotions had been badly cudgeled by her bout with Harriet, and now that the moment of Clare's arrival was here, Lady Thane found herself momentarily unable to move. Pressing her snowy handkerchief to her lips in a futile effort to stop them from trembling, she started to her feet and stared at the door.

Then, a lifetime of training impelled her forward, and she started across the Blue Saloon. She reached the foyer to see Darrin inviting in a slender girl not quite of average height, with gold ringlets and a modish traveling bonnet. Her traveling coat was dark and of severe cut. But the smile trembling on her lips, the apprehension in her dark blue eyes, had already won over Darrin, Lady Thane noticed, and was conscious of a warm spreading feeling in the region of her own sensibilities.

"Clare, my dear!" Lady Thane hurried across the foyer to clasp the girl in her arms, kissing her on both cheeks, and wiping a tear away from her own. "How very welcome you are!"

3.

London was as far removed from Penryck Abbey, Clare decided, as though she had unaccountably been flown to the moon. Penryck Abbey was an almost forgotten backwater in Dorset, the Penrycks long out of the swim, mostly, of course, because of the aging Lady Penryck's painful infirmities, but even before that, because of the failing fortunes of the family.

The most excitement that Clare remembered was when the squire and his wife, Sir Ewald and Lady Melvin, came to call, bringing their house guests from Northumberland, a maiden lady of mature years and her inarticulate brother.

But London! It seemed to Clare that she had never heard such noise. When her coach had rumbled into town, over the cobbles and into the square, she had been too excited to notice, but now, a week later, as she stood in the square portico at the top of the front steps of Lady Thane's house, she could hear in the far distance a hum as of innumerable hiving bees. Closer there were cries, rumble of carriages, sharp *clop* of horses' hooves—the immensely varied sounds of a busy city at work.

There was so much to do in London! Clare stood for a moment trying to realize that she was at last there. The hub of the universe—and although Clare's education had been impeccable, including the elements of natural sciences and the use of the globes, and she was aware that there were other worlds beyond London, yet she was realist enough to suspect that the city would engross her sufficiently without worrying about the rest of the world.

There was much that she wanted to see. She had on her mental list the Tower, with its lions and certain other animals in the menagerie that she darkly suspected existed only in hearsay. A Greenland bear, for example—all white, so it was said. A small ant bear, too, and a creature listed in the guide as a "White Fox from Owhyhee." Most intriguing!

There was the great river, that in her grandmother's time had furnished much transportation for ladies and

18

gentlemen, but was now populated mostly by freight barges.

There was the prince regent's residence, Carlton House, looking out over St. James's Square, only a short distance from where she stood this moment. And out of sight, but not out of mind, lay the park, the rendezvous of the fashionable world, and the most exciting, colorful spot in the world!

She must remember, she told herself, not to give way to her enthusiasm. It was not quite the thing, she had already learned, to let one's feelings show, at least very much. And Lady Thane's strong injunctions to her to watch her decorum, lest she betray her extreme youth, had made an indelible impression.

She sighed deeply. There was so much to learn in the fashionable world, and she dreaded putting her foot wrong. Lady Thane's advice had included the dire warning that one mistake could easily mean the end of her pretensions to a place in this world.

"But surely they are not so uncharitable?" protested Clare, unwilling to believe that such unkindness existed, particularly in the glittering world of England's aristocracy.

"Fashion, my dear. That is all it is. But if you experienced a breath of criticism, you would be sadly out of fashion, and there would be nothing more I could do for you."

But Clare's misgivings, while lurking just out of sight in her thoughts, nonetheless had to give way to the tremendous activity that began to fill her days. She was used to riding, and Lady Thane's stables provided an unexceptionable hack for her to mount. With Wells, the groom, discreetly behind her, she rode nearly every morning in Hyde Park. The morning was reserved, so it seemed, for those on horseback, while the late afternoon found carriages of all descriptions joining the outing.

Lady Thane, usually rising just before noon, managed to restore her vitality in time to ride out in her barouche, the top laid back, to allow the fashionable world to catch a glimpse of her pretty protégée. The tactics had worked when she was presenting Harriet, three years ago, and while Harriet's generous but meddling offer to stay and help chaperon Clare had been promptly and decisively vetoed by her indignant husband, Lady Thane was convinced she knew well enough how to go on without her daughter.

Lady Thane's efforts were rewarded with a decided increase in invitations, and Clare soon found that the wardrobe that had been made and packed with such care to accompany her to London was not nearly sufficient for the round of parties that was her lot.

So, taking her small hoard of money with her, she and Lady Thane repaired to the silk mercer's, the dressmaker's, and the milliner's, where she fell in love with a wide-brimmed bonnet of straw, the brim bordered with a ruching of pink satin ribbon, which extended to allow a big bow to be tied under her chin. On their way home, they passed by Covent Garden, where Lady Thane promised to take her to the theater one night.

Clare had not been in London above a week when she realized one of her childhood ambitions. At Penryck Abbey, the long gallery held portraits, of varying quality, of members of the family. They were by artists of uneven ability, but one feature all had painted clearly. The Penryck eyebrows.

Black and straight, like bars across the face of both lady and gentleman, giving the Penrycks as a family an air of stern foreboding. And Clare, from the time she had first glimpsed them, could not believe that such eyebrows existed.

"I shall believe them when I see them," she had told grandmama brightly.

There were few enough Penrycks left, so Grandmama had once told her. "Your poor papa was the last. Except for a distant cousin, and she died young."

This particular day, Lady Thane found she had exhausted her supply of reading material. Repairing to Mr. Lane's library in Leadenhall Street, she explained to Clare, "I know I shall not have much time to read now that you are here, but I do like to settle down in the afternoon after lunch with one of Miss Burney's novels. I have read all that she has written, I believe. And some, more than once. I do believe I have read *Clarentine*—one of her books, you know—three times. Do you read a great deal?"

"We do not have a bookseller near us," said Clare. "But I did borrow from Lady Melvin a novel called *The Fatal Revenge*." She laughed a little, and added, "I have never cried so much in my life."

Lady Thane nodded approvingly. "You show great sensibility, my dear. I do not blush when I say that I have wept more at Maria Edgeworth's hands than I did when my dear husband died."

The carriage turned into Leadenhall Street, to find they were not alone in seeking the latest from the Minerva Press. There were two barouches ahead of them, and by the time that Lady Thane's carriage reached the door, and her footman, Charles, leaped to the ground and disappeared inside with his mistress's list in his hand, the owner of one of the vehicles was emerging from the door of the library.

It was, so Lady Thane announced, Miss Marianna Morton, one of the brightest lights of society, betrothed a year since to Lord Benedict Choate.

But Clare had eyes only for the exceedingly well-dressed gentleman who followed Miss Morton toward her carriage. He was dressed in trousers of gray, a morning coat of impeccable fit and quiet cut, and a top hat. His "highlows" were polished till they outshone the sun, and, if Clare had known it, they were among Hoby's newest creations.

The gentleman had a distinct curl to his lip, and the glance full of faint contempt with which he swept the street could have daunted the brashest person. But Clare bounced in her seat and said, "I know him!"

Lady Thane looked at her with unveiled surprise. "You do? Lord Benedict Choate? How can that be, child?"

The conversation had not taken into consideration the open window of the carriage. Clare's voice had carried as far as the nonpareil standing on the sidewalk. Lord Choate turned in their direction, and then, recognizing Lady Thane, descended the steps and crossed the sidewalk to speak to her.

Somewhat flustered, Lady Thane managed the introductions, including Miss Morton, who joined her affianced husband.

"But then," she said in a rush, "I needn't have introduced you, should I? For my goddaughter, Lord Choate, tells me she knows you!"

Lord Benedict bowed civilly. "I fear I have the wretchedest memory," he murmured.

"Of course you don't remember," said Clare, seeing that she had made a mull of things. "It is only your eyebrows . . ."

Lord Benedict lifted one of the items in question, and Clare rushed on. "In the long gallery at home, you know," she stammered. "All the portraits of the Penrycks . . ." Her voice died away, as enlightenment dawned on Lord Choate.

"My mother was a Penryck," he said musingly. "But I fear I am not acquainted with her family. She died, you must know, when I was very young."

Clare thought of several things she wanted to say to him, but before she could decide upon one of them, she met the quelling eye of Choate's betrothed. Miss Morton was dressed in a simple elegance that reduced Clare to dumbness. Her gown of gray, with the new full sleeves, was topped by a bonnet of primrose yellow, setting off her raven curls. Clare felt at once dowdy and awkward. Miss Morton's kindling eye did nothing to put her at ease.

"So you are related to Choate?" said Miss Morton in a tone calculated to fob off pretenders to intimacy. "I don't believe I knew much of your connections, Benedict. At least I do not know the Penrycks."

Clare was moved, injudiciously, to fence with Miss Morton. "An old family," she said innocently, "from Dorset. Of course, we prefer our own quiet life to the tumult you have here in this city. You don't find London dirty? I must confess I am moved to dust everything I see." Realizing that her words could be interpreted to mean that she herself plied the duster, she added, even more unfortunately, "My own staff at the abbey would be struck with horror."

Lady Thane said with a suggestion of tartness, "I am sure, my dear, that you have not found a mote of dust in my house."

"Oh, no, dear Lady Thane, but you have such hard-working servants."

"But," said Lord Choate suddenly, "this is your first season in London?"

"Yes," said Clare languidly. "I wished not to come at all to London, but I was told that I should come before I grew too old to enjoy it."

Miss Morton, who had decided at first that Clare was an importunate, childish connection of her affianced, whom she would make sure to see very little of in the next years, now decided that Clare must be older than she looked. Miss Morton, an only child, had little humor, and a strong tendency to take a literal view of all things.

Enough of this was certainly enough, she thought, turning to Benedict. But her betrothed had a queer look in his eye, one that she had not as yet been privileged to see, and could not decipher.

"I must regret that our families have grown apart," he said soberly. "Perhaps Lady Thane will permit me to call upon you one morning next week. I should enjoy pursuing the ramifications of our relationship."

Lady Thane, overcome, said faintly, "Of course, Lord Choate."

But Clare, conscious of a strong surge of dislike for the mocking light she discerned in his dark eyes, objected. "I fear, Lady Thane, that we will find it difficult for some days to come to find time. With much regret, Lord Choate."

Miss Morton's eyes took on a glitter. Benedict, catching sight of her tucked-in lips, thought better of baiting the girl in the carriage. She was far out of her depth, he realized, if she wished to tilt with Marianna. And he himself, surprisingly, did not wish the child to be publicly shamed.

And, he thought ruefully, Marianna could do it!

"Come, Benedict," said his beloved. "I cannot think why we stand here on the street, when I have told you I wished to go to Botibol's. Countess Lieven says he has a new shipment of ostrich feathers, and I must see them at once."

Bowing civilly to Lady Thane and to Clare, Benedict followed his Marianna to the fashionable black barouche just ahead of them.

"For all the world," said Clare, nettled, "like a small lapdog."

Lady Thane was horrified. Even more, she was stirred to the bottom of her conventional soul. "Do you know who he is?"

"A cousin, I daresay," said Clare. She was beginning to realize now that she had made an error: one of the ever-present pitfalls of the world of Mayfair had sucked her in. She would have, if she could, crawled into a small hole. But she was open to the world in Lady Thane's barouche, and must of necessity put a good face on things.

"He is," said Lady Thane in a stifling manner, "a non-pareil. A notable whip, an arbiter of fashion . . ." Words failed her, not surprisingly, and she fell back upon the cushions. "Well," she said finally, as the coachman began to draw ahead, "perhaps all is not lost. I doubt that Choate himself will talk, and Miss Morton, I wager, has already forgotten you. But, child, do not be so *forward*. It does make you look very young, you know."

In part, Lady Thane was mistaken. Marianna Morton had not forgotten Clare. She, like her late father, was well-versed in the ramifications of every family of consequence in the kingdom. She knew to the fourth cousin all of Benedict's family, meaning, of course, the Choates. But she became conscious now of a lack in her information. The Penrycks had nearly dropped out of sight. Nothing derogatory was known of them—in fact, little at all was known of them. Benedict's mother faded gently from the scene, after presenting her lord with the heir, and the lord's subsequent remarriage, to a Fenly from Derby, and the regular succession of additions to the nursery had obscured the Penryck connection.

Marianna intended that the connection remain unnoticed. Looking sidelong at Benedict, she thought better of broaching the subject to him. He had taught her, politely but with decision, that opposition could in no way alter his mind. She resolved, not for the first time, to tread warily until after their wedding. He would not cry off now, she knew, but still . . . forty thousand pounds a year was not a sum to take the least chance on.

She could not help but say, however, "Such a charming child," in an interrogatory tone of voice.

There was a frown between Lord Benedict's black brows. Absently he reached a finger up to smooth his left eyebrow. Suddenly he laughed. "Imagine! Being recognized in London only because I resemble a portrait in Dorset! And not even I, in fact, but my eyebrows!" he said, genuinely amused.

"I believe they are considered very distinguished," said Marianna, adding, "although of course, it is not the thing to discuss such a personal matter."

"But, knowing my friends, I am assured that it is done. But rarely, I will admit, with such frankness."

"I wonder," ventured Marianna, "how she will take."

"At the rate she has started," said Benedict, "I dread the thought of further association with that child."

"I feared," said Marianna, "that she was going to make

a claim upon you." She added archly, "And if so, I should be very jealous."

"Jealous of a child, Marianna? I confess I thought better of you than that."

"I trust your honor, Benedict."

With that not-quite-subtle reminder, Marianna tugged gently at the silken rein by which she led Benedict Choate in the ways she wished him to go.

Dutifully Benedict bowed. "Your servant, my dear, as always," he said automatically. "But not, I fear," he added in quite a different tone of voice, "as far as your *plumassier*'s. I see Lady Courtenay approaching, and I have remembered that I must meet friends at White's."

"At eleven in the morning?" protested Marianna.

"Pray give Lady Courtenay my best duty," he said, ignoring her protests, and, tipping his top hat with grace to her, and a bow to the fast-approaching Lady Courtenay, who, he had time to notice, had her plain, eager daughter with her, Benedict vanished with all possible speed in the direction of St. James's Street.

4.

If Clare believed Lady Thane's comfortable assurance that the recent interview with Miss Morton and Lord Choate had already been forgotten, she could agree at least so far as those two were concerned.

But as for herself, she found that as they drove away from Leadenhall Street the eyebrows engrossed her to the exclusion of all else.

It was unsettling to see the portrait come down from the wall of the long gallery and walk about the streets of London. And while she must be perfectly honest, knowing that the portrait of Lord Benedict Choate himself did not hang on the gallery walls, yet the family resemblance to their mutual great-grandfather was more than striking.

She was finally able to put Lord Choate out of her mind, when Sir Alexander Ferguson and his aunt, Lady Warfield, made up a party to see the Tower of London. Sir Alexander was knowledgeable about the ghosts and the executions and the famous and ill-fated prisoners, but his prosy gloom vanished from her mind when she saw the snowy bear from Greenland with his coal-black nose, and the lions, and the improbable zebra—what was once called a painted ass—and the strangest of all, the two kangaroos. Never before had she seen such marvels!

Clare was gratified, during the next few days, to know that she was becoming more and more acquainted in the circle of her godmother's friends. As well she might, since Lady Thane was invited nearly everywhere, and Clare was of course invited too.

At length came a day, three weeks after her arrival in London, when Lady Thane came in search of her in the small back sitting room, called, from the color of its furnishings, the Yellow Room. It was now a favorite retreat for Clare, not so grand as the Blue Saloon or the green brocade drawing room, or even the somber-hued back room.

She had with her this day the second volume of *Bewildered Affections, or All is Not Lost,* a novel of some years

26

past, but Clare had much reading to catch up on, for Grandmama had not subscribed to the latest novels.

Lady Thane opened the door and hurried in, the swish of her taffeta underskirt marking her progress. "My dear, there you are! I will not stay long, for I know that I hate to have my own reading interrupted, but I just have had a revelation."

Clare promptly put away her book, secretly noting the page number so as not to be delayed when she could take it up again. "What can that be?"

"I have just been counting up the parties we've attended, my dear. Routs, and afternoon teas, and a card party at the duchess's, although I fear that must have been a very dull evening for you, since you do not play cards. And Lady Warfield's invitation to the Tower, and Lady Courtenay's being so good as to invite you into her barouche last week Friday in the park . . ."

"Your friends have been most kind."

"Well," said Lady Thane complacently, "I do have friends, and I fancy that I still have credit in society, even though dear Harriet has been married these two years, and rarely comes to London now. But my idea, Clare, is to have a ball."

"A ball?"

"We owe so many people. I thought we could open up the ballroom—you know, it hasn't been used since Harriet's last ball. I remember it was such a sad crush!" Lady Thane's eyes sparkled. "Two hundred and fifty cards . . ."

That was the beginning of what Clare could only regard as pandemonium. There was system in it, somewhere, she was sure. But she could not discern the pattern. Lady Thane, far from being the indolent, lackadaisical woman that Clare had thought her, responded to the challenge she had set herself as an artillery horse hearing the trumpets.

There were lists, and tradesmen, and Darrin the butler dealing with ever-increasing details, and Lady Thane in a blissful state of confusion.

Clare was allowed to do nothing—and in fact, she would not have known where to begin. Berry Brothers were consulted for wine, and Gunter's for the ices they were famed for—at a most reasonable price, too, said Lady Thane, for a new shipment of ice from Greenland had just arrived and been buried beneath the cellars of their establishment in Berkeley Square.

At length Clare decided she needed some new ribbons to run through a new skirt, and with Lady Thane's permission she set out with Budge for Oxford Street. It was the first time that Clare had been shopping alone, and the unexpected sense of freedom was exhilarating.

But Budge did not share her feeling. Budge did not like London, and Budge was vocal enough about it so that Hobbs had been quite sharp with her in the servants' hall. "Be it that you don't like it, that's you that's not up to snuff. But don't come cracking to us about it. *We* didn't invite you here." And Budge continued with a darkling feeling about the perils of the streets of the wicked city. For, she reasoned, if you can't count on friends where you live, then where are you?

Her grumbling finally gave out after Clare had finished her shopping. "Never mind, Budge," consoled Clare. "We're done now and we'll be back home in a trice. I'm sorry I ever brought you to London, Budge. I shouldn't have done so had I thought you would be so desperately unhappy."

Budge tucked the parcels under her arm and, mollified, grunted, "But I'd a been worrying all the while about who was taking care of you, Miss Clare, and that's a fact. But we'll be going back before long, won't we?"

"You mean back to Dorset? I should hope so."

Budge reached to clutch her shawl closer to her chin. Even though the air was mild, she had a fixed impression that the air of London was full of evil. Her gesture loosened a parcel, and the brown paper object fell to the pavement. Clare exclaimed, and turned back to aid her maid, when a small ragged urchin darted out of the crowd, snatched the parcel from the pavement, and took to his heels. Clare, instantly indignant, cried out, "Stop, thief!"

Her only thought was pursuit. The boy must not be allowed to escape. She feared to lose sight of him, in the mill of people, and ran after him, heedless of the passersby, ignoring the comments of surprised onlookers.

But the boy was too fast for her, and disappeared within a few yards, and Clare, intent upon seeing where he had gone, did not notice the uneven cobbles beneath her feet. She felt her smooth-soled slipper skid, and instantly fell to her hands and knees, her breath knocked out of her by the impact.

Budge, at her heels, saw her mistress felled by what in Budge's alarmed fancy could only be foul play. Her nightmare fears at last realized, she dropped the rest of her parcels and opened her mouth. The screams she emitted at first had no shape, but within seconds, as a curious crowd gathered, she was able to form the word "Murder!" which she expressed in one long, high-pitched note.

"Budge!" cried Clare, but due to her position, still on the cobbles, and a sharp pain in her knee, the sound came out as a whisper, far too faint to reach Budge's ear.

Clare's heart sank. Of all things, a scene in Oxford Street was the worst possible thing that could befall her. She tested her knee, but decided, as pain shot through, that she was not ready to try it.

"Ah, the lady's down. Somebody shoved her. Stop that caterwauling! Did someone really stab her?"

It was the sense of the crowd that murder had indeed been done, and although Clare was sitting up, clearly still alive, she wished she were dead. But if she could just get Budge shut up, and on their way home without anyone seeing them . . .

It was a vain hope.

Clare watched, as in a dream, the crowd melting away. As in a vision, Budge closed her mouth and fell silent, her ruddy cheeks an unwonted pallor.

A strong hand under her elbow and a note of concern in his voice, as Lord Benedict Choate said, "Are you much hurt?"

Of all people to come to her rescue! But Clare managed to say, even though a little shakily, "I think not. My knee, I think, will be all right."

She stood erect again, and tested her knee, holding to Benedict's hand. "It will serve," she said at last. "I must thank you, sir, for your assistance. It was a foolish accident—"

"What happened?" said Benedict. "Your maid has some idea that murder is done?"

Clare looked up at her rescuer. In his dark eyes she could see a queer mixture of amusement tinged with something else she could not identify. Suddenly the enormity of her action came home to her. To run shouting down Oxford Street after a thief, for all the world like a pennypinching greengrocer—she could not have done anything more vulgar!

"A small boy ran into me," she improvised hastily. "I trust he was not hurt."

"It would seem no more than he deserved. But I cannot believe murder?"

"Budge dislikes London."

"As you do, I think. If memory serves me, you have already told me as much."

He offered her his arm. "It is but a step to Lady Thane's house," he pointed out. "Perhaps you can walk that far?"

"Oh, yes," said Clare. "Truly I was not hurt. Only mortified."

"As well you might be," he observed. He said nothing more until they were admitted to Lady Thane's house. He desired Darrin to bring tea, and he stood over her until she had downed a cup of the restorative.

"Now, then," he said, "I must point out to you that certainly to cause a scene in Oxford Street is folly."

"I am to blame for a small boy?" she countered.

"No matter how it happened. Doesn't Lady Thane have a carriage you can use? Doesn't it suit your country ways to have a little decorum?"

Clare was recovering rapidly from the jarring fall. She had expected—and received, temporarily—sympathy, but suddenly Benedict had changed. "I truly am grateful to you," she said with effort, "for rescuing me from my accident. I do not see, however, how one is to go on and never fall afoul of the least mishap. Surely London is not so well-regulated as that?"

Benedict was prey to more than one emotion. He had been alarmed when he thought she might have been hurt, and he was fully aware that he was unjust to blame her for what could, after all, have happened to anyone. But still another piece of information had reached him recently, in response to his seeking it out, and it was paramount now in his mind.

"I can't think what you are doing in London, at your age," he said with crisp disapproval. "At fifteen, you should still be in the schoolroom."

"And how do you know my age?" she said with rising anger.

"I've made it my business to know," he said savagely. "At fifteen, it is folly to come out in London. I am totally surprised at Lady Thane for bringing you out when you haven't the least notion—"

"Lord Choate," said Clare in a shaky voice, "I have said I am grateful for your assistance. I am grateful for your bringing me back to this house. I am, in addition, grateful for your ordering tea, although I do feel that my years in the schoolroom have prepared me for such a task as desiring a servant to attend to my wishes. But I do not think that by your assistance in the street you have earned the right to read me such a riot act!"

She had not finished, but she dared say no more, for tears lurked just behind her eyelids.

"Someone should," continued Benedict inexorably.

"I perceive you do not approve of me," said Clare.

"You perceive correctly," said Benedict.

"I must be sure to tell my grandmama," said Clare, "for she will be glad of your opinion, I am sure."

Benedict now realized he had perhaps allowed his rage to overrule his extreme good sense. He had carefully fostered an attitude in his life of allowing no emotion to overrule him. The oldest of a brood of half-sisters and half-brothers, he had learned early in his life that emotion was wearing. And since nothing he had experienced so far in his life had led him to change his opinion, he was overset as much by the intensity of his rage as by his strong opinions themselves.

This winsome child, to his surprise, was possessed of a will of steel. And he had been trapped into fencing with her. But his pride would not let him admit defeat at the hands of a mere slip of a girl.

This child who now said to him, "I must beg you to enlighten me, sir. I had thought that my grandmama's approval was all that I need concern myself with. But now, I seem to be required to gain yours as well. But really, Lord Choate, I fail to understand your concern with me."

"I thank God daily," said Benedict, savagely, "that I am no longer concerned with females. My sister Primula is married and off my hands, and my youngest sister is just out of the nursery."

Clare turned away, more upset than she would have thought by his strictures. She found a great deal to think about in the pleating of the fringe on the golden damask draperies—except that she could see them only dimly through her tears.

"If I had to deal with such a female as you," Benedict continued, "I would—"

Clare had had enough. Her pride, of which she had a good deal, prodded her now, and she took a shuddering breath and turned to face him.

Eyebrows or not, Penryck or not, he had no right to scold her as he did. And she would not allow it. She forced a smile, and crossed the room to stand before him, the marquetry table between them. Leaning forward, hands on the table, she told him with all the sweetness at her command, "But you don't."

A tiny muscle worked at the corner of his mouth.

"You do not have to deal with me, Cousin," she said, "and believe me, you never will."

Through clenched jaws he gritted, "Thank God for that!"

5.

Upon this tense scene, the two participants glaring fiercely at each other over the small table, entered Lady Thane. She hesitated almost imperceptibly at the sight, before sweeping in with her hand extended to Lord Choate.

"My dear sir," she exclaimed, "Darrin told me you had called, and I must apologize for keeping you waiting."

"It is no matter, Lady Thane," said Benedict stiffly. "I did not expect you to trouble yourself. I merely restored Miss Penryck to you."

"Restored?" echoed Lady Thane. "How is this?"

Clearly Benedict was seething, she thought, and a feeling of dismay smote her. What had the child done now? The fact that her earlier forebodings looked in a fair way to be justified did nothing to mollify her.

"I am sure Miss Penryck will wish to tell you herself," said Benedict, looking directly at Clare.

Clare had every intention of doing so, but she would not embark upon her narrative of the afternoon's doings upon Benedict's direction, as though she were a delinquent pupil dancing to the tune of the schoolmaster. But Lady Thane just now noticed Clare's torn dress. "My dear child," she cried out, in real concern, "what does this mean?"

Outrageously, Benedict said, "Just so, ma'am." With a few more words, and strongly repressing a wish to box the child's ears, he took his leave. Not until much later that day, while examining a box of books that had been delivered from Egerton, did it occur to him to wonder just why his anger had flared up to such a pitch. The accident had not been the child's fault, and he had been gothic in his reaction.

The wide blue eyes that had very prettily looked their thanks swam before his eyes, but memory instantly transmuted them into the flashing sapphire glance that had next put him in his place.

Was it merely the shock of finding someone—a mere chit of a girl at that—who told him to mind his own affairs? He didn't think so. But no other reason occurred to him. His servant discreetly reminded him that he was due in Mount Street to dine with his betrothed and her mama in an hour. It was a duty he did not relish, considering that a lifetime spent having dinner with Marianna was sufficient, without anticipating. But he sighed, and began to dress.

In the meantime, Lady Thane had succeeded in eliciting from her goddaughter the details of her accident. "And you came home in tatters!" cried Lady Thane. "With Lord Benedict Choate!"

"I am dreadfully sorry if that was wrong, Lady Thane, but truly I did not know quite what to do, with Budge in flapping hysterics, and I could not calm her. I could not even think what to do!" Clare collapsed into a chair, and occupied herself by drawing together the edges of the rent sustained when she toppled to the pavement.

"I wish you would send Budge back to the country," said Lady Thane crossly, diverted by a subject on which she had strong feelings. "The wench is less than useless, dear Clare, for she does not know the best way to dress your hair, and she trembles when one speaks to her. I daresay that is the way of Penryck Abbey, but I cannot think it is good for her to go in such fear."

"I agree," said Clare. For a moment she played with the thought of telling Lady Thane that she too would return to Penryck Abbey, and rusticate in consoling silence. She had not felt so low in her mind since she had come to town. And it was not quite clear whether it was the unaccustomed gaiety or the constant anxiety lest she put a foot wrong that preyed on her so.

But Lady Thane had already forgotten Budge, and moved again to the subject that engrossed her. "Choate is a stickler, you know. And he has such credit—you will not believe this, but I know of three cases where he simply gave *such* a look, and quite put the girls in the shade. Too bad of him, of course, and not quite kind, but . . . my girl, facts are facts, and we would be wrong not to face up to them."

But Clare was listening with only half her mind. "Then there is your ball, Lady Thane, and I must not fail that."

Lady Thane, unaware of Clare's brooding upon a return home to Penryck Abbey, where she was known and loved, misunderstood. "Of course you must not. But depend upon me, we will not see Lord Choate in this house that evening. Unless, of course"—she furrowed her brow in thought—"unless he takes pity on your innocence."

"I do not think him capable of pity," said Clare firmly.

"No more do I," said Lady Thane mournfully. "Depend upon it, my dear, you have made a formidable enemy in him."

Clare's heart sank to her satin-shod toes. She had not mentioned to her godmother the spirited repartee that had occurred just before her entrance. She could not imagine what Lady Thane's reaction would be had she known of Clare's outright defiance of the arbiter of the fashionable world. An enemy, indeed! If Benedict had had his way, Clare had no doubt that she would even now be blasted into a pile of cinders.

There were still several days before the ball. Depend upon it, Lady Thane had warned, we will not see Lord Choate here again. How embarrassing it must have been for that Corinthian to pick up a young lady from the public walk. And escort her home, with a great rent in her gown, and her bonnet sadly alop.

But if he had been the kind of man Clare admired, she thought darkly, he would not have minded that.

Lady Thane's pessimism did not lie deep. Of a cheerful disposition, but something of a realist, she had not held much hope that Lord Choate would distinguish her god-daughter in any way. Now, upon wishful reflection, she believed that Lord Choate also could not be troubled to exert himself to put down Clare's possible pretensions.

Marianna Morton had a hint of hardness in her face, thought Lady Thane, that indicated that Lord Choate would find she required all his dutiful attention. And that, Lady Thane decided with satisfaction, would keep him from refining upon Clare's youthful awkwardness.

In due time the incident dropped from the thoughts of both Lady Thane and Clare. The preparations for the party still took Lady Thane's attention. One full day was spent with Mrs. Darrin and the man from Gunter's on the confections to be served. And another day arranging for flowers and a plethora of potted palms.

Clare was glad enough, therefore, to receive an invitation from Lady Warfield to go riding in the park with her and her daughter. Quite likely, Sir Alexander would escort them. "Pray say that I might go," begged Clare. And Lady Thane, somewhat surprised that Lady Warfield wished to contrast Clare's pretty face with the plain face of her own daughter, agreed at once.

But she had misjudged Lady Warfield. That lady was not planning to marry her daughter to anyone except a distant cousin in Scotland, who was not of the fashionable world but who had what Lady Warfield considered an indecent number of sheep and five castles, or was it eight? She never could remember. At any rate, Clare's undoubted fresh beauty stirred no jealousy in Eugenia's heart, and Lady Warfield smiled benignly on them both as her coachman tooled the black barouche into the park.

It was nearing five o'clock in the afternoon, the most fashionable hour to be seen in the park. She was already acquainted with many of the famous beauties, the Duchess of Rutland, Lady Cowper. Lady Hertford bowed to them both as they met, and Lady Jersey, the regent's great friend, passed by on the other side.

It was a balmy afternoon, the mildest of breezes lifted Clare's curls, and soon she began to feel more comfortable. It would be too much, she thought, to expect her to feel at home in this world, but apparently Benedict had not passed the word that she was hopelessly naive. At least the Countess Lieven smiled kindly at her, she noticed, and Lady Warfield, by her countenancing of Clare, gave her as much credit as she could.

"There's Lord Alvanley," said Eugenia, her plain face lighting with impish amusement. "Do you know that he likes apricot tart so well that his cook makes one a day, and there is always a fresh one on his sideboard?"

"Doesn't he get tired of it?" marveled Clare. "I vow I should not want the same taste day after day."

Lady Warfield laughed. "So one should. But Alvanley, you know, never eats it. And yet he is the most good-natured man in the world and I dote on him."

"Then why . . . ?"

"Because he might want to," said Eugenia, "eat it, I mean."

Lady Warfield demurred. "I think he has simply forgotten to tell them he no longer wants the tart. He's terribly absentminded, you know."

Diverting as was the gossip of Lady Warfield, seasoned by the unexpected humor of Eugenia, yet the constant spectacle of dandies and more sober gentlemen, of ladies in their superb carriages, provided much entertainment for

Clare. She forgot her own troubles in marveling at Lady Melbourne's proud demeanor, when everyone knew she had borne children by several different fathers.

Or learning that two gentlemen had wagered five hundred pounds the night before at Watier's on the outcome of two flies climbing up the wall—the bet fell through when one of the flies buzzed away, leaving behind him an acrimonious dispute as to whether the bet was still valid.

Her enjoyment faded when she saw, with sinking heart, Marianna Morton cantering gracefully toward them. Clare's glance slid past Marianna to the sober-clad horseman behind her. Choate, of course.

A flush mantled Clare's cheek as she fell into confusion. What could she say to him? How would he greet her? Like the hoyden that he must have thought her? She clenched her hands together in her lap and waited for the blow to fall.

It did not fall. She heard Lady Warfield and Eugenia greeting Miss Morton, and knew that Benedict spoke to the Warfields. And to Clare. She forced herself to look up, unable to conceal the apprehension in her eyes.

Lord Choate, however, seemed to regard her with indifference, and spoke only the merest commonplaces, and soon she began to believe that she had refined too much upon the incident the other day. More proof, if it were needed, of her *greenness*.

Before she could bring herself to answer Benedict's remarks, Marianna had nodded to them and moved off, Benedict dutifully in her wake.

"She does remind me," said Eugenia thoughtfully, "of my old governess. Remember Patterson, Mama? Such a disciplinarian, Clare. I was quite afraid of her."

"Miss Morton has far too much *ton* for you to speak of her thus," said Lady Warfield repressively.

"I'm sorry, Mama," said Eugenia. But she gave Clare a glance brimming with amusement, and Clare smiled back. It was helpful, she thought, to consider the splendid Miss Morton in the irreverent light that Eugenia cast on her. Clare decided, suddenly, that she did not like Marianna Morton in the least.

The barouche now turned, on Lady Warfield's order, and began the return journey. Harry Rowse cantered up and spoke to them, his eyes lingering on Clare. He was a friendly face among many impersonal and indifferent ones, and Clare felt a grateful warming toward him. But Lady Warfield spoke coldly, and did not stop. Toward the corner, just before they were to leave the park, a late-comer to the promenade hurried in on a fresh horse, tit-tupping as it caracoled onto the drive.

"Cousin Alexander!" cried Eugenia. "I thought he would not wish to be late, when he knew who was riding in our carriage," she added with an arch glance at Clare.

He was an undistinguished man, with a plain but kindly face, and since he knew he could not approach Corinthian sartorial splendor, he chose not to try. Clad in fawn riding breeches and a black coat, he managed to look unexceptionable, which, to do him justice, was all he wished.

Now, reining in beside the Warfield barouche, he doffed his top hat and spoke pleasantly.

"I was delayed," he said importantly, "because Catalini was arriving at the opera house just as I went past. By the stars, there is a fine woman, and they say she has a voice that could charm the angels. I should wish to hear her, for you must know that I have heard the greatest singers in Italy, and I consider myself no mean judge of the voice, you know.

"While I feel that *bel canto* is by far the most delightful sound, yet I must confess there is something about the im-passioned drama that impels one to continue listening, no matter what the music."

Turning to Clare, he made a bow. "Perhaps, if Lady Thane would like it, I could make up a party to view the opera. Should you like that?"

"Of all things!" cried Clare, suddenly enthusiastic. "Shall it be soon?"

"I will see whether my sister, Mrs. Totten, will come with us. Totten has a box, you know, and he has offered it to me any number of times. I think I shall certainly take advantage of the opportunity, don't you know."

Leaving him with many expressions of civility, the War-field carriage moved on, past the corner and through the streets until it arrived in Grosvenor Square. Entering the house, Clare glanced behind her to the park in the center of the square. Behind the iron fencing, several children played a game with a brightly colored ball, and a barking dog capered, delirious with excitement.

Life here in London was beginning to take a turn for

the better, she thought. The great ball of Lady Thane's was approaching, Sir Alexander was being very attentive, and she truly liked him, even though she had dark thoughts about his prosiness, and Lord Benedict Choate had not deliberately snubbed her, this first meeting after the incident. Cousin Benedict—she thought with amusement. How he would hate for her to call him that—the connection being remote, but unmistakably there! She resolved not to yield to the temptation to sting him further.

Lady Thane's approval was easily obtained for the theater party, and in three days the carriages joined others in the Haymarket, where the King's Theater was brilliant with gas lights. Its arched facade in the Italian style glowed in the darkness.

Catalini was reported to have received two thousand pounds for her first season in London five years before. The proceeds of two benefit performances and some private concerts, so said Sir Alexander, more than doubled her salary in that first year.

"Since then," he said, "of course she is recognized as the highest-paid prima donna in the world."

Mrs. Totten and her brother escorted Lady Thane and Clare to their box. Totten, so his wife said with a wry twist to her lips, suffered from the headache, but probably was this moment sitting down to a green baize table at Crockey's to gamble the night away. "Fortunately, he is often lucky," said Amelia Totten.

"The auditorium here is a particularly fine one," said Sir Alexander, taking upon himself Clare's entertainment. "It was designed, I believe, by Novosielsky, and you will see it is in the shape of a giant horseshoe. Although, I suppose you are not much acquainted with such mundane affairs as horseshoes?" Sir Alexander gave his peculiar snorting laugh.

Not waiting for an answer, he said, "I believe the five tiers of boxes represent the largest structure of its kind in the world—they tell me . . . I have made particular inquiries about this—it can hold more than *three thousand persons* at once!"

Clare soon found it was beyond her ability to sustain a lively interest in Sir Alexander's well-informed speech. She fixed a smile on her face, but her eyes wandered over the beautifully gowned ladies in the boxes, the jewels flashing as their wearers moved, catching the light.

One in particular caught her eye. "Pray tell me," she said when she found an opportunity, "who is that very attractive lady in the box just outside? She has been watching you this long time."

To her great surprise, Sir Alexander ignored her question. But a telltale flush crept along his cheekbone, and she knew she had made an error. Not until the intermission did Lady Thane enlighten her.

"That is Harriette Wilson," she told Clare in a whisper. "A Fashionable Impure."

Suddenly enlightened, Clare realized that the woman dressed in white, perfectly at home in a box that let for more than two thousand pounds for the season, with diamonds at her throat and in her ears, was, for all purposes, invisible to the ladies of Clare's acquaintance. But not to the men, Clare noted with sudden amusement. For there was Frederick Lamb, Lady Melbourne's son, and the Duke of Beaufort's heir, whose name Clare couldn't remember, behind Harriette.

And surely Sir Alexander, flushed of cheek still, knew her well!

Not until Catalini had sung her last note and taken her last bow, still with the fixed smile with which the singer greeted tragedy or ecstasy in her singing, did Clare rouse from the trance that the performance had engendered in her.

There was a sad crush while the audience gathered in the foyer and waited for their carriages to file the length of the short street and arrive at the arched portico. In the jostling throng Clare was thrown off balance, and a strong arm steadied her. She turned to smile her thanks, and the smile faded on her face.

Lord Choate said, with the ghost of a smile, "A sad ending to a delightful evening."

Clare stiffened. "To meet me, you mean?"

He lifted a quizzical eyebrow. "Not at all. I am glad once more to be of service to you. I merely meant such a shocking squeeze."

His words had been pitched low, but not low enough to escape the sharp ears of Miss Morton. Smoothly she joined the conversation. "How comforting it must be to you, Miss

Penryck, to find a gentleman always at hand to set you straight again."

Clare paled. Marianna clearly referred to the episode in Oxford Street, and she could only have known it from Benedict. How dared he discuss her with Marianna? His rage was strong, but she had thought his behavior not so degraded as to gossip about her, but clearly she was wrong. She glanced at him with a kindling eye, but he had become once more unapproachable and remote.

Marianna had not finished. "I do wish, Miss Penryck, that you wouldn't find it necessary for Choate to rescue you at every hand. It does look so . . . strange, don't you think?"

Mrs. Morton, on her daughter's other side, said quietly, "Marianna, my dear . . ."

Marianna's tongue fell silent at her mother's reproof, but her eyes still glittered, and Clare was glad when Sir Alexander's carriage was called.

But the damage had been done. Clare fell asleep that night not listening in her mind to Catalini's rich voice, but to the realization that Choate found her a nuisance.

Or—said a lurking imp—is it Marianna that finds you a nuisance?

6.

It was nearly mid-June. Clare had, in less than two months, become well-acquainted in the fashionable world of London society. She had come to London at her grandmama's bidding to see something of the world, and if all went well, to make an advantageous marriage. But the time had flown by, and while she had certainly seen something of the world, no marriage was in sight.

To be truthful, Grandmama had not given much instruction on that head, even though it was a source of anxiety to Lady Penryck as to what would happen to her darling granddaughter when she would be left alone.

"But you have no call to worry," urged Clare. "You told me that Great-Uncle Horsham would be my guardian, and I am sure I know how to behave. I shall give him no trouble."

Grandmama shook her head. "I fear he would not be quite up to bringing you out in London. I should like to see you settled, child."

Clare thought a moment. "Even if Great-Uncle Horsham is disinclined to anything but a retired life . . . well, he is all there is, and I will just have to conform."

"All there is?" said Grandmama musingly. Then a sudden thought struck her, and she dismissed Clare from her presence. "I have things to settle," she said, and called for writing paper.

It was later that Clare learned that one of the letters was to Lady Thane, and before long she was on her way to London.

Two months, and she was no farther along in fulfilling Grandmama's wishes than the day she had arrived in London. She had met many gentlemen, of varying fortunes and intentions, but none she fancied. At least, fancied enough to give any encouragement.

As a matter of fact, it took some careful finesse on Lady Thane's part to make sure that her inexperienced goddaughter was not snapped up at once. Sir Alexander Ferguson, prosy and deliberate, would have taken up all of Clare's time, had he been allowed. And Lady Thane, searching Clare's face for signs that she had at least a feeling for Sir Alex, found no comfort.

But Clare was eminently biddable. Lady Thane had to admit that. There was none of the Penryck resolution in her, so far as Lady Thane could see. Clare reminded her more and more of Elizabeth Tresillian, whom Lady Thane had much loved.

Clare tried hard to be enthusiastic about the parties that constituted their life. There were routs, and drums, and card parties. There was much talk about the series of lectures to be given by a poet called Coleridge, in the Philosophical Society's rooms in Fleet Street.

And there were the Elgin Marbles, new shipments from Greece arriving periodically to add to the remarkable frieze, the first part of which had arrived eight years before.

To view the marbles, one must travel only to Park Lane, quite near Grosvenor Square, and enter a ramshackle temporary building that Lord Elgin had erected to house his treasures until he and the government could come to terms as to price. But the marbles were open to viewing, and had been this three years past, and Lady Thane had seen them more than once.

"Sheer beauty, they tell me," she told Clare. "But sadly unclothed, I fear. And while they may have been entirely appropriate to Athens, I really feel that Lord Elgin might have done better to leave them there."

Clare dutifully inspected them, in company with Sir Alexander and his amiable sister, and regretted that she did not find them breathtaking, as she was sure she ought.

But all the sightseeing in London was cast into the shade by an event that came as much of a surprise to Lady Thane as it did to Clare.

The heavily embossed envelope with the royal crest arrived by hand, and the receipt of it nearly sent Lady Thane into a swoon. "The prince regent!" she said faintly. "His Midsummer Ball! My dear Clare, we must have new gowns—imagine his asking us, when he knows well we have been Whig this long time. But they do say he is sadly neglecting his Whig friends, and I do think it is ungrateful of him. But then, I should not criticize royalty, after all, for my dear husband would never permit it. Of course," she added reflectively, "the Tories were in great favor, and that made a difference. I daresay he might have said a word or two about the prince regent, and his highness does not easily forget criticism. But enough of that. How fortunate that the ball will come before my own small entertainment! I shall feel quite correct in sending a card to his highness."

It was the measure of the prestige of the regent's invitation to Carlton House that Lady Thane set out that very day to augment her wardrobe. Being of a kind nature, she spent rather more thought on the gift of a ball gown she was making to Clare than to her own heavy blue satin embroidered with pearls, to be worn with a delicate silk shawl of cerulean blue.

She declared herself satisfied with the result of Clare's straw-colored Indian muslin, embroidered in gold thread. "It sets off your coloring, and is not quite so young-looking as the white we looked at," she pronounced.

"Thank you," breathed Clare, entranced at her elegance.

"My birthday gift to you," Lady Thane said. "After all, you will be sixteen tomorrow. I wish we could mark the day with a special celebration, but questions might be awkward, you know."

"We'll pretend the regent's ball is my party," said Clare, with a dazzling smile.

But the new gown was, after all, not the main thing. Lady Thane, the morning of the ball, rustled in to the morning room, which faced out upon the back garden. Clare favored this room above all the others in Lady Thane's house. The walls were covered with a figured yellow paper in an old-fashioned bergère style, but gay indeed.

Clare, though, sitting with empty hands gazing out across the clipped privet that bordered the garden paths, did not reflect the cheerfulness of the room.

"My dear Clare, I am sorry to see you in the mopes!" cried Lady Thane. "Pray do not frown so, it makes the most horrid wrinkles and that ages one's face so quickly!"

"Perhaps it would be a good thing. I mean, to look a little older," said Clare, disconsolate.

Lady Thane was taken aback, but only for a moment. She had noticed a certain lack of response in Clare for some time, and she had laid it to worry about her grandmama. However justified such worry might be, yet it was Lady Thane's duty to bring her out of herself, and guide her in the ways that Lady Penryck wished the child to go.

Never one to shrink a duty, she ignored Clare's comment. "I wonder," she said guilelessly, "if you object to going to the ball with Amelia Totten. She has asked us, you know, and there will be such a sad crush of carriages that I own it would be a relief to me."

"Whatever you think best, Lady Thane."

"That means, of course, that her brother will accompany us, as well as Mr. Totten. But perhaps this is too much? Shall you like that?"

Clare, not being stupid, began to see that Lady Thane's questions were leading to an as yet unknown purpose. She fixed her eyes upon her godmother and said cautiously, "Sir Alexander is certainly unexceptionable company."

Lady Thane hesitated. She had not expected enthusiasm, but this neutrality was a bit daunting. "I have noticed," she began again, "that he has distinguished you particularly for some time. And, if I am not mistaken, he means to offer for you."

"Oh, no!" cried Clare faintly.

"The time has come for plain speaking, Clare. Naturally, your grandmother and I would do nothing to force you into a marriage you could not like. But it seems to me that there is nothing about Sir Alexander that would repel the most fastidious of ladies. He is quite wealthy, you know—not a nabob like Choate, but certainly with a respectable income. And well-informed—"

"And kind!" exclaimed Clare, and jumped to her feet. She took an agitated turn around the small room and turned back to face Lady Thane. "Oh, pray, do not let him offer!"

"And how do you suppose," said Lady Thane, startled, "that I can prevent him?"

"Oh, you must know ways to stop him!"

Lady Thane considered for a little. Surely such maidenly demureness was excessive! Unless Sir Alex had in some way presumed, and frightened the girl? Reflecting upon Sir Alex's character as it was known to her, she discarded that possibility at once.

Conceiving that the situation required either much more thought or a firm hand, Lady Thane chose the latter as being more productive of results. "My dear, you must consider the alternatives. If your grandmama is no longer able to provide for you, you must know that you will have to endure a guardian who may not be at all the way you would like. And of course, if you had your own establishment, or were betrothed so that you would be in the way of having it, things would be much more convenable for you."

Clare sighed. "I do know, ma'am. And I should not like it, to have an old man as a guardian. Uncle Horsham is very old, you know."

Lady Thane, perceiving that she had made substantial progress in the last few minutes, added a further thought that had just occurred to her. "Sir Alexander, you know, would certainly meet with my approval. And I know, your grandmother's approval as well."

"But—"

"And there is no one else, I think, who has paid you so much attention?"

"There is one other . . ." Clare said, after reflection.

Lady Thane's heart sank. "If you mean Harry Rowse, my child, no one in her right mind would encourage him. He is not at all the thing, you know." She looked intently at her charge. "You surely have not developed a *tendre* for *him,* have you?"

"I have talked with him not above three times," said Clare, "but he is amusing. And he was kind, to take the trouble to see that I was not left out. That was at the duchess's card party, ma'am, while you were playing cards."

"Kind" was not the word Lady Thane would have used, but she thought better of explaining exactly what her opinion of that rake was. Instead, she chose to expand on the virtues of Sir Alexander Ferguson, and at length achieved a result which, while it was not exactly what she wished, yet would serve to allow Sir Alexander to press his suit.

"Well, then," said Lady Thane, rising and shaking out the folds of her morning gown, "I am glad to see that you will be agreeable. I confess I had not thought, to begin with, that you would be such a success, your first season, and getting off on the wrong foot with Lord Choate to begin with, too. But all's well that ends well, I say. Best get some rest before tonight. You will want to look your best!"

With a surprisingly roguish glance, Lady Thane tripped out, leaving her goddaughter behind. It was as well that Lady Thane, believing firmly in the wisdom of her own words and congratulating herself on her good fortune at being so successful in her obligation to Clare and to Lady Penryck, did not see the results of her information.

For Clare had dropped her head into her hands, and began to sob as she had not done since Miss Peek, her governess, had been called home to tend her ailing sister, Sara, two years before.

7.

Carlton House, so Sir Alexander informed Clare, had undergone a remarkable transformation in the past years, since the prince regent, then Prince of Wales, had taken it over upon the death of his grandmother, who had let it fall sadly into disrepair.

"Didn't have the columns then," interposed Mr. Totten, rousing himself from his dreams of vast winnings at Crockford's. "Holland put them on."

Henry Holland had rebuilt the Pall Mall facade, added a long colonnade of Ionic columns, broken by two gates, in order to screen the royal residence from the curious passerby. Inside, Clare was informed by Amelia Totten, who had never seen the interior, there was a hall that was eight-sided, and a double staircase, and the most marvelous cabinetwork and ornamentation, in the latest fashion, altogether making a wondrously harmonious appearance.

"But," continued Amelia, "it is the gardens that I long to view. There, the regent has given full reign to the picturesque, with great sensibility, I am told. There are bowers and grottoes, and of all things, one might expect at any time a wicked nobleman to appear!"

"You read too much," said Mr. Totten, roused to comment by his wife's fantasies. "Hard on your complexion."

"I cannot imagine why you should say so," retorted his Amelia. "You told me only this evening," she added complacently, "that I was looking in high gig."

"Want to keep it that way," said her husband, unruffled. "Forget the wild tales—the Minerva Press has done more damage than can be calculated."

His wife joined battle, and Clare was glad when the coach turned into Pall Mall, the new gas lights making it, she declared, as bright as day.

When they arrived at the entrance, and were assisted to descend by a myriad of footmen and other satellites, Clare was on tiptoe with excitement. Ushered into the entrance foyer, and beyond into the famed Octagon Room, she realized that the extravagant praise lavished upon the regent's residence was only the truth. Not a spot but what had some kind of finery on it, not a cabinet but what was inlaid with fine parquetry, its shelves filled with such a multitude of snuffboxes, tankards, bibelots of all kinds, so that she thought she could never tire of looking at them.

But Sir Alexander and Lady Thane urged her forward to make room for the press of arriving guests.

Dinner was served in the great conservatory, lit by five hundred flambeaux. She gasped with delight at the sight. The table stretched the entire length of the room—a distance of at least two hundred feet, said Sir Alex, who was possessed of an endless supply of information. Before the prince regent's place at the table she saw a large basin of water from which flowed a stream of real water, of lights, perfumes, wavering candle flames, the music of sand, moss, and rocks—in miniature, with elfin bridges spanning the stream.

Incredibly, there were gold and silver fish swimming in the water, and Clare eyed those nearest her uneasily, fearing they might leap their watery bounds and splash into her soup.

The evening moved on for Clare in a vague impression of lights, perfumes, wavering candle flames, the music of stringed orchestras, and a steadily rising sensation of heat.

The prince regent himself made her welcome, and while this was not the first time she had seen him, yet at close quarters he was more than stupefying. Taller than the average, and displaying abundant proof of the prosperity of his life, the broad chest of his field marshal's uniform provided room for the many decorations that he chose to wear. He smiled down at Clare, restrained a swift impulse to pinch her cheek, and allowed Lady Thane to carry her away.

Sir Alexander set himself to amuse Clare, and pointed out the various celebrities he thought might interest her. Beau Brummell, the son of a clerk, who now was regarded with awe by the regent himself. John Nash, the new architect, who probably would add to Carlton House a new Gothic garden, which would be completely hidden from the Haymarket.

Thomas Moore, an obscure poet who had the regent's ear, at least for a short time.

"There is to be dancing later," said Sir Alexander.

Clare's heart sank, for Sir Alexander, heavy with virtue, was equally heavy on his feet. The tragedy, she felt, was that he did not seem to be aware of his lack of grace.

In the Chinese Room a small orchestra played, and Clare, always susceptible to music, moved toward the sound. It was a shocking squeeze, and before she realized it she had been separated from Sir Alexander. She was able to make her way toward the column at the door, which would protect her somewhat.

At least she could breathe. She began to worry about her gown. Truly it seemed such a waste to dress with such care, and then be in a crowd so dense that your gown could not be seen! But at least she would be grateful if the fragile gauze overlay sustained no damage.

She examined it as well as she could, and was gratified to find no great rent in it. A snag, where one of the spangles had caught on something, but—

"I am gratified to see," said a well-known voice in her ear, "that this time at least your gown has remained whole."

"Lord Choate!" she breathed, mortified beyond measure to be caught in such an undignified posture. But even more so to remember the incident that was clearly in his mind.

"I had not expected to find you unescorted," he said. "But perhaps you will trust me enough to give me your hand for the next dance?"

Scarcely knowing what she replied, she found herself led out on the small dance floor by Lord Benedict Choate, surely tonight the handsomest man in all of London!

He was dressed in black, with snowy ruffles edging his sleeves, his satin breeches and striped hose in the first line of fashion.

She soon discovered that he danced as elegantly as he looked, leading her through the intricate steps with ease. She found that she was nearly floating on the strains of the stringed viols that were hidden in an alcove.

His accomplished grace soon lured her into incautiousness. She did not have to mind her steps as much as usual, and her thoughts strayed, arriving sooner than advisable at impishness. "I do know, Lord Choate, that I am very young, and inexperienced in the social ways of London . . ." she began.

"I have no wish to argue that point," he said with grave civility. "We are agreed."

"And yet it seems to me that I have been told that it is customary to exchange a few words while one dances?"

His eyes flashed, telling her that he understood her. But he was not inexperienced in flirtation. "I feared to distract your mind from your dancing," he said. "I see now," he added handsomely, "that I need not have been anxious. You dance well."

She did not know precisely what a great compliment she had just received, but she did think he probably did not give such praise to everyone.

If she had been content to bask in the attention of Lord Choate, letting him take her back to Lady Thane when the set was finished, all might have gone well.

Lord Choate himself precipitated events unwittingly. "You will be returning to Dorset soon?" he said smoothly.

"I will?"

"Of course I would expect that you would. Your grandmother must be satisfied, now that you have had a taste of London society, even though I wonder at her sending you at such a tender age."

"It is your affair?" said Clare, biting her lip to hold back a retort that she feared might be tear-laden.

"Insofar as I am of some kin to you, I take an interest."

"Believe me, nothing could make me regret our kinship more than you do. But at least my Uncle Horsham will be easier to get along with than you are."

She had succeeded in startling him. "What does he have to do with this?"

"If Grandmama is unable to deal with my affairs, as I fear may soon be the case," said Clare, her eyes shiny with tears, "then Uncle Horsham is to be my guardian. And so, you see . . ."

Benedict suddenly fell into thoughtful silence. The set ended, and he made his mistake. Leading her back toward the conservatory, where he expected to find Lady Thane, he said to Clare, "I don't envy Horsham a whit. But if you take care, and don't step over the line again, I think you may do very well. Once you have a bit of polish, that is, and begin to look as though you had left the schoolroom behind."

Clare, stung, retorted, "I can't help the way I look!"

"True, but very unfortunate," said Lord Choate. "Although time will mend all things, so I am told."

Clare breathed heavily. She knew no one who could make her quite so angry, with just a supercilious lift of his heavy black eyebrows. She wished above all things to throw something—something very hard and unbreakable—at Lord Choate. But the thought that he would consider such an action as juvenile was distinctly lowering. Perhaps he was right!

The squeeze at the door gave her the chance that she had, without knowing it, been looking for. She eased away from Benedict's hand on her elbow, and allowed someone—Mrs. Morton?—to intrude between her and her escort. And in a moment she had made her escape in the crowd.

Seeing in the distance Sir Alexander, taller than most of the men, peering nearsightedly around the room, doubtless in search of her, Clare edged away in the opposite direction. Suddenly she found herself in front of a window that came to the floor, and stood ajar. The welcome thought of fresh cool air drew her like a magnet, and she eased the window open sufficiently to pass through.

She was outside the house. Carlton House, since the Prince of Wales had set up his separate establishment in 1783, had undergone transforming changes. She was not aware of all the building, the restoring that had taken place after the dowager princess had departed, leaving the house in sad condition, according to Sir Alexander.

But she was fully sensible of the magical quality which pervaded the gardens and grounds. Beyond her sight, now, in the darkness, were flowerbeds under the great old elms, statues of varied description, a waterfall, a temple with a floor of Italian marble, in the Florentine fashion, and, she remembered hearing, an observatory, where the regent fancied himself an astronomer.

Now there were flambeaux beyond counting glimmering in the dark, marking the walks, illuminating—but not too brightly—marble benches in the shelter of blooming shrubs that scented the air.

If Clare had thought about paradise, she decided, she would have eventually come to imagine just such a place as this. The cool air refreshing on her hot cheek, the soft luminosity of the artificial lights, from far off the strains of sweet music, and nearer at hand little bursts of muted voices.

And, below the terrace where she stood, looking up at her with admiring laughter in his face, stood Harry Rowse.

"Stand there," he advised her, "while I drink my fill of the sight. A veritable marble maiden, a beauty from another world."

A small part of her mind suggested that Harry Rowse should be thoroughly snubbed. But another part of her mind, fortified by resentment against Lord Choate's overbearing superiority, and irritated by his assumption that she hardly knew how to go on, overruled, and she stepped to the marble balustrade and smiled back at Harry.

"If you call Dorset another world," she said, "then you are right. But not otherwise, I fear."

He appeared to consider. "I think we need to discuss this," he said, amusement in his voice. "Shall I come up, or will you come down?"

She had no illusions about Benedict. He would not take it kindly that she had strayed before he could bring her safely to Lady Thane. She realized that the first place he would search for her was right here on the terrace. "I'll come down," she told Harry.

He held his hand up to help her down the last broad steps that led between rock gardens to the graveled walk below. Once on the walk, she withdrew her hand from his, and, she noted with gratitude, he did not try to hold it. In fact, as they strolled away from the building, down the walk leading farther into the gardens, he put himself out to be amusing. There were other couples and groups on the path, coming and going, and surely, Clare thought, there could be no criticism of her strolling in company with anyone she chose, even Harry Rowse.

He was, she knew, a gambler and a rake, but he was hanging out for a rich wife, so everyone said, to mend his fortunes, and she was clearly not suitable. So she set herself to enjoy his company—frankly admiring, and in sharp contrast to that of the forbidding nobleman she had eluded.

"Did you ever see anything so vulgar," he said, "as that veritable river wandering down the middle of the table? Nothing like it in the world, I am convinced."

"I could not believe that those were real fish," said

Clare. "But I do not quite see how one could contrive such real-looking creatures."

"No need to contrive," said Harry. "They were real fish. I can tell you this is the truth, for a lady seated near me found one leaping into her glass of champagne."

Clare gurgled with laughter. "Truly?"

"Truly," he affirmed. "I can tell you I haven't seen such a sight since my brother and I took a dislike to our tutor and . . . well, that's not germane to the issue at all."

They reached a turn in the path, but beyond, the flambeaux flickered reassuringly, and she allowed Harry to urge her gently forward. "Should you like something to drink?" he asked at last. "I should have thought of it when we were closer to the house!"

"Oh, I would!" she exclaimed. "But—"

"No buts," he said. "Here is a bench. If you will wait here for me, I shall bring you . . . What shall I bring you? A lemon squash?"

"That will be fine. But had I not better come with you?" She looked around her at the bench, the shrubs.

"And have Sir Alexander whisk you away?" said Harry in assumed shock. "To dance?"

"I'll wait here," said Clare. But in truth it was not Sir Alex she feared, but Lord Choate. Perhaps he had given up searching for her. She devoutly hoped so, for she was too restless and upset to endure further strictures from a man she barely could tolerate, and who, thank goodness, had no right to tell her anything.

But sitting alone on the bench, she began to consider her position. Surely she was wrong to allow herself to be lured so far from her friends, and while there were voices beyond, and now and then a footstep on the gravel, yet she felt suddenly very much alone.

But she did not have time enough to become truly frightened. Harry returned, bearing a tall glass of lemon squash. "I'm sorry to have been so long," he said. "I had trouble finding a waiter."

The glass was cold, and welcome. She began to sip it. "Were you frightened here?" said Harry, sitting beside her on the bench. "Did . . . anyone come?"

"No," she said. "Not precisely frightened, although I confess I did not like it very much. It was darker than I thought at first. But . . . Isn't this delightful! I do appreciate your bringing me the drink."

It tickled her nose. "This is quite the best lemon squash I ever had," she told him in a rush. "It is so tingly!"

Harry laughed softly. "They do not stint on the soda water. The regent, you know, thinks in large terms!"

She had half-finished her drink before she spoke again. "I really think this is more than I want. Mr. Rowse, I think . . ." She truly thought the drink was too much for her. After her exertions on the dance floor, perhaps the cold drink was upsetting her stomach. At least, she was feeling very strange.

"I think," she began again, "that we had better . . ."

Mr. Rowse's arm, which had stolen along the back of the bench, now encircled her shoulders, and turned her toward him. Instinct told her to throw the drink in his face, but her fingers would not obey her.

Mr. Rowse, with his free hand, took her chin firmly in his fingers and tilted it up. His smile was still admiring, but there was a quality in it now that turned her blood to ice.

How foolish—how very *stupid*—she had been!

8.

The drink was too strong—she realized that now. The drink had been laced with alcohol, and she would be lucky to get away. She had no hope of escape.

Harry Rowse's arm now moved downward from her shoulders to her waist, and his clasp was as one of iron. She should have been suspicious, said a scolding voice in her mind. Any lady of any countenance would never have allowed herself to stroll even in broad daylight with such a one as Harry Rowse.

The liquor exerted a paralyzing influence upon her. She knew vaguely she should struggle, but there seemed to be a great gap between the wish and the deed. The world reduced itself to Harry—his hold on her, his hand caressing her throat . . .

"Pray do not, Mr. Rowse!" she managed to say at last. "Only think of the consequence—"

"The consequence, my kitten, will be an unalloyed delight." Harry chuckled deep in his throat. "For me . . . even if you disagree. But I have been thinking of naught else since I first saw you. And—"

"And I was stupid enough—"

His lips on hers muffled any further protest. She could not breathe. She felt strangely as if a part of her had left her body and looked on from a place somewhere above her left shoulder, with exceedingly great displeasure, but a torpor spread throughout her limbs.

And suddenly she was released. Harry's arm was snatched away, and she nearly fell backward on the bench. The drink was beginning to wear off, she realized with gratitude, for she could move again, and her legs obeyed her. To a point; they would not allow her, yet, to flee.

But Harry was not able just now to return to his original design. He was standing on the gravel path, face to face with a man who clearly had come to Clare's rescue, in the nick of time, she had no doubt.

She was wild with relief, and even welcomed her rescuer—Lord Choate. She was grateful beyond measure, but still she could have wished it were someone else who had found her.

Wishfully, a complete stranger!

Choate was seething with fury. He had hurled Rowse away from Clare, and now stood in the gravel walk, artfully between Clare and her attacker, lightly dusting his fingers. "I wonder whether I shall feel clean again?" he said thoughtfully, looking at his hands. "Probably by tomorrow. But I confess to a bit of curiosity, Rowse. How did you think you would come out of this with credit?"

"I imagine," said Harry, drawling, "that you will give me all the credit I shall need on this."

"I fail to see your reasoning," said Benedict. The flambeau nearest them flickered—or else it was the tiny muscle along the end of Benedict's jaw that tightened—and then gave every sign of dying. Neither man on the walk so much as noticed.

"Surely," Benedict added, "if this story got abroad, you would find it difficult to so much as speak to any respectable female. And then, of course, you would probably find it more comfortable to sojourn abroad."

"Now, I wonder why you would think that," commented Harry. "When I doubt that you will find much credit yourself, were you to tell the story abroad."

A little silence greeted this remark. Clare was on her feet by this time, and was fully occupied in overcoming her dizziness.

Harry laughed softly. "I wonder why you took such interest in the lady. Surely you have no reason to follow her through the paths of this most enchanting and seductive garden? Or have you? Perhaps a certain lady of our acquaintance would be well-advised to look to her affairs, lest her rightful interests be infringed upon."

"I should call you out for that," said Benedict with a studied air of carelessness. "Too bad that dueling has lost its *ton*." Then, with a savage intensity he added, "But I warn you, Rowse, one more word from you and I will deal with you, swords, pistols, whatever your choice. Although my own choice runs more along the lines of horsewhipping."

Harry Rowse was shaken. He had no wish to confront Benedict Choate at the opposite end of a dueling ground, no matter what the weapon. He had lost the game this time, he reflected, but it was not the end of things. As with many another man, failure meant only determined pursuance, and while he had lost this round, there would be another time. And perhaps, another time, he could deal a double blow.

For he wanted Clare—not to set her up in any kind of establishment. For one thing, he didn't have the money, and for another thing, his fancy was very soon diverted. But want her he did. And perhaps, if he played his cards right, and luck was with him, he could in that same ambition deal with Lord Choate as well. He would have to give it thought.

Just now, he declined any offer of a duel with Choate. "For I think the quarrel is not worth such an effort," said Rowse carefully. "And a duel could not but reflect upon your motives, my dear Choate. And if I am right—and I'm not usually mistaken about this kind of thing, you know—you would not come out of the affair scot-free, either."

So saying, he stepped around his adversary on the walk and vanished in the direction of Carlton House, leaving Benedict, a prey of mixed emotions, alone with Clare.

Clare had mastered her undependable knees, and was reduced to a small trembling that she could not stop. She looked up at Benedict, and began to speak, but could not utter a sound.

It was as well, for Choate was not in the mood to hear anything she said. Turning on her, now that Rowse was out of sight, he said, "You *idiot!*"

She drew in a quick breath. She knew she had been an idiot, but she didn't relish hearing it from anyone else.

"I cannot think what possessed you to allow yourself to take three steps in public with Harry Rowse. Surely you knew what he was? . . . You don't answer? Well, at least you know what he is now." He peered at her. "Don't you?"

Suddenly her spirit returned to her. "Well, since you ask," she said in a rush, "yes, I do. But at least he was amiable."

It was an unfortunate choice of words. "Amiable! Is that your term for it? Does that mean that anyone who smiles at you is going to lead you down a dark path and—"

"No!" she exclaimed sharply. "But you are always such a great scold, and I confess I am weary of hearing about my faults. You came to rescue me as though I were a stray puppy on the street."

"I came because you had left my protection—"

"Your protection!"

"And," he pursued darkly, "I think you must agree that my protection is not to be scorned? What would you have done?"

The question was one that Clare herself was beginning to consider. It did not help that it came from Benedict at this moment. She could not answer.

"So I thought," he said.

His anger was holding at its high pitch. He had a few items on his mind, and, so far from being an urbane man with complete control over his baser instincts, he simply gave his tongue loose rein.

"While you feel that any escape from a dull escort— such as I gather you consider me—is justified, let me tell you that in society it is not the thing. A well-brought-up lady stays with her dancing partner, or her escort, until she is restored to the chaperon with whom she came. She also says, as prettily as she can manage, thank you to the gentleman who partnered her. And—should the occasion arise, as, I am sure you need not be told, does not happen often—she says thank you to her rescuer as well. Perhaps you think it would be exciting to have two men duel over you? Let me tell you, it is not. I should feel soiled were I to duel with Harry Rowse, and if I did call him out, it would not be over you."

Clare mustered her dignity. "Then why, my dear sir, did you follow me out here?"

"Because you haven't the sense that a goose has!"

"Indeed?" Clare quaked inwardly, but she knew instinctively that if she meekly allowed Benedict to read the riot act over her, she would collapse, and—probably—die on the spot. While it might prove embarrassing for Benedict were this to happen, yet she did not feel it wise. "And I suppose that no lady ever found herself weary of your company in such a degree that any escape would serve?"

The flambeau guttered and gave out at that moment, but not soon enough so that she missed the glitter in his eyes as he leaned toward her. At that moment she was almost afraid of him. But still, she thought, she would welcome whatever happened next.

Nothing happened. "My firm belief," he said, ignoring

her outrageous remark, "is that you ought to be kept close—preferably in a cloistered convent—until you get some sense."

She already repented of her provocative outburst, but she would not apologize. She was suddenly infinitely weary of this whole evening—of Harry Rowse, of Benedict Choate, of Alexander Ferguson, of London itself.

Without a word she turned and started back toward Carlton House. Benedict's footsteps sounded on the gravel behind her, and soon he had caught up to her. He offered her his arm, but she pretended not to see it. He took her, at last, to a door different from the one she had come out of. It opened onto a smaller room, which at the moment was not occupied.

They crossed the room in silence, to the door opposite, which led onto the grand octagonal entrance hall with the great double staircase leading to upper rooms.

"Go upstairs," he told her, not quite roughly, "and straighten your attire. I will make your excuses to Lady Thane."

Without a word she did as she was bid. Across the room and up the stairs. Halfway up, she turned and looked back. Benedict was standing where she had left him, seeing that she was safe as far as he could.

He had saved her from a fate she did not want to think about. She managed a wan smile, and then continued up the stairs.

Benedict's conscience smote him. He had been too rough on her, he believed. It would have been enough to send that scoundrel on his way, and then let the child cry herself back to normal. Why had he gone after her, hammer and tongs? Something Harry had said—that Marianna Morton might be jealous—came to him, and with it the reflection that he knew too well that lady's capacity for lacerated feelings.

It was a ridiculous affair, of course, and he for one would never breathe a word of what had just transpired. Harry was wide of the mark, of course. Benedict had not the slightest interest in a schoolgirl. Or even this maddening female just out of the schoolroom.

And yet, as he remembered her stricken look just now as she ascended the stairs, a queer misgiving passed over his mind. And her look of forlorn loneliness stayed with him as he moved through the crowd to find Lady Thane.

9.

In the meantime, Clare, unaware of how powerfully her appearance had worked upon her distant kinsman, entered the retiring room, a delightful confection in the French fashion of a decade or so before, in gold and white.

Hardly noticing her surroundings, she longed above all to lay her head down so that the room would not swim so distractingly. The outer room held half a dozen modishly gowned women, including the severe Lady Hertford, whose taste, it was said, had commanded the prince's purse in furnishing Carlton House. Lady Hertford, tall, blond, and possessed of unmoved poise, glanced at Clare, and Clare felt that that powerful woman could read her thoughts.

She passed on into the next room, one of several that opened from the little gilt salon. A little bergère chair stood near an open window, and Clare sank into it gratefully. Her head swam alarmingly, and for a few moments she feared she was about to be disgracefully sick. She was the victim of more than the emotional aftermath of that dreadful scene in the garden. The liquor that Harry Rowse had poured—with a free hand!—into her drink addled her wits and churned her stomach. She was, she realized with horror, half-foxed! She closed her eyes in despair.

But her thoughts, while her head rested upon the back of the chair, swam quite as much as her head. She had made a mull of the whole thing—all of Grandmama's hopes for her had come to naught. She was distressed to believe that Benedict had been right: she was too young to go on in London. Everything was new and exciting, and she had lacked the balance necessary to deal with what was after all a very tempting life.

She finally believed that she had two choices. Fortunately, Benedict had rescued her—twice, as it happened, in recent days—and she had no very great disaster to overcome. She could go home to Penryck Abbey, and come back—if Lady Thane could be persuaded—next year. And having a taste of London, she thought she could spend the intervening months with profit, preparing for a life she knew better now.

Or, she thought, closing her eyes, she could marry Sir Alexander. If Lady Thane were right—and she usually had a very fine sense of social nuances—then Sir Alexander would be offering for her very soon. And Clare, disgracefully, was not ready to give an answer.

She was not sure whether the advantages of her own establishment, with ample funds in hand, would outweigh the disadvantage of listening everlastingly to Sir Alexander's constant flow of untimely information.

I wish I had not come! she thought fiercely.

But at least Harry Rowse's attempt would not be common knowledge. She could count on Benedict to keep such an incident to himself.

Almost as though her mind spoke aloud, the words came to her. "But Benedict is so disgusted with the brat— that's what he calls her, you know, the Penryck brat. . . ."

An eavesdropper never hears good of herself! But Clare could not have pulled herself away, or made her presence known, for half of Dorset.

A murmur from the unseen listener was indistinguishable, but the nearer voice spoke again, and this time Clare recognized it. Marianna Morton was holding forth, and Clare realized that the ladies were in the small room next door, with the window open, so that Marianna's words came out one window and could be clearly heard through the next.

"Well, my dear," said Marianna to her unseen audience, "it is a privilege of family, you know. Benedict has some remote connection, so remote he hasn't thought of it for years, with the Penrycks. But of course, with the child underfoot in London everywhere you go, he can't help but be aware of her."

Underfoot! Clare squirmed in her chair but could not muster enough character to leave.

"One can't blame her, I suppose," continued Marianna, "in hanging out for a rich husband. She has the kind of beauty, you know, that fades quickly. One season, or at best two, and she'll begin to show signs of wear. These blonds, you know, always look faded . . ."

Clare finally summoned enough anger to get to her feet, ready to leave. But she did not leave quite soon enough, for Marianna had one more word to say, and that proved to be the worst.

"Choate told me about an incident in Oxford Street, where the foolish child caused a dreadful scene. It is too bad she hasn't learned a little decorum. Benedict was so disgusted—and I must say I agreed with him when we discussed what is best to do. Just ignore her, I told him. But he said, and I confess I must agree with that too, that he would never know what dreadful thing she will next do. I trust I am not around—and yet Benedict finds such release in talking to me that it is selfish of me . . ."

Clare's feet were released from their paralysis on that last word. So Benedict had discussed Clare in detail with the raven-haired beauty he was to wed. And Clare had thought him the soul of honor, a man who could and would keep his own counsel, and not spread her missteps abroad. Well, if he had made much of the Oxford Street incident, then how much more would he need consolation from his Marianna when the Harry Rowse incident was aired between them?

But one more word came through the window. Marianna said, with a certain vindictive edge to her carrying voice, "I wish I had the rule of that brat for a month!"

And for the first time the listener spoke intelligibly. "I wonder whether I detect a bit of jealousy in you?"

Clare did not wait for an answer. Suddenly fearing that the speakers would emerge and catch sight of her, Clare fairly flew across the small salon and down the stairs. Surely, if Marianna Morton had her way, no one would ever forget Clare Penryck's disastrous first season. Clare herself had thought her escapades were unfortunate, but certainly not scandalous, yet, with Marianna's peculiar twist to them, Clare would never be able again to show her face in London.

She paused halfway down the staircase. The ballroom below was, to her great surprise, still full. It was almost as though no time at all had elapsed, or as though the participants had remained frozen for an hour, until Clare came to set them in motion again.

But she realized that it was only that she had not been gone long. She glanced over the crowd, searching for a face that she might know. The only one she saw at first was Benedict, who caught her eye fleetingly before clearly looking away. So, she would not avoid him this time, since the last time she had been sadly ill-advised. But she would not ask his escort to Lady Thane, either. In fact, all she wanted in this world was not to see Lord Benedict Choate, ever again.

She reached the bottom of the stair, to find Ned Fenton at hand. "Good evening," he said with a warm smile. "I feared I had missed you in the squeeze. The regent certainly knows how to entertain, doesn't he? Are you enjoying yourself?"

He reached his hand out to help her down the last step. She faltered some kind of response, and he added, "Choate told me you were here."

So Benedict did not confide in Marianna alone! Here was his good friend, Ned Fenton, and Benedict had obviously (thought Clare) told him all that had transpired in the garden.

"Indeed?" said Clare stiffly. She dared not follow her instinct and rail at Ned. Not just because he had always been kind to her—her state of mind was too riotous to consider such niceties—but simply because if she did not hold tight rein on her tongue, she would fall into disaster. "He couldn't wait to confide in you, could he?"

Ned looked bewildered. "I don't know exactly what you mean," he said, puzzled, "but I assure you, he said nothing untoward."

Clare flushed. Perhaps she had been wrong, and Benedict had not told Ned. Yet. But she surely judged that Benedict was a rattle instead of the man of integrity she had thought him. And if he had not told Ned already, then it was only a matter of time until he did so.

"I am on my way to Lady Thane," she said, her voice trembling in spite of all her effort. "Pray let me pass."

And then Sir Alexander arrived. Unfortunately, he was a man, at best, of little sensitivity, and now he blundered as badly as possible. Ignoring the signs of brittle anger in Clare, and the hurt puzzlement of Ned Fenton, Sir Alexander greeted them both ponderously.

"I have been looking for you, Miss Penryck, this long time," he said. "I thought we might stand up for the quadrille. A lively dance which I do enjoy, even though I know the steps only imperfectly." He beamed impartially on them both. "But I fancy the next sets are all made up. We shall try again later."

"Have you seen Lady Thane?" Clare faltered, not knowing how else to answer Sir Alex.

"Yes, she is in the Chinese Room," said Sir Alex. "I left her there when I began to search for you. Someone," he added in obvious disbelief, "said that you had ventured outside the house, into the garden, but since Lady Thane and my sister are upstairs, and I knew you weren't with me, then I took leave to counter such a canard. Never, I said, would Miss Penryck stoop to such a disgraceful action—"

Clare had been sorely tried, and now she reached the end of her limited patience. She cried, "Oh, be quiet!" in an unfortunately carrying voice.

The measure of her error lay to her appalled eyes in the faces of her two companions. Sheer horror lay in Sir Alexander's blue eyes, the color of a Scottish lake in winter. But Ned Fenton's brow creased in grave concern.

He said quickly, "Let me take you to Lady Thane. I fear you are ill."

She was aware of a little circle forming around her and the two men, just before tears came quickly to film over her vision.

"Ill!" she cried out. "I am! I wish you will not bother me!"

"As you wish," said Sir Alexander stiffly, stepping back, unfortunately treading on the toes of a curious onlooker. "I fancy that I was mistaken, then, in thinking that you could not be outside the house in the gardens. With whom were you, then, Lord Choate? In that case, I collect that he was the soul of honor."

"Don't speak such fustian!" she cried, and started blindly away. She scarcely knew what direction she was traveling. Her eyes had misted over, and even if she could have seen, it is most likely that her mind could not have taken in what she saw. For she was near fainting, and sobbing wildly.

Making her way with difficulty through the crowd, she ran into a veritable brick wall, only to find herself against the vast abdomen of the prince regent.

"Here, here!" said that astonished man. "What's all this! What's all this!"

Since there was no answer, she did not try to explain, but only cried out inarticulately, and went on her way. Her progress was marked by a murmur of swelling disapproval behind her. She did not care, even though she thought, bleakly, that one day she would care very much.

She scarcely knew how it all happened, but at length she was in the Tottens' coach, alone with Lady Thane. Sir Alex had directed the coachman to take his passengers to Grosvenor Square at once, and then return to collect Sir Alex and his sister. It was a welcome respite for Clare, leaning back against the velvet squabs and letting her head throb as it would.

For the liquor that had been in the lemon squash had at last worn itself off, and, while Clare was not sure of everything she had said, she was quite positive that however bad she had felt before, she had now put the cap on her desolation.

Her first—and only—season in London was now an unmitigated catastrophe. And if she had not realized it herself in her rapidly sobering mind, Lady Thane was able to confirm it.

"Never have I seen such an overweening display of rudeness! I cannot imagine what can have possessed you to act in such a fashion! My dear child, only my love for your mother prevents me from putting the event in the proper light, but I can say that it will be weeks before I can raise my head in society again."

"I'm sorry."

"And *sorry* won't do it, Clare. I shall not even go into society until next season. What on earth can have occurred to set you off in such an ill-bred way?"

Clare could not think over her throbbing head. She might have mentioned the liquor in the lemon squash, but that would lead to Harry Rowse. Or she could have commented on the comments of Marianna Morton, but then she would have to confess to eavesdropping, and then to the reason why she was in the retiring room at all, and that would lead to Harry Rowse.

"My head aches," she said, knowing it was only a feeble extenuation.

"I should think it would," said Lady Thane. "I vow I cannot face tomorrow with a calm set of nerves myself. But I should have known this would happen."

Her curiosity aroused at last, Clare said, "How could you have known this, ma'am?"

"It is my fault," announced Lady Thane as the carriage turned into Grosvenor Street and debouched into the square. The rectangular park in the center of the square was dark, and the iron railings glimmered faintly in the lights flanking the doors of the houses lining all sides of the square.

"My fault," she continued. "I should have responded to your grandmother at once, telling her that she simply did not understand how things can go awry in London. It's been fifty years since she set foot in town, and manners have changed greatly. But it is never amiss to acquire a little polish, and perhaps that is what has happened tonight."

"I'll never go anywhere in town again," muttered Clare.

"Of course not," said Lady Thane, having talked herself into a more comfortable frame of mind. "We must bid farewell to Sir Alexander. That sister of his is such a stickler for the proprieties that I fear she will never get over this evening."

"I did not want him," said Clare, through a lump in her throat that threatened to overset her.

Lady Thane affected not to hear. "But perhaps a life in the country might appeal to him. Surely to be Lady Ferguson would be a pleasant state, and no one in Scotland will care about your decorum," said Lady Thane, dismissing an entire nation out of hand.

"I won't see him," said Clare. "Even if he were so . . . kind as to forgive me, I won't see him. I couldn't!" She turned a tear-streaked face to Lady Thane.

"Well, well," said Lady Thane, falling a victim to unjustified hope, "perhaps it will all look better in the morning. We'll just have a good night's sleep. I find that a glass of hot milk often calms one's nerves, and we'll see what is to be done."

Such a restorative plan was destined not to take place. For inside the foyer there was bad news. Swann, the coachman from Penryck Abbey, waited on the chair usually occupied by the stripling footman, and sprang to his feet when the door opened.

"Miss Clare . . ." he began, and then could go no further. Darrin took pity on him and said with oppressive solemnity, "I fear this is bad news, and cannot wait until the morning, my lady. Lady Penryck has died."

It was too much. Clare sank to the floor in a swoon. When she came to herself, she was in bed. Lying propped up against pillows dampened with her unstemmed tears, she thought, with meager consolation: Now at least Grandmama will never know how I've failed her. How I've disgraced her and the family name, as Miss Morton said. How right Marianna was! The thought did nothing to raise her spirits.

She would leave for home tomorrow morning, and never, never show her face in London again. She was a failure, a disgrace, a hopeless country clod, and a chit too soon out of the schoolroom.

But at least she would not have to marry Sir Alexander, she thought. She would go home to Penryck Abbey and live a quiet, retired life, doing what Great-Uncle Horsham told her to do, and minding everything that she was bid.

And I won't regret London for even one minute! she thought fiercely, just before she fell asleep.

10.

Penryck Abbey stood on an eminence overlooking the River Stour and bore little resemblance to the monastic establishment which gave it its name. The monks had lived in what was now a disused wing until Henry VIII's time, when they found their ordered life in shambles.

Later Penrycks had added to the original structure, none daring to tear it down, even though they would not have admitted to the least superstition. Yet the monks' cells had fallen into ruin, as had the fortunes of the Penrycks themselves.

Made of mellow brick, the main part of the new building had been erected in Queen Anne's day, and it was these spacious rooms that Clare loved the best. She had now been home for three days and had settled back into the old familiar life as though she had never been away. The strenuous days in London were only a memory already, and even though in the middle of the night Clare would wake suddenly with the scene at the regent's ball vivid in her mind, it too was losing its urgency.

Her own bedroom looked down across the hills toward the river, past the little clumps of trees and the sheep upon the grassy slopes. Far below was the church spire, where bells were rung on Sunday, and if the wind were right, she could hear them from here.

She wandered aimlessly those first days from room to room. Budge was happy, back in the land she loved, and put on airs in the servants' hall. For the first time in a long time, Clare longed for her parents. She had learned from Lady Thane that her mother had been a great beauty, a girl of biddable temperament, and sweet of disposition.

But Clare herself knew that she partook more of the Penryck heritage than she did the Tresillian. Her father, the late baron, was improvident, and optimistic, and a gambler. This had often been pointed out to Clare as a bad example. But yet he had been full of charm, and laughed a lot, and suddenly she longed for him with all of her heart. She had been only five when her parents had been killed and she had come to live with her invalid Grandmama. But the portraits in the upper gallery had served to keep her memory green.

She had not gone up to the gallery since her return. She knew why, too, although she would not quite put it into words. She kept away from any reminder of Benedict Choate.

There was one thing she could rejoice in, she told herself. Never again would she need to see that tattling, superior, arrogant, and thoroughly unlikable man!

But still, until she heard from Uncle Horsham, she could not settle down at Penryck Abbey. He might hail her up to Wiltshire, where he lived in some grand state, according to what Grandmama had told her. "My own brother," said Grandmama, "my only relative, one might say, and I hate to say it of him, but he is living up to the limit of his income. There will be little enough left, and no doubt what he will leave you is small enough, but added to what I can give you, there will be a respectable dowry."

The dowry didn't matter to Clare. But Uncle Horsham's wishes did. Well, she would soon enough find out what Uncle Horsham wanted her to do, for Mr. Austin was coming to the abbey this morning to tell her how she was to go on.

She was sitting in the salon, her thoughts vacant, when he was announced. He came into the room with his curious crablike gait, almost as though his wish was to turn around and leave at once. But he was a kindly man, mostly bald, with a gray fringe around his shiny dome, and an air of mustiness that invaded his chambers and seemed to have become part of the man himself.

She rose to greet him warmly, and ordered tea for him. Setting down his empty cup, he looked around him.

"My, my," he said with a sigh, "it surely doesn't seem right not to see Lady Penryck sitting in that green chair, her little dog at her feet, and holding her cane."

"I suppose you will miss her nearly as much as I," said Clare. "I feel sorry that I was not here when she died."

"Now, now, young lady," said Mr. Austin, wagging a square-tipped finger. "It was her wish to have you go. And she was so pleased with the reports that Lady Thane sent back. An invitation to the prince regent's ball, I think she told me. Is that right? My, my, I surely envy you. Tell me, is the regent as . . . well, obese . . . as they say?"

Upon Clare's assurance that he was indeed as portly as rumor had it, Mr. Austin moved smoothly on to her own future.

"Now, just let me find my spectacles, and we will get down to business. I know that you have a head for this kind of thing, not like most females, I am sure. But Lady Penryck could not take care of all things here, and I know she relied much upon you." He put on his spectacles and at once peered at her over the top of them. "Is Lady Melvin here? Would you like me to call her for you?"

"No, Mr. Austin," said Clare, puzzled. "I cannot imagine why I should wish her here. This is, after all, my business, is it not? Perhaps you can tell me at once what my great-uncle wishes me to do?"

"Your great-uncle." Mr. Austin let the words rest in the air. "Now, I fear, that is just what I can't tell you."

"I wonder why not?" said Clare. "Hasn't he been in touch with you?"

"Actually, my dear," Mr. Austin sputtered, "I have not been in touch with him."

Clare looked her puzzlement. "But I don't understand . . ."

"Of course you don't," he said heartily. He seemed to be in two minds—one was to pat Clare on the head as one does a small tot and go on his own way, and the other was the necessity to deal with her as a reasoning person. He swung pendulumlike between the two.

"You remember your great-uncle?" he said.

"No, I never saw him. He was Grandmama's half-brother, I know that." Clare eyed Mr. Austin with skepticism. There was something odd about Mr. Austin's manner, and she wished he would get to the point. But he was off again on another tangent.

"Lady Penryck was the daughter of the second wife. This made Lord Horsham—your great-uncle—her half-brother. A man of great eccentricity, you know. Lived on his capital," Mr. Austin said, gamely exposing the iniquity of Lord Horsham. "Why the estate wasn't entailed, I don't know. Or—do I remember?—he was able to break the entail. At any rate, there was nothing left."

His odd phrasing struck Clare. "You say *was*."

"That was why your grandmother wrote her new will."

"New will?" Clare echoed faintly.

"Just three weeks ago, she gave me the instructions," he said, "and she signed it one week before she died." He beamed in satisfaction that at least one loose end was neatly tied up.

"So," he added, "you must not count on much of a dowry. There will be money enough to keep the abbey going as it has been. *If* you exercise strict economy. But of course that won't matter, since from what I hear, you will not be living here long, is that right?"

Archly smiling, he waggled his finger again. "A certain wealthy man has been charmed by your pretty face, your grandmama told me. But I am far from surprised," he added, "for you must have set the world of London a-reeling with excitement."

A shadow crossed her face. Reeling, perhaps, but not with admiration. And Sir Alexander's offer was as good as whistled down the wind. Mr. Austin's perambulations were disconcerting, to say the least.

"Not quite," she said with a faint smile.

"Well, your guardian will see to your swift wedding, I am sure. He is a man of great integrity, and of the highest ton, I am told, so we needn't worry about that, need we?"

"But what about Uncle Horsham?" she persisted, trying to get at least one end of this bewildering skein into her hands. "You said there was nothing left. Does that mean he died?"

"Oh, yes. A month ago. Just after you went to London. Didn't your grandmother write to you about it? No, I can see she did not. Well, it is not fitting for me to say what I think, but females in business . . ." He left his thought unfinished, but it was clear to Clare.

"Well, then, if Uncle Horsham is gone, there is nobody else to turn to," said Clare. "But I don't understand. You did mention my guardian. Please, Mr. Austin, I must beg you to tell me at once how I am left. If I have a guardian, then I am not on my own?"

"Oh, no, no. It would be most improper for that to be the case, you know. I could not have approved a will leaving you without a legal guardian. He must sign the papers, you know, for your marriage settlement, when it comes time for that. And I must expect that any moment, mustn't I? And your guardian will have full control of the funds and of the farms here at the abbey, and of course of the household here, until your husband takes over. And I am sure that he—your guardian, that is—will see that you have a proper establishment here."

"But I have an establishment here!" said Clare, resorting to a barely concealed mutiny to cover her growing dismay.

"But not quite *comme il faut*, as they say. But then, it is not my province to instruct you on this. It will be your guardian's obligation, and I am sure he has a strong sense of responsibility toward his duties."

Clare rose to her feet and took a turn around the room. "Mr. Austin," she said, turning to face him, "it would be best, I think, were you to tell me directly what my grandmother's will provides. I collect there have been great changes in her plans since she made me acquainted with them a few years ago."

"Oh, my, my, yes!" exclaimed Mr. Austin. "And I confess that I am much more pleased with them than I was before. I could not quite like, you know, a man of Lord Horsham's age, so unsuitable, you know, so—so to speak—out of tune with a young person."

"Then who?" demanded Clare. Something in the tone of her voice must have warned Mr. Austin.

"You will be pleased to know that you will be subject to the guardianship of a member of the Penryck family instead of your grandmother's."

Even a growing suspicion did not prepare Clare for Mr. Austin's fateful announcement.

"Your guardian is Lord Benedict Choate!"

The room tilted and straightened again.

"Now, what do you say to that, young lady?"

Stonily Clare answered him. "I wish I were dead!"

11.

Clare's expressed wish for an instant demise would have found an echo in the town house of Lord Benedict Choate on Mount Street. His secretary, Ronald Audley, had been in two minds about presenting the fateful letter to his employer.

Of a certainty, it would cause a tempest. Ronald's only question was choosing a time to present it when the storm might be minimized. Certainly the morning the letter arrived was not the most propitious time, for Lord Choate had spent the night at Watier's, and while, being usually lucky at cards, he had apparently won a great deal of money—his valet, Grinstead, had reported a profusion of bills and vowels in his master's possession—he had also drunk deeply and not wisely.

So it was not until the next day that Ronald inserted the letter neatly between an invitation from the Countess Lieven, the new issue of *The Quarterly Review,* and a note from Choate's betrothed, Miss Morton. Ronald had not opened the latter, but he was astute enough to guess at its contents, and he thought that his employer's response to it would be wrathful enough to overlook the closely written epistle from Mr. Austin in Dorset.

Fortunately, before Choate could open his mail that morning, Mr. Ruffin, his legal man of affairs, called upon him.

"Good morning, Ruffin," said Choate lazily. "Pray have some of this coffee before you tell me whatever dire news you have."

When Choate had fortified himself with a second cup and civilly allowed Ruffin to finish his own, he asked, "What brings you to see me so early, Ruffin? I have not yet opened my mail, as you see. But I shall postpone that delight, since I expect nothing of value in it. There will be no letter from Lady Lindsay. At least . . . Is there a letter from my sister, Audley?"

"No, my lord. You will remember that she is due back in London at any time now."

"Yes, yes, of course I remember it. Although I must admit that I am glad Lindsay has Primula in charge now, for a young female can have a devastating effect on one's own life, you know, Ruffin."

Ruffin, well-acquainted with Lord Choate, permitted himself a smile. "Very much so, my lord. Although I might venture to suggest that you find your life without excitement since Lady Lindsay's marriage?"

"Ruffin, you know me too well. But I apprehend that there will be further changes in store for me." Clearly, thought Ronald Audley, seeing the frown between the heavy black eyebrows of his employer, he was thinking of his intended marriage with Miss Morton, a lady whose advent into the household would terminate Ronald's very pleasant employment. He could not endure the future Lady Choate peering over his shoulder all the time.

But Ruffin said abruptly, "I collect then that you are willing to accept the charge?"

Abruptly brought back to ground, Choate gave Ruffin a swift glance and said, more to himself than to his companions, "Is there a choice?"

Mr. Ruffin shook his head. "I see none, my lord."

"After all," said Choate, "it was arranged when we were both infants."

Ruffin looked blankly at him. "I beg your pardon, my lord. It was arranged scarcely a month ago."

Choate looked at his man of affairs and then at his secretary, who suddenly looked acutely uncomfortable. "I do believe," said Choate, "that we are traveling upon different roads. I was referring to my marriage with Miss Morton. And you, Ruffin?"

"I was referring to this letter from Dorset," said Mr. Ruffin, producing a paper from an inner pocket. "I collect that this information was conveyed to you at the same time."

Choate looked at Ronald Audley, one black brow lifted in inquiry. "The information, Audley?"

"In your mail this morning, my lord," said the secretary in a neutral tone.

There was silence while Lord Choate riffled through the cards of invitation, the short notes, ignoring the one in Miss Morton's narrow, spiky hand, until he arrived at the letter in question. "Pray forgive me," he said mechanically, "while I possess myself of the information that both of you seem to know already."

He missed the glance that the two men exchanged, a glance of apprehension and anticipation of a storm to break over their heads. They were not disappointed.

"Impossible!" said Lord Choate. "Ridiculous! I wonder what kind of hen-wit this Austin—is that his name?—is, to think I'd . . ."

He rose and in unwonted agitation crossed to the sideboard and poured another cup of coffee for himself. He emptied his cup before he felt himself sufficiently in control to speak again. But while his eyes flashed fire, yet his tone was civil enough.

"Well, Ruffin? How can you get me out of this coil?"

"My lord," said Mr. Ruffin, having anticipated just such a demand, and prepared himself, "it cannot be done. At least with propriety."

"Propriety? There can be nothing more improper than to set a bachelor like myself as guardian over that girl!"

Mr. Ruffin remained silent, and Lord Choate read the signs. He was in many ways arrogant, and often unfeeling, but no one had ever accused him of being unintelligent. With as good grace as he could muster, he said ruefully, "Perhaps you will explain it to me, Ruffin. I myself do not quite see the inevitability of this development."

"Well, of course," said Mr. Ruffin with a deprecatory cough. "No one need point out that you are related to the Penrycks, on your late mother's side of the family." Choate nodded impatiently. "And of course, there is no one of that family left." He thought over his statement, checking it for accuracy, and then added, "Except this child. Miss Clare Penryck."

Mr. Ruffin's life did not lead him into society, and he was unaware that Miss Clare Penryck had indeed come to town, and was in unmistakable fact not a child.

Choate, for his part, was searching his brain for a fact that had so far eluded him, but now he remembered it. "What about Horsham? He is the guardian of that girl. She told me herself. Horsham! Not me. Ruffin, I have never known you to make a mistake, and we must now lay the blame upon this Mr. Austin from Dorset. Let us hope that his shoulders are broad enough—"

But Mr. Ruffin was dogged. "It is no mistake, my lord. Lord Horsham was indeed to have served. But of course now he cannot. He died a month ago, just before Lady Penryck wrote her new will."

Choate was thunderstruck. "Dead? I had not heard that."

Mr. Ruffin's conservative soul could not refrain from adding, "Just in time too, my lord, else he would have been on the rocks."

Benedict took a turn around the room. At length, he came to a decision. "I cannot take the guardianship. Some-one else—"

"There is no one else of the family, my lord," said Mr. Ruffin firmly. "A great pity, but there it is. And of course, when the happy event of your marriage occurs, there would be no suggestion of impropriety. I should imagine Miss Morton would be just the right influence for a child."

Benedict had thought swiftly while his man of affairs was prosing on. A great pity, was it? But nothing as to the consequences that lay ahead. Although Benedict had no very clear vision of those consequences, no man of sense could deny that putting an impulsive and wayward girl into the hands of Miss Morton, whose opinions were well known to him, could lead only to disaster.

But suddenly Benedict relaxed his grim frown. One corner of his mouth tilted momentarily, and to the surprise of Mr. Ruffin and also of Ronald Audley, Benedict smiled, the rare smile that transformed his face and was part of his unexpected charm.

"I have the answer," said Benedict. "Mr. Austin shall receive a letter from you, Ruffin, accepting this charge, as one of the duties I owe my family, and telling him that Lady Lindsay will travel to Penryck Abbey within a few days."

"Lady Lindsay!" said Mr. Ruffin, beaming. "Just the thing, my lord. She will know what to do."

"At least I am sure I hope so," said Benedict. "Marriage will have settled her to a degree."

However, Benedict was destined to sustain yet another shock. Two days passed, and the letter from Ruffin to Dorset was on its way. Benedict considered that his problem—which had quite daunted him at first, he admitted privately—had been handsomely solved. Surely Primula, having benefited by the strictest of governesses and a tight chaperonage when she at length came out into society, would curb the wayward tendencies of the slip of a girl from Dorset.

Only momentarily did Benedict reflect that it might be a

shame to subdue Clare's freshness, turning her into simply another young lady, as like to all the others as peas in a pod.

When Lord and Lady Lindsay returned at last from their prolonged honeymoon in Italy, the first call they made was on her elder brother, Benedict. He was a half-brother, of course, but Primula loved him dearly, and she greeted him now with an openhearted embrace.

"Well, Primula," said Benedict. "You have certainly become more handsome in the past half-year. Lindsay, my congratulations."

Lindsay, his eyes holding a secret twinkle, acknowledged the compliment, watching his beloved and her brother settle down to a prolonged visit.

Sometime later, when he judged the moment propitious, Benedict dropped his bomb. "I daresay you are out of touch with the *on-dits* of the town," he said.

"Very much so," said Primula. "You are, I collect, about to tell me something shocking. If it is that your wedding is off, pray tell me at once!"

Benedict repressed a slight grimace. "No, it is not off. Postponed for a while, however."

"Her choice?"

"I suppose not. She had spoken, you know, of a spring wedding, but now she has fixed the date of October. But . . . we shall see. However, that is not what I wanted to tell you."

"Benedict, I cannot like your marriage to that woman. She will rule with an iron hand—"

"Are you suggesting," said Benedict softly, "that I am to submit to petticoat rule without a struggle?"

"Not without a struggle," agreed Primula. "But you are betrothed, and you cannot tell me that that is by your own wish. And if not your wish, then whose?"

"You know very well that the marriage was arranged when we were children . . ." Benedict caught himself up short. "No reason to rehearse all this. Lindsay, I wonder that you haven't been able to control your wife?"

Lindsay laughed outright. "I do, Choate. Just the way you controlled her when you were her guardian!"

Benedict gave a rueful grin. "Well, this is all not to the point."

"But if not your marriage, then what is the point?" said

Primula. "Do you want me to insult her so that she cries off?"

"Good God, no, Primula!" exploded Benedict.

"Well, I should not like to do so, but if that is the only way . . ."

"Primula!" said Lord Lindsay, and the tone of his voice had the desired effect.

"All right, Benedict," said his sister. "I collect that you have something of moment to tell me."

"Well," he said in studied indifference, "yes. But it is not as shocking as I suppose you expect. The fact is that you could do a great favor for me."

Imperceptibly, Lindsay stiffened. But whatever he might have expected, the fact was far different.

"I'm a guardian again—oh, no, not to anyone you know. But old Lady Penryck, a distant kinswoman of my mother's—at least, Penryck was—has died and left her granddaughter to my care."

"A mere child? What do you have to do with children? Simply engage a governess."

Benedict shook his head. "I would not inflict such a task on anyone. Even your Mrs. Duff—not this young miss."

"What is she like? You know her, then?"

"She came to London to stay with Lady Thane, her godmother. And Lady Thane brought her out."

"Well, then?"

"But she only turned sixteen a month ago."

Primula frowned. "And *out*? What were they thinking of?"

"I imagine it is old Lady Penryck whom we have to thank for this. She wanted to get Clare settled. And of course it might have worked out. Ferguson was about to offer, I think."

"Alexander Ferguson? My goodness, Benedict, would that serve?"

"At any rate, it didn't."

Primula watched her brother for a few moments, and then in an altered tone said, "What is she like, Benedict? Shall I like her?"

Benedict said, "I think I may as well tell you. She is the kind of girl who, when an urchin steals her purse on Oxford street, runs after him through the crowds calling 'Stop!' "

Lindsay said curiously, "Did she catch the thief?"

Benedict grimaced. "No. She tripped over a cobble and measured her length on the street."

Irrepressibly, Primula giggled. "And you saw this?"

"I picked her up," said Benedict grimly. "Her foolish maid was screaming at the top of her lungs, and . . . well, something had to be done."

"And you read her a great scold." Primula nodded.

"I pointed out to her . . ." began Benedict, and then thought better of it. Clare's flashing eyes still stayed in his memory, and while she had deserved it all, yet he was of the opinion now that he needn't have been so harsh.

"But she is not in London now," suggested Lindsay.

"No, not after the regent's fete."

"I am not sure that I want to hear," said Primula reflectively, "but I know I can't rest until I do. What happened then?"

"I had to rescue her again—never mind from what. It would do no good to rake that over. But she is the most foolish, green, impulsive, *troublesome* child I have ever had the misfortune to know!" said Benedict, rising to savage heights.

Primula favored him with a roguish smile. "I never thought I would see the day," she said obscurely. "You call her a child, Benedict, and yet I think she has managed something I did not expect."

Suddenly suspicious, Benedict frowned. "What do you mean?"

"I think," she said judiciously, "that Providence works in mysterious ways. And I am beginning to see a bit of hope."

Repressively, Benedict said, "I do not understand you."

Primula said airily, with a gay smile that revealed her dimples, "You will, one day. And I will say I told you so."

Baffled, Benedict turned to Lindsay, but that gentleman shook his head. Benedict turned back to his sister. "So, then, you will do it?"

"Do what?" she asked, suspicious in her turn.

"Go down to Penryck Abbey and see about this troublesome child."

She glanced at her husband. Lindsay said, "Sorry, Choate. Out of the question."

Seeing Benedict's stricken look, Primula took pity on him. "I'm increasing," she said gently, "and I am to go directly into Wiltshire."

"And stay there," said Lindsay firmly. "She is allowed to travel as far as Shenton Hall, but no farther. The doctors in Italy were very firm."

And Lindsay himself was as firm as any, Benedict realized. His plans were going astray with speed. Lindsay forestalled Benedict. "Nor is she to have any anxieties," he said. "I will see to that."

"Send for the girl to London," suggested Primula.

"I fear for the capital," said Benedict fiercely.

Surrounded by the shards of his near-perfect scheme, Benedict reflected. At length, watched by his apprehensive relatives, he said grimly, "That infant belongs in the country until she's grown up."

Glancing ruefully at both Lindsays, he said, "You're right. She is my responsibility. She must stay at Penryck Abbey. I shall go down myself, and believe me, I shall set her straight!"

12.

So it was that on a day near the end of July, Lord Benedict Choate was tooling down the road leading from London in the direction of Dorset. His thoughts, gloomy at first, insensibly began to rise with the fineness of the day and the growing perception that he would be free for a short space from the importunities of his London existence.

Certain of his half-sister's representations had struck closer home than he liked. For one, the idea that his betrothed would rule him as with a rod of iron. While he knew that would not be the case—for no man or woman ruled Benedict Choate—yet those of his staff and his household could not escape as easily from the vicinity as their master. And surely it would be too much to place Clare Penryck in the ungentle hands of Marianna Morton.

Benedict had no illusions about Marianna. But he was strongly aware of the duty he owed, both to his family and to a lady who had long considered herself as the next Lady Choate. But for now, behind his four matched grays, Benedict was responsible only to himself.

The object of his journey sat in the small drawing room at Penryck Abbey. Clare was not alone, although she longed for solitude.

Lady Melvin, the squire's wife, had come to keep her company.

Lady Melvin viewed herself as of a maternal bent. It was unfortunate that she and Sir Ewald had no children, at least any who lived beyond infancy, and she had a great store of sympathy and advice left unused, until now.

"What a pity," she said, not for the first time, "that your grandmother did not live until you had become settled in life. I am sure that you must have had offers in London. After all, you were there for two months and I am sure the beaux are not less attentive today than they were in my time. Why, I hadn't been there above six weeks when I had refused two offers! Two, of the most eligible kind imaginable!"

Unfortunately, Clare's mind had wandered and she spoke absently. "And then you married Sir Ewald."

"Well, it was not that I didn't have other chances, my dear. But of course, I have always had a comfortable feeling about living here in the country. I daresay I should have rubbed along with the baronet. I wonder if I mentioned him?"

"Oh, yes, yes, you did," Clare assured her earnestly. "I wonder what Lady Lindsay will be like?"

Lady Melvin, knowing Clare well, wondered too. The child was in such a state that the slightest curb on her impulses might run into such consequences as Lady Melvin shuddered to think of. Fortunately, it would be a young woman of *ton* and address who would make what arrangements Lord Choate felt necessary. Lady Melvin set great store on Lady Lindsay's tact, even though she did not know her at all.

Clare lapsed into melancholy thoughts. She was apprehensive about Lady Lindsay's arrival. She had no word from Benedict or his sister, but only the letter from Mr. Ruffin that informed her that Lord Choate found himself unable, due to his approaching wedding—thus ran Mr. Ruffin's improvisations—to come to Dorset, but he was sending his sister, and so on, and so on. Clare dismissed the legal roundaboutations and fastened on one thing. Benedict hated his responsibility for her, and seized upon any excuse to get out of it.

Well, she was glad enough of that! If she had not lost her head at Carlton House, she could, perhaps, have been betrothed to Sir Alexander Ferguson, and while it was not quite what she liked, to look forward to a long life of listening to Sir Alex, yet she could not deny that such a life would be very *educational*.

And besides that, she would never have to look at Benedict Choate again. It was above all things what she wanted.

But, as often happens with strong wishes, hers were to be denied. For just as she had formulated her devout wish, her hopes were dashed. From the window of the drawing room she had an excellent view of the long drive that came sweeping up to the front door of the abbey, through the old oaks, and past the sunken garden that had once held the carp ponds for the monks.

And the smart rig that now came spanking up the drive,

behind beautifully handled horses, was driven by a man, with a groom beside him, and there was no possible hope that Lady Lindsay was arriving.

Wisby announced, in an awestruck voice, "Lord Benedict Choate, Miss Clare."

Benedict entered, to find his ward backed against the long table that stood against the far wall. She was eyeing him with a look that would not be inappropriate were she to be facing the Devil himself.

Lady Melvin advanced to greet him. "We did not expect you, Lord Choate," she said with a smile. "But of course, I must say you are very welcome."

He lifted one heavy eyebrow. "I must thank you," he said, not sure to whom he was speaking.

Clare murmured something in a stifled voice, and Lady Melvin turned chidingly to her. "Come, now, Clare, you must not show your disappointment. You see, Lord Choate, we were expecting your sister, and we have the rooms upstairs in readiness for her and her maid. But of course it is totally ineligible for you to stay here. I must make you welcome at my own home. Across the woods there, you know. I am Lady Melvin, and perhaps you know my husband, Sir Ewald Melvin? But then, it isn't likely you would."

Lady Melvin's speech flowed gently on, but Lord Choate found, as many a listener had found before, that it was not necessary to heed the content.

Finally he broke in, "I have made arrangements at the inn, the Swan, I think? Since I will be staying for only a couple of days, I thought I could manage there. And they do seem to know horses." He glanced at Clare. "I shall only stay long enough to see about what business I must, and then . . ."

"Then," said Clare, emerging from the state of paralysis that his appearance had cast her into, "you will return for your wedding. When is it to take place, sir?"

"My marriage?" echoed Benedict. "No doubt it will be quite soon."

"I am sure you must be anxious for that happy day," said Lady Melvin. "I remember how Sir Ewald simply would not brook any delays in our wedding. At once, he said; and at once, he meant. But then, you will not be taking Clare back to London, I must suppose?"

"No, I shall not," said Benedict. "I have given the

matter much thought, and it seems to me that the best thing for my ward is to live out the period of her mourning here at the abbey."

Clare still stood where she had been when he entered. But there was a certain uprising within her that was not visible to her companions. She had hoped never to see Benedict again. Now, she realized, she was very wrong. She wanted to see him so that she could remember just how much she detested him. She could not imagine submitting to the high-handed ways that she saw were such a part of him that he was nearly unaware of them.

To talk to Lady Melvin as though she herself were not in the room, to discuss Clare's affairs with Lady Melvin as though the squire's wife had something to say in the matter, was outside of enough.

And while Clare had been in awe of Benedict in London, where she had felt uncertain ground beneath her feet, yet here she was in her own house on her own ground. And she was accustomed to directing her servants—in lieu of her grandmother's invalid hand—and altogether knowing full well what she was about.

And Benedict did not seem even to see her.

The Penryck *resolution*—as Lady Thane would have said—was stirring, and Clare was willing to give it full rein.

"But you have not welcomed Lord Choate," said Lady Melvin, belatedly remembering that she was here to do her duty to the bereft girl, and not, however delightful it was, to chat with a nonpareil from London.

Clare stepped forward, casting her eyes demurely down. She half-expected Benedict to say something about the fiasco at Carlton House, but instead, he took her hand in his and held it for a moment before releasing it. "My dear Miss Penryck," he said, "I collect that the situation in which we find ourselves is as repugnant to you as it is to me, and therefore we will do well to deal with it quickly."

"I am certain, Lord Choate, that you can be no more surprised than I was," said Clare with commendable poise. "Poor Uncle Horsham!"

"I imagine he is well out of his troubles," said Benedict, referring to the state of Horsham's finances.

Clare misunderstood. So Benedict thought he was heir to Uncle Horsham's troubles—with Clare Penryck as ward? An obscure feeling stirred within her, one that she did not recognize. It might have been resentment, she thought later, at his high-handed ways of talking to her— even in Lady Melvin's hearing—as though she were a package of no account, which could be set on a shelf or taken down, at will.

Or it might have been a mixture of grief and loneliness, a deep need to matter to somebody, even to her obnoxious guardian, whom, of all people in the world, she disliked most.

No matter, she thought now. She watched Choate with finesse and ruthlessness get rid of Lady Melvin, and then they were alone.

Benedict said, "Do you have to put up with that woman a great deal?"

Clare said very softly, "She has been very kind to me. And I have learned to value kindness above all things." Although her appearance was innocuous, although she seemed to be exceedingly biddable, yet anyone who knew her very well would have been aware of a certain feeling of uneasy apprehension. Clare on her home ground was not quite the same as Clare on her best behavior in London.

Benedict, however, did not know her that well. Not yet, although in the folds of the future, he was to learn.

He studied her now, congratulating himself on his handling of the situation. He had gained her submission, he thought, for she had not ripped him up the moment he came in, as he might have expected, since she had been furious with him at their last meeting.

He would be able to put things into train at once, and then, apart from frequent reports, no doubt, by the garrulous Mr. Austin, he could consider his duty to the Penrycks accomplished.

"Of course it is ineligible for you to continue here alone. That woman is not the kind of person to guide you, and of course you must have someone to stay."

"I have my servants," said Clare evenly. He was not warned by the calm authority with which she spoke of her staff.

"Ineligible," he repeated. "I have thought much about this, and I am persuaded I have the solution."

"Indeed?"

"My sister, Lady Lindsay, is unable to travel to Dorset, as you may have surmised. But she has given me the address of her old governess-companion, who is, I think, quite properly qualified to come to you."

"To stay?"

Benedict's eyebrows rose. "Of course. You must have a female to lend you countenance here. You must not live alone."

"I do not wish to be a trouble to you," Clare temporized.

"No doubt," he said dryly. "But somehow you do seem to attract trouble, do you not? And I am persuaded that my sister's companion will be able to take charge of your training so that the next time you come to London, you may be able to control your impulsiveness."

"I shall not come to London."

"Oh, yes, you will," said Benedict with a half-smile. "I shall certainly see that you are given every chance to marry well."

Clare found employment for the moment in pleating her skirt with her fingers. Benedict continued, "So, then, it is all settled."

"Pray tell me," she said, lifting an innocent face to him, "what is settled?"

"Why, that Mrs. Duff will come to stay with you. I shall write to her directly."

"Do not trouble, Lord Choate, for I shall not receive her."

Benedict stood aghast. Almost his jaw dropped, but his training stood him in good stead and he simply glowered at her. "What did you say?"

"I said that I shall not receive Mrs. Whatever-her-name-is."

"And I say you shall!"

Clare smiled. "And I say that if she does come, she will not stay above a fortnight. For her life here will be miserable, I can promise you that!"

Benedict took a deep breath. He was about to lash out at her, but caution, tempered by a certain experience, held him back.

"You doubt me?" said Clare silkily.

A long reflective look at her made up his mind. "No, I don't doubt you. This behavior is no more than I would expect from someone as badly schooled as I found you to be in London."

"You will remember that your own behavior was far outside what I would have expected from you."

He took a tight rein on his tongue. It was an unaccustomed feat for him, since he was not in the habit of modifying his remarks to anyone. "Come, now. We must muddle through this guardianship as best we can. I know what is best for you, and I have the power to make you obey me."

"By force? Will you tie me down? You will go back to your Miss Morton, and I should imagine that your villainous ways would be better employed with her than with me."

"This is not to the point. . . ."

"Quite right, Lord Choate. The point is that I shall not allow any governess-companion to come and tell me what to do. I am mistress of Penryck Hall, and you will do well to remember it."

Benedict's thoughts jostled each other on the tip of his tongue, but he could think of no way to put them into language polite enough for a female's ears, nor could he be sure that his growing rage was not exactly what she was trying to provoke.

He had a gnawing suspicion that the weapons he had found effective in the past in dealing with the ladies of his family or of his acquaintance might not serve him here.

A good soldier knows when it is time to advance. And when to retreat. Benedict, although no great student of military tactics, yet found that he did know when to pull back. This was certainly the time.

"I find you astonishingly juvenile," he said cuttingly, "for one who was ambitious enough to attempt a London season. I had thought to deal with you as though with a reasonable individual. Now, I see, I have only a hysterical female to deal with."

It was unfair, for she was far from hysterical. But in a few moments, she thought darkly, she could well be.

"I bid you good day," he said with punctiliousness. "Pray give the matter some thought. I trust that in the morning I shall find you more amenable to reason."

"I doubt it," she told him.

He drove off down the drive, and it seemed to her that even the set of his shoulders spoke of his unbridled anger. It was the first time that he had been defied, as far as he could remember, and she suspected that she would be hard put to come out of this encounter with any kind of credit.

Her eyes filmed over, and she could no longer see her guardian. She brushed past Lady Melvin in the hall, as though she weren't there, and hurried up the stairs. She barely reached the haven of her own room, bolting the door behind her against interruption, before she burst into racking sobs.

13.

Although Benedict was out of sight down the drive, he was far from forgotten. Clare's sinking feeling did not lighten with her guardian's absence. Rather, it grew stronger the more she thought about the great fix her grandmother had left her in.

Uncle Horsham might have been a stuffy old man, but he would never have been as odious, as repellently *odious*, as Benedict Choate!

What was she to *do*?

Lady Melvin followed her up the stairs. She tried in vain to lighten her spirits, touching unerringly upon the very things that most lacerated Clare's feelings. "How very handsome he is, to be sure! And such elegance of demeanor. I vow, Clare dear, that you could not find, I am positive, another such gentleman in England!"

Clare nodded vigorous agreement, and bit back the words on the tip of her tongue. *Fortunately for England*.

"How much wiser Lady Penryck was to give you a guardian who is up to snuff—now, where did I learn that vulgar phrase?—in all details. Your affairs will march very well with him in charge. I recommend to you that you thank God every night on your knees for such a fortunate delivery!"

Since Clare's thoughts ran along entirely different lines, and since she could share them with no one—not even in her prayers—she allowed Lady Melvin's rhapsodies to float past her, unheeded, and Lady Melvin, secure in the belief that she had given Clare a good deal of sensible advice, left her.

But Clare was not comforted. Even that night, her sleep was not so much broken as nonexistent. She gazed out onto the sleeping landscape, her thoughts darker than the night. The hours passed, the moon's rays moved across the window, and still she could not sleep. Was ever anyone in such a fix?

She knew that Benedict was right. He was powerful in himself, of course, and by sheer force of his intimidating character he could bend her to his will. But in addition to that, he had the entire force of the law behind him. He was truly her legal guardian, and his authority over her was limitless.

He could shut her up in a cloister, he could provide her with so little pocket money that she could not buy a ribbon without his consent. And this was what Lady Penryck had thought was best for her granddaughter!

Clare's thoughts moved on, then, to turn over and over the plans that Benedict had already made. To bring his sister's companion-governess to live at Penryck Abbey, without so much as a word to Clare, was intolerable. Clare believed she had scotched that plan of his, but she knew Benedict well enough to know that he would prevail in the long run.

And the devil of it was, he was right! She could not live alone here. Such a plan was totally ineligible. But if Benedict had schemes afoot, Clare decided, he would not be alone. She herself was as determined as he was, and it was her entire life at stake.

Benedict could simply wave a hand—so he thought—and people would spring to do his bidding, and he could then hasten back to London and the arms of Marianna, leaving Clare to manage whatever was left to her—a companion, a lowering series of instruction on whatever Benedict thought she lacked.

One thing, she decided, she did not lack, and that was a determination not to let Benedict dictate to her. To arrange her affairs in a lordly fashion and then forget about her—that was outside of enough! Clare came to the conclusion that the one thing she could be sure of in the days ahead was that Benedict would not be allowed to forget her existence.

Surprisingly, she found great comfort in her decision. She left the window and climbed into her bed, and drifted off to sleep, a satisfied smile still lingering on her lips.

The next day, when Benedict returned, he found her in a surprisingly amiable mood. He himself had mastered his anger overnight, and greeted her with great civility.

"Will you take coffee?" she offered. "Perhaps some chocolate? I am not quite sure what kind of refreshment you take in the morning, but you have only to command me."

For a second, surprise showed in his face, but it was

gone at once. "Nothing, I thank you," he said. "The landlady has given me an excellent breakfast."

"Then I imagine you would like to take a tour of the grounds?"

"It is not at all necessary," he began, but she was already moving through the open door onto the terrace that faced south.

"I am sure you will wish to understand the properties with which you will be dealing," Clare said, turning innocent eyes to him. "You are not a person, I collect, who turns over his duty to an underling."

Since Benedict had precisely that in mind, he did not reply. He followed her onto the bricked terrace. "My father had this terrace built," she said. "He said it was to give the local brickmakers employment, but I believe it was more likely to have been designed to provide a comfortable spot for an afternoon nap, in the shade of the beech trees."

She moved across the lawn, toward a pergola in the Italian fashion, embellished by a rose vine bursting into red bloom at the top. Talking over her shoulder to him as she went, she pointed out the herb garden beyond the low hedge, and, to the left below the crest of the hill, the stables.

"Poor Papa would have hated to see the stables in such disrepair, and sadly empty. But I am sure you will put all in order before you leave. I must make Purvis known to you."

"Purvis?"

"Our farm manager—I should not say *our*, of course. *Your* farm manager."

"I make no claim to Purvis," said Benedict, ruffled. His hard-won aplomb sat uneasily. "I imagine that your Mr. Austin will tell Purvis how to go on."

"Oh, do you think so?" asked Clare, looking up at him seriously. "I had not thought he would know anything about farming. But surely, as my guardian, you must see that my income is assured? And since it all comes from the land . . ." She left the thought dangling, and turned again to lead the way toward the service buildings.

Purvis was at hand, as she knew he would be, and she presented him to Lord Choate. Benedict, making the best of it, engaged Purvis in conversation, which soon turned more technical than Clare could understand. Choate was surprisingly knowledgeable about agriculture and livestock, and Clare stood amazed until she remembered that he had vast lands of his own, and he was not a man to overlook necessary duties.

When at length they left Purvis and walked again to the house, Clare felt her spirits soaring. It would turn out better than she had at first expected, she thought, and she was almost in charity with her guardian by the time they reached the small morning room again.

"Purvis is a good man," pronounced Choate. "You may safely leave your farm management to him. I have promised to put my own man in touch with him. There is a possibility, Purvis thinks, of improving your strain of sheep, and it would be well to look into it."

Benedict, too, was pleased with his morning. It looked to him as though his ward had come to her senses, after all, and decided not to kick against the pricks of fortune. In a year or two, he would see about a suitable marriage for her, and then she would be off his hands. So he devoutly hoped. And misled by his sanguine prospects, and by his ward's demure charm, he blundered.

"I have written the letter I spoke of yesterday," he announced, almost with geniality.

"The letter? I don't remember that we spoke of a letter," said Clare, feeling a tightening in her throat. He could not mean what she thought.

But it seems he did indeed. "The letter to Mrs. Duff, my sister's old companion. She will, I am sure, come to you at once."

Clare's hands clenched and unclenched before she spoke again. What could she do? The morning had been a rainbow dream, and all was as it had been at first—ruined.

"I believed we had settled that, had we not? I will not receive her."

"You must."

"If I must, I must," Clare said in a dangerously quiet voice. Panic swept over her. She fought down the tide of anger that threatened to overwhelm her, and added in a voice that didn't sound like her own, "But I promise you, she will not stay."

"But . . . you cannot live here alone!"

"My Uncle Horsham would not have treated me so!"

"I quite agree," said Benedict smoothly. "However, your Uncle Horsham was never unlucky enough to be charged with the responsibility of a badly spoiled, totally irresponsible child. For my sins, I find myself in the unenviable position of having to decide what is best."

"And you, of course, know what is best for everyone in the world!"

"Let us not exaggerate wildly," said Benedict, seething. He was quite as angry as she was, but being more experienced, had more control over his emotions. But this child had tried him far more excessively than anyone else in his recent life, and he was hard put to hold a tight rein on his tongue.

"Very well," she said after a long moment. "I bow to your authority. For the moment. But I cannot like this scheme. To set a woman over me, one I do not know, and one I am sure I will dislike—it is infamous!"

Her lower lip quivered in spite of all her efforts, and Benedict was quick to notice. With a laborious attempt at fairness he said, "What, then? You have not informed me what you wish to do, that is true. And perhaps I was wrong not to consult your wishes first." He came to where she stood at the window. "Tell me what you wish."

His sudden gentleness left her without the support of the anger that she had been leaning on. She had no answer for him.

"Perhaps you would go to stay with my sister? It might be just the thing."

Clare said, "Certainly I would not wish to be an added burden on her. Nor especially since she is so newly wed."

Benedict agreed. And indeed he was glad she refused the suggestion, for while he had every confidence in his sister's generosity, yet to burden her with a total stranger for some months was not the thing.

"Well, then," said Benedict, "pray tell me if you wish to go back to Lady Thane in London. I believe I could persuade your godmother to accept you into her household."

Clare reflected. Nothing he suggested recommended itself to her. Nor could she think of anything she truly wanted of her own. She was sadly torn, not knowing what she wanted, only knowing what she didn't want. And the latter category embraced a wide variety.

If she went to Lady Thane, she would hear more and more strictures upon her behavior, and she was quite sure that nothing she could do would quite meet with that lady's approval. And an obscure part of Clare longed, quite strongly, for at least one word of approval, for a word that denied that she was a spoiled brat, that she was overly ambitious, overweening in her impudence . . .

"I cannot go back to London," she said sadly. "You must see that, Lord Choate. I could not show my face in society again, after that last evening there. You of all people should know that!"

"I do know that," he said. He found that her sad little voice worked powerfully on him, and of all things, he knew he could not afford to have pity on her. She was a legal obligation, and that was the only way he could handle her. If he gave in once to her, he felt strongly that he would continue to give ground on the most reasonable of excuses.

The determination to do what was best for her turned him grim. Every way he turned, she put an obstacle in his path, and he was not accustomed to such rebellion. For although her demeanor was demure, yet she was inwardly defiant. She had not fooled him at all, he told himself, and it was time to put an end to any pretensions she may have had.

"But," he said, returning to the attack, "I think that I know how it can be carried off. You were worried about your grandmother, and such commendable anxiety led you into an emotional excess."

She opened her eyes wide. "But I didn't know about Grandmama until I got home that night."

Nettled, he said sharply, "You would do well to go along with my suggestion."

She sensed her advantage. Quickly she smiled. "I should indeed be glad to do so, Lord Choate. How kind you are to arrange all for me! But I am such an addlepate that I cannot promise not to let the truth slip out. And then . . . I am persuaded I would not do you credit!"

"No matter," he said. "I had quite forgot you are in mourning. I confess it does not show in your demeanor, but it would be wrong to appear in London."

"You are quite right. But then, all will think I am too young, just a nuisance," she said hotly. "I would no doubt cast disgrace on the family name, wouldn't I?" Warming to a sense of her wrongs, she continued, "I wonder that you would consider letting me loose in London—I think that is the term, is it not? You must refresh my memory!"

"I don't know what you are talking about!"

"Oh, you must know! For I have been the subject of many a conversation where you have calmly torn apart my character, and done all you can to cast me down. You cannot deny it!"

"I do deny it! And where you got these nonsensical notions, I do not know! It is quite illogical of you to remember that, more than once, to my own discomfort, I extracted you from one mess after another, and then tell me I have wronged you."

If she were to speak, she thought darkly, she would quite simply burst into tears. And that, she vowed, she would not do—not where Benedict could see.

Benedict, however, was a man of considerable intelligence and a certain amount of experience with the female variety of logic. He thought he could discern, now, a deliberately planned ambush, where he might become enmeshed in the toils of accusation and counterattack, and lose his way. That, he vowed, would not happen to Benedict Choate.

"I consider that you have solved my problem. I confess I had not seen my way so clearly until now, but it is just the thing."

She looked up hastily at the altered note in his voice. Apprehensive about what was to come, she hastened to divert him. "You do consider me a nuisance and a disgrace, you know. Miss Morton said so."

The sudden revelation came as a shock to him. "She could not have told you so!" he exclaimed.

"Then it is true," she said. "You do not deny it, I notice."

Too late he saw the pit beneath his feet. "I did not quite say that, you know. You should not believe all you hear."

"She was not speaking to me," said Clare. "But it is clear that you have discussed me, quite unnecessarily, with Miss Morton. And since I know that you have so little honor as to talk about me—long before you were my guardian—I see that I cannot depend upon your setting all straight in London. No, I think I shall not go to London."

She looked absurdly young, under the dignity that she wore like an adult's cloak on a child. But yet, beneath it all, he could see that the dignity was not something she donned for the occasion. She was a well-bred young lady, old beyond her years in some things. And he remembered with a twinge his own first year in London, acquiring some town bronze while his fond parent believed he was at Oxford, engrossed in his study of Greek.

He had been wrong in talking to Marianna, of course. But he had been mistaken in her, too, if she had repeated his words to anyone else. He must be more careful, and as a prospect for a harmonious married life ahead, it lacked appeal.

But Clare—strangely!—was smiling. "I have the answer, Lord Choate. You asked me what I wanted to do, and I know now. I'm going to go and live with my own old governess. Miss Peek lives with her sister, and I know she will be glad to have me. You can rest assured—"

"Where does this Miss—Peek, is it?—live?"

"It will be such fun, and nobody will care that I am in mourning. For they won't heed that, you see. Not in Bath!"

Aghast, Lord Choate could only echo, "Bath?"

14.

Benedict took a grip on himself. "*Not* to Bath!"

"Oh, it will be delightful!" she said, as though he had not spoken. "I cannot think why I did not think of it before!"

"Disabuse your mind of the plan," said Benedict grimly. "It will not do."

"Miss Peek is quite as good a governess as your sister's, I am convinced. And surely if I am to have a companion, then I do not see why I am not to have my choice in the matter. She will be glad to see me, and the salary you would give your sister's companion will surely be welcome to Miss Peek. For I think they are perhaps a little *pressed*."

"You will not go to Bath," said Benedict, and she recognized with satisfaction the note of final authority in his voice. "That town is a hotbed of intrigue and even vice, and it is totally out of the question that you set foot there without a better chaperone than a governess."

"Do you think it is really *wicked*?" she demanded, and then artlessly added, "I suppose you are right, for I am persuaded that you would know about such things."

He laughed harshly. "You suppose right. Not that I have indulged in all the lower forms of activity, but I know enough to steer my way clear of them. But to go to live in Bath without a woman of some credit in the world to show you how to go on is totally ineligible. Do not think that I will relent, for I warn you, on this point I am adamant."

She sighed hugely. "And I had so hoped to see Peeky again."

He reflected momentarily. "I am glad to hear you say so, for I feel that all may be settled comfortably after all. Suppose Miss Peek were to come here to live with you? She has the advantage of having your regard, and until your period of mourning is over, you will wish to lead a retired life."

Benedict was uncomfortably aware that he was spouting fustian, but if Clare did not feel as he suggested, she *ought* to feel so, and he was not ready to countenance any vagaries on her part.

His ward was just now looking at him as though he had produced a vision of angels for her entertainment. "How marvelous!" she cried. "Just the thing! I wonder how you came to think of that!"

He had an uneasy recognition that he was losing control of the situation. He had had a severely trying few days since Ruffin had come to bring him the dire news of his guardianship, and he had never felt so like a chip adrift on the waves as now when he tried to cope with the ceaseless changing of his ward's mind and moods.

He thought automatically of the quiet backwater he expected of his marriage. His duty by the family and his duty toward Marianna, who had been promised to him from her cradle, weighed heavily on him, and he had thought that, in wedding Marianna, he could rejoice in the quiet security of duty well done, of heirs assured, of freedom to live, as so many of his married acquaintance did, in the clubs of Brook Street or in the outdoor sports that lay to his hand on one or another of his estates.

He had not truly thought of the quality of such a life. Suffice it to say, he had considered it as inevitable, and with certain advantages. Marianna would not be importunate, bewildering, devious, scheming—as this girl before him clearly was. She was a challenge, this girl, and he would rise to the occasion. She smiled at him, transforming her face enchantingly.

"How good you are to me!"

The sound he gave then could be described as a snort, or even a bark of laughter. It held a wealth of skepticism in it. "I wonder," he said wryly, "what I have done this time."

"You have straightened all out for me," said Clare sunnily.

"I have the strangest feeling that I have somehow blundered. But I suppose that I must await the unfolding of events to tell me where I erred."

Clare favored him wih a sidelong glance, in which he was startled to see a totally mature female peeping out of the kittenish face.

"I cannot understand what you mean, sir," she said innocently, "but I shall do my best to cause you no discomfort. You will be anxious to return to Miss Morton," she added, "and I will watch the journals to have news of your wedding."

"The happy event is to take place in October, I believe," he said briefly. "I shall convey your compliments to Miss Morton."

"Pray do!" Clare urged. "I am sure you will do famously together."

"Thank you," said Benedict repressively as he took his leave.

His next stop was at the office of Mr. Austin. Mr. Austin was overwhelmed at the dazzling appearance of Lord Choate. Dressed correctly in country buckskins, with high top boots, and a simply folded cravat, he contrived to make all pretenders to elegance fall into the shade.

"Now, then, Mr. Austin," said Choate, "I must tell you what I have arranged. I have sent for Miss Penryck's former governess, a Miss Peek, I think. She is to reply to you, and I trust you will send her traveling funds." He spoke further about salary to be paid, and directions to Purvis.

"Lord Choate, if you will permit me," said Mr. Austin, beaming upon his visitor, "you have done a magnificent job. I confess I did not see how it would work out, since Miss Clare . . ." His voice died away. He thought better of bringing forth any doubts he might have as to Clare's surprising acquiescence in what would be, after all, a dull existence.

". . . is accustomed to making her own decisions," Lord Choate finished for him. "It was a great shame that Lady Penryck was such an invalid. The child has grown up beyond her years."

"Just so, my lord. But her father was just such another one. Couldn't wait to spend his money. He had a pair of grays in his stable—not the ones that ran away on the Bath road, but some that were sold after the breakup. They were real goers!"

"Well, we must between us see that his daughter does not have an opportunity to spend her money. I rely upon you, Mr. Austin, to keep me informed of any events that you think I should know of."

With many an expression of goodwill, Mr. Austin ushered his elegant visitor to the street and stood watching after him as he walked the few steps to the coachyard of the White Swan. He shook his head dolefully. He recognized his responsibility toward Clare's small inheritance, but in no way was he going to be held responsible for what that young lady did.

As long as her grandmother was alive, he reflected, Clare had done nothing to reflect discredit upon her. In fact, she had often astonished him by her grasp of business details. He had sometimes felt that he was the child and she the efficient director of affairs. No wonder Lady Penryck had judged her mature enough to venture upon a London season. And from all he had heard, she had reflected great credit on the family. At least, no other rumor had reached him.

But he remembered her father, and he shook his head dubiously as he watched Clare's guardian walking innocently down the walk. But if anyone could make her see reason, it would be Lord Choate. And Mr. Austin envied him not at all.

Miss Peek, leaving Bath behind her without a qualm, rode toward Penryck Abbey. She would be so happy to see her dear Clare again, to say nothing of the abbey, which she had loved during the years she had presided over Clare's schoolroom. Clare would be quite the young lady now, having the elegance that only London could provide, and it was with great gratification that she touched, inside her reticule, the letter that Lord Choate had written to her: "Miss Penryck tells me that her dearest wish is that you come to share her life at Penryck Abbey. . . ."

And she was on her way. Her sister, left behind in Bath, had prophesied mournfully, "That girl always could turn you around her little finger. You had better watch your step with her."

But Miss Peek knew Clare far better than Sara did, and while Clare had often been unpredictable, yet she had never, never done anything the least *improper*. One phrase in Lord Choate's letter did lend itself to a feeling of misgiving. "Miss Penryck is to lead a retired life while she is in mourning." Miss Peek hoped that Clare had agreed. Otherwise . . .

Her arrival at Penryck Abbey was all that she could have wished. Clare flew out of the door when the carriage stopped, and threw her arms around her governess.

"Dear Peeky! How good of you to come! Here, let Budge take your bandbox—bandbox—Budge! Peeky, I'm sure you will want tea. Come into the living room—no, no, I know you will want to take off your bonnet first. You are to have your old room, and I am in mine! What fun this will be!"

"Fun, my dear?"

"Oh, I know I should be sad because Grandmama is gone. But only think how much pain she had, Peeky, and I couldn't wish her back. But I do miss her."

"Of course you do. So do we all. But now you must tell me all that has happened since I've been away."

But all did not come out that first day. It was more than a week, and Clare had told Miss Peek about the newest fashions in London—much newer than appeared in the *Lady's Journal*—and the Greek statues that everyone said were wonderful, but that Lord Elgin was no better than a thief for taking them away from Greece. "But the Greeks, you know, weren't fond of them at all, not until they thought they were leaving the country. But the government, you know, wants to buy them now, and someone says that they are buying the statues only to take them back to Greece. Which is a great waste!"

"It is a nice question of honor, my dear," said Miss Peek mildly.

"I confess I agree that it was wrong. But then . . . I wish you could have seen them!"

Lady Thane's house had been described in detail, and the shops in Oxford Street—"that was where Lord Choate rescued me."

"Rescued you?" said Miss Peek, blinking. "From what, my dear?"

"There was a small boy, and I did not see him. He made away with my parcel, running past me and snatching it, and poor Budge—she hated London, you know—stood there screaming, no good at all, and I had to run after the boy myself. I knew I shouldn't, but what was I to do?"

Miss Peek said with a cough, "Did you get your parcel back? Was that what Lord Choate rescued?"

"Oh, no. I don't know precisely how to tell you this. But, you see, I stumbled. And fell."

"Oh, dear!"

"And Lord Choate came along just then, and Budge was still screaming, and my gown was torn . . ."

"And Lord Choate rescued you. I see how it was."

"Oh, but you don't. He was so odious. He told Budge off proper—so she told me later—and read me a scold all the way home. And even after that, he"—her voice trailed away—"said some very unpleasant things."

Miss Peek could well imagine Lord Choate's chagrin at seeing his kinswoman stretched her length on the cobbles of Oxford Street. But, glancing wisely at Clare, she held her peace. Clare had already felt the sting of that episode, and it was not needful for the governess to ring a peal over her too.

"Well, my dear, it could have been much worse, you know."

Clare's face reflected her unspoken question.

"Why, surely you must see that if Lord Choate had not come along at that precise time, only think what dreadful things might have happened to you. I do know," continued Miss Peek in her thoughtful, gentle voice that nonetheless evoked a biddable mood in her charge, "that you were mortified beyond belief, but at least—so I collect—your injuries were not serious? And how unfortunate it would have been for you to be at the mercy of a mob!" Miss Peek managed to invest the word with all the horrors of *The Invisible Hand*.

"Perfectly gothic," echoed Clare, slightly subdued. "I do know that I owe him gratitude for his timely rescue. But he didn't have to trumpet that . . . that *accident* all over town."

"Oh, my dear, he could not have done so!" Miss Peek looked up in horror. "He is of such exalted *ton*, I am persuaded you are mistaken!"

"No? Let me tell you, then, dear Peeky, how mistaken you are in your judgment of that villain."

She had been in two minds about revealing her disgrace at the regent's ball. And as to the disgrace, she knew that fleeing in tears would be considered almost as bad as retiring to the shadowed garden with a known rake. But the habit of confiding in Peeky was strong, and in fact she longed to lay bare her guardian's iniquities. And he had such a multitude of them, Clare believed, that they would serve to occupy her for some time.

She told her first about Benedict's claiming her for a dance, and taking advantage of her captivity in the set to urge her to travel home again. "Since I was clearly upsetting the world by my *green* behavior."

She eyed Miss Peek severely. But the governess knew her charge well, and allowed not the slightest quiver to appear on her mild face.

"And so, at the first opportunity, I left him." In an effort to be fair, she said, "He was taking me back to Lady Thane, but there was such a crush that I . . . I got separated from him. And then I went out on the balcony for a bit of air, and then . . ." She fell silent.

She knew full well she had been an idiot to allow herself to engage in conversation with Harry Rowse, to say nothing of allowing him to show her the garden—a transparent excuse, if there ever was one. And she disliked confessing to what after all did not place her in a glowing light of virtue. But, basically honest, she forged ahead.

She passed over the glaring faults lightly; by listening to her, one might imagine that strolling down a badly lit path was understandable, to be left sitting alone on a marble bench in the dark was unexceptionable, and to drink lemon squash laced with champagne was no more than a rector's daughter might do.

She fell silent, contemplating her own errors. But Miss Peek, believing in the virtues of confession, urged her gently on.

So it was that Miss Peek heard the story of Benedict's furious rescue, his equally furious escorting her back to the lighted house and sending her upstairs to straighten her gown.

"But that does not seem so villainous to me," she said. "But perhaps I do not rightly understand this. It seems to me that you owe Lord Choate a great deal, my child—your reputation at the very least."

"But that is not the half of it!" exclaimed Clare. "Just listen to this. While I was upstairs putting myself to rights, I heard through the window my own name. And of course I must hear what was to follow. And that woman said that Benedict could not abide me, that I was a nuisance and a spoiled brat, and he was sorry that I was related to him, since I brought such sh-shame on the family name!"

Clare dropped to her knees beside Miss Peek's chair. The tears had begun to flow now, and the face she turned up to her governess was streaked and reddened. Miss Peek was put forcefully in mind of the first time she had seen Clare, who was in disgrace with cook for making off with the raisins for her cookies.

"My dear Clare," she said softly. "It was that bad? Who on earth could have been so *misguided* and so vulgar as to tell such untruths?"

"But it was not untruths!" insisted Clare. "For you must know it was Miss Morton who said so, and she was quoting Benedict, and she is his betrothed! Surely she told the truth?"

Miss Peek coughed gently. "Surely she is ill-bred to pass on what after all must have been a very private conversation between Lord Choate and his intended wife. Very wrong!"

"So you see, if he is so misguided as to say all those things, knowing that she is a sad rattle, then I cannot believe that he knows what is best for me!"

Detecting signs of overt rebellion, Miss Peek hastened to extinguish the first sparks. "But, my dear, he is your guardian, and no matter what you think, he is responsible for your welfare. And you must be guided by him."

Clare leaped to her feet and took a quick turn around the room. Then, with swirling skirts, she faced her governess, and clenching her fists, delivered herself of her final judgment: "Lord Benedict Choate is a wicked, *wicked* guardian!"

15.

Clare's confession had unburdened her soul, and Miss Peek's practiced methods provided the unguent to heal her wounds. But it would be wrong to believe that Clare had now agreed to submit to the cruel destiny that had brought her Lord Benedict Choate.

Resignation was not a vital part of Clare's character, and Choate, driving back to London, was mistaken in his satisfaction at the way things had turned out. Clare Penryck was settled in her ancestral home, with her governess, and since she had gotten her own way, he believed, she would now subside and bide her time until, with Miss Peek's further governance, she would be ready to make her appearance once more in London society.

A lurking thought told him that London would not be quite the same without Clare, but he steeled himself to facing a world of order and security, without unpleasant alarm every time he caught sight of her, wondering what she would do next to set the world by the ears.

But while he moved in a rainbow world of his own false hopes, Clare retreated into her own thoughts, and they were far from iris-hued.

She was not harried by Miss Peek, and she had been right to wish for her company. Miss Peek, glancing from time to time at her dear Clare, forbore to reopen the subject that she was quite sure was uppermost in the girl's mind. But, she thought comfortably, if time were allowed to shroud the untoward events with its healing veil, it would be the best cure of all.

Miss Peek found sufficient employment in turning out closets, since Clare had given her freedom to do what she would, and setting the household to rights. So there were linens to mend, china to wash, carpets to be beaten, herbs to be gathered and dried, holland covers to be installed in the rooms that were consigned to idleness.

And while Miss Peek hummed through her day, totally contented, Clare employed herself with turning over every slightest incident of her sojourn in London. It was a mistake to have acceded to Grandmama's wishes, she believed now, and yet she would have longed for London had she been kept at home.

But no matter in what direction her thoughts ran now, she found that sooner or later the thin, elegant face of her guardian swam into her mind's eye. The heavy black brows, the suggestion of a faintly curled lip, the dark eyes blazing with pent-up fury, and the slightly contemptuous expression with which he regarded her when he was in charity with her—all this weighed heavily upon her.

She could not forgive him for what he said behind her back. He had told Marianna Morton that Clare was hanging out for a rich husband!

And while part of that was true, riches meant little to her. To be without a feather to fly with was, of course, a way of life abhorrent to any female. But to give her heart away for a fortune was equally derogatory, and untrue. And Marianna was spreading Benedict's words around London with the speed of a grass fire.

It was too callous to be borne!

And although she gave due consideration to Miss Peek's glossing over the overheard words as exaggerated and in any case not relevant, yet they had wounded her far deeper than she would admit.

And especially now. For her guardian had dealt with her summarily—or he would have, had she not defied him in the matter of Miss Peek—and made sure that she would not come to London to be in the way, before his marriage to Miss Morton took place.

Of course, Grandmama's death required the year of mourning, and Clare was too realistic to rail against that. But it was Benedict's clear satisfaction at getting her settled in the depths of the country, his obvious relief at disposing of her so easily, and the clear prospect of forgetting her as quickly as he left the White Swan in town—Clare felt all this as deeply as a saber wound.

She was not reconciled to her situation, nor, she promised herself darkly, would she ever be. It was while she was still moodily turning over the London affair that Lady Melvin came to call once more.

"I've brought you some reading to keep you occupied," she said gaily. "I subscribe, don't you know, to the circulating library in London, and they send me books. I vow I do love to read, and here is the new one from Mrs. Meeke, and there's a great selection. I have read them all, so you need not hurry with them. But only see what riches are here!"

She set her basket on the table, and delved with both hands into its capacious depths. Talking all the time, she gave rise to doubts in Clare's mind as to when she could find time to read, with her tongue wagging thirteen to the dozen. But the basket contained some gems, Clare noticed, and soon the two were deep in discussion of their favorites.

Clarentine, and Miss Edgeworth's *Leonora. Midnight Weddings. Bewildered Affections. Irish Girl*. And a foolish novel that Clare had read at Lady Thane's—*Self-control*.

"A promising month of reading ahead for you," announced Lady Melvin triumphantly. "I told your guardian I should look out for you. But you will tell Lord Choate when you write him that I kept my promise, won't you,"

"I do not plan to write him," said Clare in a muffled voice.

Lady Melvin looked blank. "Not write to your guardian!" exclaimed Lady Melvin. "I should think you must! How else will he know that all is well with you? While Mr. Austin is all very well, yet Lord Choate should not take the word of a man of affairs! It would not suit. But then, I am persuaded that you are merely funning, and you really intend all the time to behave just as you ought."

Clare could think of no reply to this. Fortunately, it was not required, for Lady Melvin had more to say. "He is such a man, of the first consequence. You must know that I have a cousin in Kent, at Sevenoaks, near Choate's main residence, and she is full of the most exquisite examples of Choate's kindness. His tenants, all in the village, speak of nothing but his great condescension."

"It is too bad that they lead such meager lives that all they talk of is their landlord."

Lady Melvin frowned. "But of course you know him better even than they do," she recovered rapidly. "Pray tell me—I know I haven't had a chance to visit with you without interruption since you returned from your gay visit to the capital—I imagine you had many many offers, did you not!" She smiled archly.

Clare resolved to play the part to the hilt. Recklessly, she said, "It was such a gay life, you know. Several parties a day. Routs, drums, card parties. Sightseeing." She was doing it too brown, she thought, ashamed. Lady Melvin really meant well.

"But I did miss Grandmama," she added with a rush.

"Of course you did. But you didn't mention any eligible men. Of course, Lord Choate would be a magnificent match, but there is no chance of that?"

"No, no. He is betrothed, you know, to Miss Morton. A very fashionable lady." But one who will lead him a merry chase, she thought darkly. A veritable shrew.

"Well, too bad your mourning will keep you in Dorset, but I expect that before too long we will be hearing news of your marriage."

"There is no one in sight, Lady Melvin."

"Lord Choate will see to it that there is. Believe me, he will want you settled in your own establishment, and there is no one with more influence than Choate and his sister, Lady Lindsay."

"I would rather seek my own destiny," said Clare, unconsciously quoting one of the books in the basket. "There was," she added mendaciously, "a wealthy baronet about to offer for me. But I haven't made up my mind about him yet."

Lady Melvin nodded wisely. "Oh, yes, I see. But you will, you little minx. Anyone as pretty as you will have them swooning at your feet when you return to London."

As pretty as I am, thought Clare in despair, my beauty will fade fast—I have Marianna Morton's word for it.

She visited for a longer while with Lady Melvin, and when Miss Peek came to join them, she rang for tea and macaroons.

Her thoughts romped away again, while Miss Peek and Lady Melvin mulled over the respective merits of Fanny Burney's heroines and those of Miss Maria Edgeworth. And her thoughts, this time, moved on to bear some unexpected fruit.

Her frustrations and her regrets came to a sharp focus. She realized that Lord Choate loomed too large in her thoughts for comfort. And, always the realist, she decided that the only way to deal with Lord Choate's presence in her thoughts was to put him in his place.

It would take some doing, she knew. First she would have to decide exactly what his place was, and then . . .

His place was at present atop a pedestal. While she had no part of putting him there, yet there he was—witness Miss Peek's admiration, and Lady Melvin's rhapsodies. But Clare herself knew him to be arrogant and selfish, unfeeling and ruthless.

She did not need a large audience to witness her victory. She shrank from a public humbling of Lord Choate—she at least knew how it felt to be, even unwittingly, a public spectacle. Nor was she a cruel rattle like Marianna Morton. But she longed to point out his various grave flaws to Choate himself.

She had told him before, but her words had had as little effect as a gnat. But if he could *somehow* be brought to *admit* his grievous faults . . .

The humbling of Lord Choate! It was a capital scheme! She began busily to put her mind to it, and by the time Lady Melvin rose to take her leave, Clare was committed to the project.

Just how she could accomplish this would have to wait upon further thought. But for the first time, she looked to the future.

After Lady Melvin's departure, Miss Peek fell upon the books in the basket. "My goodness, this is going to be a fine read," she said, critically surveying a three-volume edition of *Woman, or Ida of Athens.* "Only, I do wish Lady Melvin did not feel it necessary to sip chocolate while she reads. Look here at this great brown smear."

"Let us hope," said Clare absently, "that she does not accuse us of carelessness. She is quite apt to do so, you know."

Miss Peek looked thoughtful, and then decided, "It will make no difference now. She would never believe us if we told her we had not read it. I am sure no one could resist Miss Owenson."

Then, something in the quality of Clare's silence spoke to her. "My dear?" she queried gently. "Did Lady Melvin say something to you to bring you so low?"

"Well, in a way she did. She had nothing but the most *fulsome* praise for Choate. And I do feel it unhandsome in her to try to tell me just how I should regard a man whom I know much better than she could ever hope to!"

"I quite agree, my dear," said Miss Peek promptly. "I suppose she spoke of his address, his impeccable courtesy?"

"Of course she did, Peeky. She knows nothing else of him. Her cousin knows him, and of all the flat-headed toadies her cousin is. . . !"

Miss Peek smiled gently. Her cap was awry, from her efforts in sorting out the books, and she put up both hands now to set it straight. "But you, of course, told her of his sterling character and his eminent fairness? His meticulous attention to your welfare?"

Clare stared at her. She had not suspected her companion of such a mischievous sense of humor, but to her great surprise, she saw that Miss Peek was entirely serious.

"I should have asked you to declaim upon the subject of his character. You see much more in him than I do."

"Well, no doubt you are right," said Miss Peek indulgently. "But I do think, my dear, that you would do well to cultivate such thoughts of him as would show off to advantage. It is no use to swim against the tide of popular opinion, you know."

"But popular opinion does consider him cold, you know. And full of his own importance."

But Miss Peek was already glancing surreptitiously at the books that she had chosen for her first afternoon's reading, and gave only scant attention to Clare. When Clare took a book of her own, and the two ascended the stairs to the upper floor, each went to her own room, to revel in solitude—Miss Peek to plunge into the vicissitudes of *Woman*, and Clare to set her book down on a table and walk to the window.

She found herself too much in sympathy with the beleaguered heroine of the romance to read about her with any enjoyment. But one thing she did know—and that was that any young female so placed that her guardian rode roughshod over her sensibilities was a poor thing if she did not retaliate in whatever way occurred to her.

Schooled in romance, Clare's first thoughts were of a kind to make Miss Peek, had she known them, turn pale and grasp at a nearby chair for support. Clare could not elope to Gretna Green—there was no one to elope with. She could not flee the country, going to lose herself in Paris, for Napoleon was still at war with England. And the ever-present remedy in the books she knew well—to fall into a fit of swooning—would not serve.

She toyed, for the next few days, with various plans to rout Benedict. But when the wildest of her ideas were subjected to a realistic light, she saw the flaw in them.

Each of the plans she had in mind was aimed at escape from the hateful yoke of the wicked guardian—to live without the burden of his decrees that limited her into a close confinement.

But she already had that. There was nothing that Benedict had arranged that she wouldn't have arranged herself, had she had the power. She was living in her own home, and if her life was constricted, it was not Benedict's fault, but only the fault of the required year of mourning. She did not resent the mourning for her grandmama, but she could not blame Benedict for it, either.

She had her dear Peeky to keep her company, she was free to roam the hills and valleys of the countryside, send for books from Mr. Lane's press in Leadenhall Street, receive visits from Lady Melvin and return them. Even to be driven into town by servants who loved her, to purchase whatever she needed, and be driven home again, without let or hindrance by her guardian.

And perhaps that was the trouble—that Benedict had given her his full attention while he dealt with her, as he would have dealt with any dependent, seeing to her welfare, and then, having settled it to his satisfaction, departing to forget all about her.

And Clare vowed to herself that she would not be left like a trunk in a lumber room, to be called for at some future time. She did not quite understand why she felt so strongly, but she believed it had to do with the Penryck pride, and surely he could understand that?

She wished to humble him, to bring him to his knees. Make him so aware of her that he could think of no one else—and then she would . . .

Her goals beyond that were dim and vague, shapeless forms in the future. Her first thought was how to gain her dearest wish. And there was nothing that she could do that would bring Benedict to his knees—the picture that lived ever in her mind.

Finally, a week later, she had almost given up the entire scheme. It was a hopeless task. Benedict was totally immersed, doubtless, in his plans to marry Marianna Morton. He would not harken to any appeal from the wilderness of Dorset.

But at this point, when the Penryck resolution lay limply bested, Fate took a hand and brought a gift in both hands to Clare. The gift, at first—as Fate's usually are—was artfully hidden in disaster.

16.

Budge and Peg had trudged up the stairs to Clare's bedroom, with the copper tub and pitcher after pitcher of hot water, for Clare's bath. This was a daily occurrence, and there was nothing this day to mark it from any other day.

Clare lingered in her bath until the water was tepid, and then added the last two pitchers of hot water, bringing the level to the top of the tub. Sliding down into the water, Clare let the warmth steal over her, drawing her into a timeless world, until suddenly she realized the water was cold.

The day was warm enough, and when she was dressed she felt marvelously invigorated. Calling to Budge, she instructed her to dispose of the bathwater, and she herself went down the hall to Miss Peek's room.

"Oh, my goodness!" declared Miss Peek. "Is it time for tea already? I could almost wish that Lady Melvin had not brought us such an assortment of new books. I can resist the temptation to read again some of my favorites, but a new book is beyond any resistance of mine!"

"But they are all alike, dear Peeky!" Clare laughed. "So many swoons per chapter, so many misshapen villains . . ." The ingenious authors had provided Clare with no help at all in her own problem.

She lingered while they discussed the merits of the various heroines of their acquaintance, comparing Evalina with Julia, and the wicked Duke of Duomo with the Marquis of Tormolino.

"And truly," said Clare, "there's not a jot or tittle of difference between them! And I wonder, Peeky, if you think they are all true to life?"

Miss Peek considered seriously. "N-no," she said at last. "For surely any young female would be able to get herself out of such outrageous scrapes! Or even better, were she well-brought-up, she would not find herself forced to flee headlong in the night. I *cannot* think that any female would have any credit in the world, if she did such a ramshackle thing."

"But sometimes," said Clare, brooding upon her own

114

trials, "the young female has nothing to say about her own affairs."

"Depend upon it," said Miss Peek sagely, "that in England matters are arranged in the best possible way. But of course, I would not be quite so sure of it in a *foreign land*."

Clare realized then that she had been hearing some unusual sounds for the last few minutes, and they now increased in volume until they demanded attention. She turned toward the door and raised her hand to enjoin silence.

There was the clamor of running feet and obscure muffled shouts, and Clare raced to the door and flung it open. Brushing aside Budge, screaming in the hall, both hands to her ears so as to shut out the sounds of her own voice, Clare quickly surveyed the scene. The floor was covered with water, unaccountably flowing swiftly from the open door and spreading across the hall.

"The tub! The tub!" screeched Budge, and Peg thrust a harassed face around the corner of the bedroom door.

"Budge!" said Clare in an incisive voice, but Budge ignored her. Leaving her to her screams, Clare, with a fleeting wish that she knew how Benedict had silenced her, lifted up her skirts and joined Peg in the bedroom.

"What happened? Never mind, I can see what happened. The tub overturned. Oh, if I had only not filled it quite so full! But then, probably the pitchers would have been overturned as well. Run downstairs, Peg, and get mops, and bring up Chugg and Goodwin. Hurry, before this soaks into the carpet too far!"

But of course, as she realized, it had already gone too far into the carpet. There was worse to come.

After strenuous mopping-up efforts, in which Budge, strongly intimidated by her mistress, took part, the tub and the pitchers were taken down the back stairs by the two footmen. Peg followed, bearing mops and pails, and Budge, spent from her emotional efforts, followed meekly.

It had truly been a mess, Clare thought. But thanks to Miss Peek, who knew precisely what to do to minimize the damage, and directed the servants with a firm hand, there seemed to be little real damage. Miss Peek retired to her room to change her clothing, sadly soiled by water and an unfortunate encounter with a dirty mop, and Clare moved toward the stairs.

There would be no comfort in her own upstairs sitting room for weeks, until the carpet was thoroughly dry. She must ask Peeky whether it would be best to take up the carpet and lay it out in the sun in the kitchen garden.

Clare was halfway down the stairs when she became aware of an unexpected consequence of the accident. She stood there on the steps, one hand lightly on the banister, while enlightenment and culmination of her week's thought came to her with a blinding flash.

The ceiling of the downstairs hall was soaking wet, and already small pieces of sodden plaster had fallen to the tile floor.

The water had seeped through to the downstairs. Perhaps . . . She ran lightly down the stairs and into the drawing room. There were telltale signs of moisture creeping over the white plastered ceiling. And her plan was complete! She had already embarked on the first step of her great plan—the humbling of Lord Choate!

The moisture had not yet done any great damage to the drawing-room ceiling. But still, having been presented with so much that would fulfill her purpose, she could certainly help it along.

She slipped out of the side door and hurried along to the stables. Glancing swiftly around to see whether she was observed, she picked up a long pole from a pile lying beside the stable. Its purpose was unknown to her, but she knew what she intended for it. She failed to see Tom Swann, the coachman's boy, emerging from the side door of the stable and stopping short at the unaccustomed sight of his mistress hurrying toward the abbey with a pole, at least seven feet long, in her hands.

Curious, he followed her, taking care not to be noticed. For there was something very secretive about Miss Clare's actions, he thought, and he was not of stern enough stuff to relegate the incident to oblivion.

Peering, at length, through the drawing-room windows, he perceived a strange sight. Miss Clare stood near the door into the hall, the pole in her hands. She was prodding at the ceiling!

Tom gulped. Miss Clare's activity was rewarded, he noticed, looking again, for small bits of plaster were sifting down to the floor. She peered at them and smiled with satisfaction. Then, to his amazement, she moved to another spot and continued, loosening the plaster and watching it drop to the French carpet.

There was something havey-cavey about the whole thing, thought Tom, and he wanted no part of it. Whatever Miss Clare wanted to do was her business, wasn't it? And if she wanted advice or help, she would ask for it, wouldn't she? Tom tiptoed away from the house, and as soon as he thought he would not be observed, fled at speed toward the safety of the stables, where horses at least acted like horses, and didn't do daft things without any warning.

But Clare, believing herself unobserved, prodded at the soaked plaster until she was satisfied with the results. There was a drift of plaster right across the carpet, and artistically she approved of the loosened piece that hung at a precarious angle, threatening to drop at the slightest breath. She looked down at the pole in her hands. Should she loosen a bit more?

The sound of footsteps in the hall made her decision for her. Swiftly she hurried to the drawing-room windows, opening onto the lawn, and thrust the pole behind the shrubs alongside the wall. Later she would have to remember to return the pole to its original location, but just now she must turn back into the drawing room to greet Peeky.

"What on earth! My dear, do you know that the hall ceiling has been loosened by the water? That foolish Budge! I cannot think what could have made her so clumsy!"

"She wasn't able to say," said Clare, trying to hide her elation. "Only, look at this ceiling, too! We shall not be able to sit here this evening. It is too dangerous."

"Uncomfortable perhaps, but hardly dangerous."

Clare stared at the dangling chunk of plaster, willing it to loosen this second and drop to the floor. Obligingly, it swayed ominously. "Careful!"

Peeky looked uneasily where Clare indicated. "Oh, my," she said faintly.

"You see? Even the slightest breath of air from opening the door makes it ready to fall."

"But," said Miss Peek stoutly, "you see, it did not fall. And while there is plaster—yes, I see it, Clare—on the carpet, we must simply have it cleaned up and then call someone up from the village to repair the ceilings."

"I suppose so," said Clare dubiously. "But I am sure it

will cost a great deal. And it cannot be done at once, can it? Won't the ceiling need to dry, and the floor above as well?"

"I suppose so. But we must take expert advice on this."

"Certainly. I do hope Lord Choate will agree that the trouble must be fixed."

"But of course he will, my dear. After all, it is your money, and not his, that must be used." Miss Peek frowned at the ceiling. She liked an orderly life, and although such catastrophes were truly a part of one's life, bringing the opportunity to set all straight again, and nothing to be considered *overwhelming*, yet there was something she did not quite like about the situation.

She could not put her finger upon any flaw in the sequence of events. Given a tub of water, overturned by clumsy maids, the natural consequence was that the unconfined water would seek a lower level, and there was eminent logic in the fact that the water had seeped through and loosened the downstairs ceilings. But yet she was uneasy.

"I am sure Lord Choate will authorize the expenditure," said Miss Peek firmly. "In the meantime, we shall simply ... What are you looking at, Clare?"

"I thought that the damage was near the door, but look here. Halfway into the room. Come on, Peeky, let's get out of here before the ceiling falls on our heads."

"Oh, I am sure it will not!"

"How can you be sure? I had thought it would surely not fall on our heads there by the door, but you see, there is a great deal of plaster already fallen."

Clare eyed her governess with apprehension. Surely Miss Peek must fall in with her plot. She knew very well that Peeky would not lend herself to an overt scheme like the one Clare had in mind. But if she could be convinced ...

"If you wish to risk your life," said Clare, "I don't. And I will move into the morning room, where at least the ceiling is sound. I hope."

Once in the morning room, joined at once by Miss Peek, Clare sat with an exaggerated sigh. "I vow I do not know what to do next. Of course, I will desire Mr. Austin to write to Lord Choate, but what are we to do in the meantime? We cannot stay here!"

"Of course we can. We are very comfortable here. A

trifle cramped, my dear, but after all, there are just the two of us, and I daresay we can make out very well indeed."

"But," wailed Clare, "where shall I sleep? I feel it is too damp in my chamber to be quite healthful, and the other rooms have not been aired recently. I am in such a stew!"

After prolonged discussion, artfully nurtured by Clare, Miss Peek had grown considerably more anxious. She did not wish to believe that there was danger from the ceiling, but there was the evidence of the plaster on the floor. And after Clare had gone from the living room, and Miss Peek had lingered, the large block of plaster that had wavered tentatively over her head had actually dropped, missing her by no more than a foot and shattering on the soft carpet. Miss Peek was convinced.

"The only thing," said Clare after a long silence, "is to remove from the abbey."

Miss Peek gaped. "Remove? From the abbey? Where?"

"We would have to be away until the damage is repaired. It may be as long as six weeks," cried Clare recklessly.

"I am sure you are wrong," said Miss Peek, but without conviction.

"At *least* that long."

"But," said Miss Peek, mindful of her instructions, "I do not think Lord Choate would consider it eligible to remove from the abbey. After all, there are still habitable rooms here, and we could manage very nicely."

"Damp," pronounced Clare darkly, "and falling plaster. I wonder at you, Peeky. Or perhaps you see this as a ruined castle or the grotto of Mandovio? Pray disabuse your mind of that, for I have no longing to emulate Julia."

Miss Peek laughed slightly. "You know you are talking nonsense."

"I do know that, Peeky," said Clare with a rush, rising to give her companion a kiss on the cheek. "But nonetheless, I do think I am right. I won't press you, dear Peeky. Let us forget the entire thing."

But when it came time for bed, Clare decided that her room was indeed too damp to sleep in, and Miss Peek agreed. For the carpet had taken up the brunt of the overturned water, and held it, in the face of determined efforts to wipe it dry.

It would have to be taken out the next morning and laid

in the sun to dry, Miss Peek agreed. But in the meantime, Clare was warmly invited to share her governess's bed.

It was a long night for both of them. And the situation did not improve. For in the morning Clare awakened to the sound of soft rain on the window. The sky was leaden, and the rain promised to last all day, and perhaps a day or two more. Wisby, a thorough countryman, gloomily prophesied at least a week of unsettled weather.

"And when it's going to clear, the land knows when," he said dourly. "And that won't help the ceiling dry out, you can believe me on that, miss."

Clare believed him. More to the point, Miss Peek also believed him. "What are we to do, Clare?" she said anxiously. "Lord Choate would want us to stay, I am persuaded."

"But not at the peril of life and limb," said Clare stoutly. "At least, not at peril of *your* life. Mine he holds of no account, but I do not care a rush for that."

"But where, then?" said Miss Peek, bewildered.

Clare appeared to think for a few moments, and then turned a sunny smile to her dear companion. "I know, although you might think I am presuming too much on you, Peeky . . ."

"Not at all, my dear. Whatever you ask me to do," she said rashly, "I shall agree."

"Then let us go to Bath and stay. I am sure your sister will be so glad to have you home again that she will not cavil over me."

"Bath!"

"With Budge, of course. Do say yes, Peeky. I vow I do not wish to spend another night in this gloomy, damp place!"

It took some persuading, but Miss Peek herself secretly did not relish the idea of sharing her bedroom for six weeks or more with Clare. And it was in fact much too damp to air another room properly, and the damaged ceiling would be weeks in drying out.

At length it was settled, so that the carriage was ordered for just after luncheon, and while Miss Peek packed and gave orders to the servants as to how to go on during their absence, and while Budge alternately packed Clare's clothes with vigor and wailed at the thought of leaving Penryck Abbey, Clare herself sat down at her little gold-and-white writing desk and drew out paper and pen.

"My dear Lord Choate," she began after much pondering, "I beg leave to tell you of the dire catastrophe that has struck Penryck Abbey. A veritable *flood* has damaged it so that it is *quite* impossible to continue to live here. I must ask you to direct Mr. Austin to see to the needful repairs. I am persuaded that you need only instruct your man of affairs to deal with things, and that you need not then give another thought to the problem. Believe me, I *do* appreciate all the time and trouble you have already expended on me, and I should be *loath* to add to your burdens, especially since you are about to become very happy. On your wedding day, I mean, of course."

She tapped her pen on her teeth while she read what she had written. Satisfied that she had put him in possession of enough facts to pique his curiosity, and no more, she added the final touch.

"If it should be needful, I should tell you that your man of affairs can reach me in care of Miss Peek, Milsom Street, Bath."

She folded the letter, ready to send. That ought to do it, she thought with great satisfaction.

17.

Clare could never tire, she believed, of walking along the Royal Crescent, looking at the elegant buildings that were inspired by Beau Nash, the guild hall, the assembly rooms, Queen Square, the North and South parades, and watching all the fashionably dressed ladies and the ailing dowagers and gouty old men who daily sought relief in the baths.

Several buildings encompassed the various mineral springs, of varying temperature and curative powers. The waters were said to be very beneficial in cases of gout, rheumatism, neuralgia, diseases of the liver, and sciatica.

Even though one was as healthy as a horse, there was a wealth of things to do in Bath, but all the assemblies and the card parties were forbidden to her. She recognized the truth of Choate's statement. Bath is a hotbed of intrigue, he had said, and he feared for her reputation.

He need not have worried, she thought glumly. She knew that Miss Peek's chaperonage, while adequate, yet did not admit her to the first society in Bath, nor could she have taken advantage of such introductions had she had them, for she was still in mourning.

But she learned that one's health provided the only excuse required for frequenting the Pump Room, drinking the ugly-tasting waters, and strolling through the Assembly Rooms in the morning.

The afternoons could be taken up with shopping, visits to mantua-makers, milliners, glovers, and other establishments catering to feminine fancies. Clare herself had no need to go far afield, for Milsom Street held two milliners, a bootmaker, and a confectioner. But only once did she enter the milliner's shop just below the Peek sisters' rooms.

She was torn between a bonnet with a great tall brim, lined with pleated silk to hold it stiff, and a smaller hat in the French style with curling feathers in a most fetching arrangement. There was another . . . But it was no use. She could not make up her mind, and truly there was no reason to buy a new bonnet, for she could not wear it for months.

She expected Benedict to arrive in Milsom Street any hour, and she dared not be from home for any length of time. Besides, she could not quite decide which hat Benedict would like, and when she realized that she was shopping entirely with him in mind, she abruptly walked out of the shop and did not return.

Benedict did not come the first day she expected him, nor the second. On the third, she took Budge with her and walked out upon the streets of Bath. She walked through Queen Street, and strolled aimlessly toward Pulteney Bridge. Looking back from the banks of the Avon, she could see the square-topped building that housed the springs themselves, and, to her surprise and dismay, strolling in front of the Pump Room were Lady Courtenay and Evalina.

There was no escaping them. "How delightful to see you," said Lady Courtenay. "I confess I had not expected to see you again until next year." She lowered her voice. "Mourning, of course."

"That is true," said Clare demurely, "but my companion, Miss Peek, has felt not quite the thing, you know, and I persuaded her that she should come to Bath to take the waters." Having cast truth aside thus far, she plunged on. "So of course I had to come too. But naturally I do not go out into society."

"Too bad," said Evalina. "For there is always something exciting going on. I have three cards for parties this very afternoon."

Clare smiled sadly. "I know you must be enjoying yourself greatly. But I must not stay away from dear Miss Peek."

She longed to ask about Benedict, but she dared not. Lady Courtenay was a dear person, kindly and generous, but with a tongue loose at both ends. And Evalina followed her mother's lead in every detail.

But Lady Courtenay suddenly had an idea. "Pray ask Miss Peek's indulgence, and we will go to the baths this afternoon. I am sure there can be no question of impropriety, don't you know, with a matter of health. We are all much concerned with our own health, you know, and while there is much gossip in a place like this, where people have little enough to think about, yet I fancy that were you to be seen with me, there would be nothing to fear."

Clare leaped at the opportunity. It would be just the thing to go with Lady Courtenay, and while she loved Peeky, she was so restless waiting for Benedict that she welcomed the diversion that Lady Courtenay offered.

So it was that that afternoon she found herself in the Pump Room with Lady Courtenay and Evalina. It was not quite what she expected, but soon she began to see faces she knew and exchanged a few words with those who came to greet her. It was the second day of her going with Lady Courtenay that she saw a face that made her shudder.

What is he doing in Bath? she wondered, thinking that she had rarely seen anyone who appeared healthier than Harry Rowse.

He saw her from across the room, and she was uncomfortably aware that his gaze fixed on her without discretion. She turned to Lady Courtenay and began to talk with animation.

"Now, then, there is the Dowager Duchess of Argyle," said Lady Courtenay. "She was a great friend of your grandmother in her early days, so I believe, and if you like, I shall take you to her."

"I should like that above all," said Clare dutifully, and carefully not looking at Harry Rowse, she accompanied Lady Courtenay around the room to stand before the chair that held the dowager duchess.

"This is Clare Penryck," introduced Lady Courtenay. "You remember her grandmother."

"Of course I do," said the duchess graciously. "I should offer you my hand but, alas, my fingers are so gnarled with this ailment that it is a pleasure I must deny myself. You do not look a thing like your grandmama. Much more like the Penrycks, I think, except for the Penryck eyebrows."

"She is much like her mother, Lady Thane tells me. A sweetly biddable girl."

Her grace looked penetratingly at Clare and said abruptly, "I should doubt that very much. But my dear, pray forgive us for talking of you as though you were not here. Sit down and tell me how your grandmother fared during the past years. You must miss her. I do myself, and I had not seen her for twenty years."

Clare answered the duchess's questions, and gained that lady's high regard for her poise. "It is hard to believe," said the duchess, when Clare rose with Lady Courtenay to take her leave, "that you are such a young person. Oh, yes, my dear, I do know how old you are, but if I did not, I would not guess you to be younger than twenty. I hope that pleases you? I always think that when one is young, one longs to be old, and of course, the reverse, as you will learn, is also true. But come and see me again. I see my foolish nurse beckoning to me, and I must prepare myself for another draft of that abominable medicine."

"I hope it helps you!" said Clare sincerely.

"I doubt it will," said the duchess, "but then, one tries everything."

It was on her way home, with Budge behind a few steps, hurrying, with the feeling that Harry Rowse might be just behind her, that she ran into Sir Alexander Ferguson.

It looked as though all London had come to Bath, she thought—all but the one man she wanted to see. But Sir Alex's honest face broke into a smile when he caught sight of her, and he lifted his beaver and greeted her.

"I certainly did not expect to see you, Miss Penryck," he said, "but will you let me escort you?" He turned and walked with her toward Milsom Street. "What are you doing in Bath?"

She told him as much of the truth as she felt necessary, and asked him in turn, "I should have thought that you would still be in London? What is the latest *on-dit* from there? I feel sadly out of things."

"Well, yes, I suppose you might," agreed Sir Alex. "But there is not much going on. Choate, you know, is still in town, but of course you would know that. He is your guardian, after all. But his marriage—"

"Next month, I collect," she said with an air of carelessness.

"No, I don't think so," he said, frowning. "I did hear, I think, that the date had been postponed. But I may be wrong. At any rate, I do not envy him. It seems to me that such a marriage is destined to be a rocky one. You know, I myself have looked for other qualities in a wife. But I should perhaps not talk of them to you. At least at this time. I know you are still in mourning, and will be for some time. But there will be a time . . ."

He smiled down at her, and drew her hand through his arm.

"Choate is not married, then."

"No. I remember Miss Morton's father. A terror if there ever was one. Heard he once flogged a footman because the meat was cold. Nonsense, of course. Not the footman's fault."

"I should say not."

"Butler should have known the meat was cold."

"Oh, dear," she said faintly. "Do you mean he should have flogged the butler?"

To her great surprise, he nodded. "Of course he should have. Bad judgment, all the way round. Somewhat of a bully, don't you know, flogging a footman because he was smaller."

They strolled farther in silence. A great bully, Miss Morton's father? She felt there was something germane to the issue in this new information, but she could not quite understand what it was. She would have to think on this further, for all things connected with her hated guardian were of compelling interest.

"I should not wish harm to anyone," she said finally, "because of course that is not right, but I cannot help but think that Lord Choate deserves flogging. Or at least some sort of revelation."

Sir Alexander looked down at her in surprise. "I should have thought that a gentleman of such prestige would be ideal as a guardian for a personable young lady such as yourself."

"Oh, nonsense!" said Clare hardily. "You do not see my guardian as I see him. He is perfectly odious, and I think"—with belated caution—"we have spoken quite enough of him. Are you enjoying Bath?"

"It is a most historical place, don't you know. The mineral springs here were first recognized by the Romans," Sir Alex informed her with all the liveliness of a guidebook. "They made their settlement of Aquae Sulis here in A.D. 44. . . ."

Her attention lapsed, until she was able, during a pause in his peroration, to insert deftly, "Tell me, you do not come to Bath for your health?"

"Oh, no. But it is the fashionable place to be just now, you know. London is deserted, and if one wants to be in the swim, one comes to Bath."

So much the better, thought Clare. Surely no one could fault her for setting aside her strict mourning seclusion on the state of her health. But if it were fashionable to be seen in Bath, then Benedict would hear of it. And even if he had not thoroughly perused her letter to him, tossing it aside without understanding it, or even—horror of horrors!—if his secretary had not shown it to him, he would yet understand that she was, as he would no doubt say, footloose in Bath!

She was much more comfortable, now that she had solved to her own satisfaction Benedict's failure to appear posthaste. She could expect now that he would surely respond to the tide of gossip that must inevitably reach his ears, in London, or at his country house.

Sir Alexander escorted her to the front door of the apartment above the milliner's shop where the Misses Peek lived in cramped quarters, even more confining now that Clare had moved in.

"I shall look forward to seeing you," he said, lifting her mittened hand to his lips, "but I must adjure you to exercise every care so that you preserve your good character. I should expect that Choate has some scheme in mind to surround you with the care that is rightfully yours. Perhaps you will instruct me," he said, essaying a ponderous twinkle, "as to how I can best safeguard you until he arrives?"

She murmured an appropriate response, but her mind was busy on a variety of subjects. Bidding farewell to her escort, she scurried up the stairs and closed the door behind her. Both Peek sisters looked up sharply when she came in.

"Peeky, I have such news! Did you know that Bath is fashionable this time of year?"

"Of course, love. But I cannot say that gives us much pleasure. Truly, Clare, we should not have come to Bath."

"No, indeed, we should not! I would *much* rather be lying in my bed with my head swathed in bandages where a portion of the abbey fell on my unsuspecting head."

"Hardly unsuspecting," interposed Miss Sara Peek. "I judge that is the reason, after all, why you came to Bath—that you did suspect such an event?"

Clare decided she did not like Miss Sara as well as she liked her own Miss Emily Peek. Miss Sara was far too perceptive, and Clare knew that the sisters' quiet life had been shattered by her arrival. But it would be for only a short time, and there was little else she could do.

"A letter came for you," announced Miss Sara. "There on the table. I had to pay the man."

Clare flew to the table to seize the letter. Not franked, so it was not from Lord Benedict Choate. An expression of dismay slipped across her face, so strong as even to move Miss Sara to a kind of pity. The miss was wayward, and this whole romp would lead to trouble, thought Miss Sara darkly, but yet it was too bad the child was so lonely.

The child, just now, was increasingly furious. The letter, while not from her guardian, yet was prompted by his moving spirit.

"My dear Miss Penryck," began the letter from Mr. Austin, in Dorset, "I have been advised by Lord Choate, your guardian, that I am to set about repairing the damage at the abbey at once. It should prove to be a small task, for the damage is hardly perceptible except for the one ceiling. There is no structural harm, I am assured. I have told Peters to rush the repairs, and they will be finished in a day or two. Lord Choate wished the work expedited, and has instructed me to tell you that you are to return to the abbey immediately upon its repair. By the time this letter reaches you, I expect all will be in readiness for your return. Pray believe me, yr. obt. servant . . ."

She sank into a chair, the letter slipping to the floor. Miss Peek, after a nervous dart forward, resolutely picked it up and read it.

"Well, then," she said bracingly. "We must make ready to return to the abbey. I think if we start early tomorrow, we shall make it by late afternoon, even in the heavy coach. I shall start packing."

She did not move, however, being arrested by some quality in Clare's silence. At length Clare burst into speech as though the words were wrung from her: "He doesn't *care!*"

18.

Clare went to bed without her supper. She had been given one of the two bedrooms of the small flat in Milsom Street for her own, and so, happily, she was able to give way entirely to her distraught state of mind, without the need for keeping up appearances before the sisters Peek.

She pulled the stool to the window and looked down into the street. It was a fairly well-traveled street during the day, for there were several shops catering to the wealthier of the valetudinarians, and there were carriages going to and fro, and fashionable women with their well-dressed escorts strolling on the sidewalk, followed by a maid or footman to carry the packages.

But at night the street was entirely deserted. The shop below had turned down its lights long since, and the aroma of cabbage that inevitably floated upstairs stirred some pangs of hunger in her.

But she could not swallow over the lump in her throat. From her window she could see the lights still lit in the Assembly Rooms, and even, now and then, a measure of violin melody telling that somewhere in that vast pile of brick there was dancing and revelry.

And she sat here in the dark, forgotten by everyone she knew—meaning Lord Choate—and resented by Peeky's sister.

Sadly she rehearsed her failures. She had made a mull of her life already and she was only sixteen. Many a girl was married by the time she was eighteen—her own mother had been, and although that had not been an overly happy marriage, yet she was sure her mother would not have wanted to depart from it with such abruptness.

She could have helped Clare through this, thought Clare, but then, if her mother had lived, she would not have gone to London, her grandmother would not have been so anxious to get her settled, and the entire affair would not have happened. Besides that, she would not now be under the uncaring supervision of a wicked guardian.

The tears came unannounced, and she wept for her

grandmother. And her mother and father, and for what might have been and was not.

But before long, the inheritance of realism she owed to the Penrycks came to her rescue. She had mourned, truly, for her grandmother many times before Lady Penryck's death, and it had done no good, nor would tears help at this juncture.

Only a plan would do—a scheme laid out in detail, to reach a point she wanted to gain.

The plan she had already hatched had misfired in her face. Mr. Austin was the delegated authority between Choate and herself. Her plan was shattered, but perhaps she could salvage some of it? Or even, as her mind began to work busily, construct a new plan?

The trouble with the previous plan, she realized, was that she would not have known what to do with Choate when she had lured him to Bath. Grandmama would have been ashamed for her, not to have thought things through.

She propped her chin on her hand, elbow on the sill, and looked broodingly out over the city founded by Caesar's legions. But the past Romans and the present invalids were alike forgotten as she set her mind on her own affairs. She had never been encouraged to believe in her own limitations, and thus it was that the failures of recent weeks weighed so heavily upon her. Grandmama had often told her she could do anything she set her mind to—within the limitations of the exigencies of society, of course, for it would not do to jeopardize her reputation—and now Clare remembered, with thankfulness, her grandmother's confidence in her.

She would bring it off, she knew. As soon as she decided what she wanted. To bring Benedict to his knees. To teach him that she was not a penniless dependent to be regarded with disinterest and cared for as a truly great man sees that his sheep are dryly penned in the winter and that his hounds are fed.

She would not simply be put on a shelf.

She stirred restlessly. Somehow these aims did not seem quite enough. But they would have to do for a start.

Now the question was, how to accomplish this much?

As she turned over in her mind the recent days in Bath, one face came to her, at last, a face that had long repelled her. Now the face of Harry Rowse continued to lurk at the fringes of her mind, like a naughty child peeping through the banisters at the festivities below.

She was already determined not to return to Penryck Abbey. Such a retreat would be a death blow to her aspirations. She had tried the simple removal to Bath, expecting that after Choate had fiercely forbidden her to travel there, he would come down posthaste to deal with her rebellion.

But he had simply turned the matter over to Mr. Austin. Instead of regarding such an act on Choate's part as giving her credit for a reasonable solution to an unexpected problem, she considered it a cowardly evasion. And she would go to any lengths, she thought, to point out his errors to his face.

And the face of Harry Rowse edged closer in her thoughts. At length she made up her mind. If there was one thing above all else, judging from her experience of him, that would set Choate boiling, it was Harry Rowse. And Rowse could be encouraged, she thought.

But that would be dangerous, she decided. She truly did not think she could trust him, and to take him into her confidence would be the outside of folly. But if Benedict *thought* that Harry Rowse was favored . . .

The next morning she informed Miss Peek that she could not possibly travel to Penryck Abbey this day. "Besides, Peeky, I know Peters from old, and he will not finish his work as soon as Mr. Austin thinks he will. I should judge another week will be soon enough to consider leaving Bath."

"I don't suppose you would consider removing to the Christopher?" suggested the dour Miss Sara.

"Sister, how could you say that? I must go with her if we consider such a change, and—"

"And it would be most expensive," added Clare quickly. "But I shall certainly give up my bed, and perhaps we could put two chairs together, and it would work out marvelously."

The discussion was still going on when Miss Peek and Clare, accompanied by Budge, at the proper hour of ten moved out of Milsom Street and onto the Parade. It was not long before they met Lady Courtenay and Evalina, and Miss Peek, pleading errands, left her charge in care of the Courtenays, suiting Clare eminently.

Scanning the faces of the crowds, she at length caught

sight of the one she searched for, and took her first step in her scheme.

"Oh, pray let us go the other way for a moment, Evalina," she begged. "I see . . . But then, I must not trouble you."

Evalina, scenting a pleasurable excitement, tightened her fingers on Clare's arm and said, "What do you see, Clare? Who is it? Lady Melvin?"

"Lady Melvin!" exclaimed Clare in surprise. "I did not know she was in Bath. Where is she?" She caught sight of Lady Melvin and Sir Ewald, the latter in a bath chair, his bandaged gouty foot held up prominently before him. They were on the opposite pavement, and Clare thought they did not see her.

Clare returned to her original plan. "Mr. Rowse, you know. I do not wish to recognize him."

"He's terrible," agreed Evalina. "Has he been . . . well, you know?" she added in a somewhat wistful tone.

Clare lowered her gaze to the pavement. "I do not wish to say more, even to you, dear Evalina."

Harry Rowse, already aprowl, altered his course to intercept the small party, and as he drew close, he doffed his beaver and waited for Lady Courtenay to speak. Since Lady Courtenay had a certain regard for Harry's mother, was sufficiently mistress of her own affairs, and possessed of a great deal of credit in society, she did not snub Harry Rowse, as many another lady would have, but nodded to him graciously.

Rowse, encouraged beyond his expectations, turned and walked a few steps with them. But, catching Lady Courtenay's speculative eye on him, he thought it prudent to recollect an errand in the opposite end of town and bade them good-day. Clare was content. Rowse had been seen with her. She could rely on gossip.

"That is enough," said Lady Courtenay comfortably. "We have recognized him and I daresay his mother would thank me for it. But we have no need to take him up, for he must know that he is not welcome in any society that prides itself on its standards."

Lady Courtenay then dismissed him totally from her mind. Catching sight of one of her cronies, together they entered the Pump Room. Lady Courtenay and her friend gravitated toward wicker chairs, and settled down for a comfortable coze. Clare had leisure to congratulate herself on the progress of her scheme.

It came time at last for Clare to return to Milsom Street, but Lady Courtenay gave no sign of leaving. Clare was uncertain as to what to do, especially since Evalina had decided to undergo a treatment that would continue for another hour, at the least.

Clare finally took her leave of Lady Courtenay, who was in the middle of a particularly exhilarating piece of gossip about the Duchess of York at Oatlands—"At least a hundred dogs, you know, and they swarmed around poor Lewis and *bit* him!"—and Clare departed from the Pump Room with only Budge to escort her.

Hungry, because she had not eaten supper the night before, she hurried down the street and turned into an angling walkway. No sooner had she left the main street than she saw, to her great dismay, coming toward her the man of all men that she did not want to see.

"Miss Penryck!" said Harry Rowse. "I had hoped to see you again. But I had not thought fortune would smile on me quite so soon. May I walk with you?"

He did not wait for permission but turned to walk in her direction. He did not offer his arm. "I want to apologize to you for that episode that I am sure you have by now forgotten—at least, I should hope you have. It was unforgivable in me to allow my feelings to guide me, and my only excuse is that my heart overruled my head. I must take care not to let it happen again," he added, watching her closely.

From his height, he could see the flush mantling her cheek beneath the feathers curled fetchingly along the brim of her bonnet.

As an apology, she thought, it lacked something—true repentance, possibly. But she was far too conscious of his company to want to prolong it. She murmured something in a stifled voice that he took to mean forgiveness, and as they reached the corner where Milsom Street crossed, he saw with surprise that she was going to turn into the street.

"But of course, you have errands. Pray allow me to accompany you."

With returning spirit, she stopped and laughed at him. "I suppose you, a very tulip of fashion, would enjoy shopping? No, I dare not imagine such a thing. I thank you for your escort this far. But now I must leave you. Good-bye."

He was not ready to give up quite yet. "But where are you staying?" he demanded. "I should like, if you do not greatly mind, to see you again."

Inspiration came to her, belatedly. She had no wish to divulge her actual residence to him, for who knew what he was capable of? She had allowed herself—even though without design this last time—to be seen with Rowse, for her own purposes, but she feared to allow him any further conversation.

"You know of course that I am in mourning," she said, gently sad, "and do not go out. But . . . you may look for me at the Christopher."

He bowed deeply, and with a satisfied smile took his leave. And look and look, thought Clare. But you will not find me there.

Nonetheless, she decided not to take any chances. She had set in train the gossip she intended, and if gossip acted as it usually did, it would be flying on wings to all corners of England. And she dared not become embroiled in any incident beyond this until she had heard from Benedict.

The next few days she kept close to the apartment, going out only when Miss Peek could go with her. Sir Alexander joined them once or twice, and while Clare noticed that Harry Rowse watched her from a distance, he made no sign of recognition.

The days wore on, and there was no word from Choate. Her spirits sank lower and lower, and as the days passed, she knew that at the end of the week she must return to Penryck Abbey.

It came to the last day she had allowed herself. One more time she would stroll on the Crescent, on the promenade, through the Pump Room. She longed for that, so when Sir Alexander called and asked whether he could escort her, she agreed gladly.

"For you must know," she told him as they descended Milsom Street, Budge walking behind them, "that I must return to my home tomorrow. You will remember that there was extensive damage to the house in the flood, and I have just been told that the repairs are complete. So that I long to be home again."

Clare continued to chatter artlessly, and soon they reached the main street and turned toward the Pump

Room. From afar they could see a heavy traveling coach drawn by four horses—not real goers, said Sir Alex, but of good blood—lumbering toward them down the street. Something familiar about the coach stopped Clare in her tracks, and they waited as the coach drew nearer.

Soon she could make out the panel, as the coach turned onto Laura Place, and she exclaimed with a sinking feeling, "Lady Thane! I wonder what she is doing here!"

But while she turned it over in her mind, Sir Alexander was pointing out the traveling curricle moving smartly behind the coach, drawn by two matched grays, the driver on the seat holding the reins effortlessly in one hand, his whip held at an elegant angle in the other.

"Choate!" exploded Sir Alexander. "I thought he had gone to the country!"

"Well, after all," said Clare, gratified at the sight of her goal attained, "his country house is not very far from here, is it?"

"In Kent, you know. But of course he does have properties everywhere." Sir Alexander nodded wisely. "A great landowner, and when Miss Morton's land and his are joined, there will be few wealthier men in England."

As they watched, the curricle began to turn, and suddenly veered in their direction. Bringing his horses to a precise halt before her, Benedict touched his hat and nodded to Alex. "I had not expected to see you here in Bath, Miss Penryck," said Benedict calmly. "I must speak to Austin about diluting my instructions."

"I had heard nothing from *you*, Lord Choate," said Clare innocently, "and I felt that I must have misunderstood Mr. Austin's letter, even though I am persuaded he quoted you exactly."

Benedict held his impatient horses easily—more easily, in truth, than he held his temper. But all he said was, "Ferguson, I would be much obliged to you if you escorted my ward back to her lodgings in Milsom Street. I must see Lady Thane settled, and then, believe me"—he glared at Clare—"I shall wait upon you directly."

Lady Thane's carriage was already out of sight. But Benedict backed his horses in the narrow way, and turning them precisely, drove into the side street and was soon also out of sight.

"Well," said Sir Alex heavily, "I must hasten to put myself in the right with him. I do not think he will object when I explain that Lady Courtenay has seen that all was proper, and certainly you have your maid with you at all times." He began to escort her back to the Peek apartment. "No, I fancy that even such a stickler as Choate will find nothing amiss."

Clare, once upstairs with the Misses Peek, was not nearly so sanguine as Alex had been. "He's here!" she announced to her hostesses. When they sorted it out, at last, from Clare's alternate fits of dread and anticipation, and they realized that Lord Choate was indeed coming to call on Clare in this apartment *within the hour*, in moments the sisters had donned their shawls and their bonnets, and, armed with an ostentatious shopping list, scuttled down the steps in a flurry, leaving only Budge to succor her mistress and support her in the coming ordeal.

Miss Peek's last words were, "Now, you know that Lord Choate is an exceedingly fine gentleman, and your guardian. There is naught amiss in your receiving him alone. But . . . I do wish we had gone back to Penryck Abbey when Mr. Austin told us that was the thing to do. I fear Lord Choate will be much exercised!"

After she was left alone, Clare agreed. She had no regrets about staying here in Bath, for she had at last gained Lord Choate's attention. She sat down on the edge of a chair to await the outcome of what she considered would be a very painful interview.

Budge at last announced him. "Lord Choate!" she said, barely staying in the room long enough to pronounce the name.

And Clare, holding to the arms of the chair with white-knuckled hands, found that the famed Penryck resolution had basely and incontinently fled.

19.

Benedict entered as the maid scuttled away. He stood in the center of the room, looking around him at the shabby furniture, the threadbare rug, and began to draw off his gloves.

He turned at last to her and lifted an eyebrow. "Well, no greeting? I must confess," he said, with every appearance of amiability, "that I had thought you not quite so juvenile as to sit gaping at me as though I were a dragon."

Somewhat encouraged by his easy words, Clare felt her self-assurance creeping back. "I do wonder at your coming to Bath," she said ingenuously, "for I had not thought you one to dose yourself."

"I am not," he said steadily. "Nor do I intend to take the waters. I rode over to Penryck Abbey three days ago, expecting to find you there."

"But you know about the ceiling, sir?"

"I do," he said, and for the first time a touch of grimness crept into his voice. "You will be relieved to know that it is entirely repaired. But Austin agreed with me that his letter to you must have gone astray. Or else," he said deliberately, "you would have returned to Dorset."

She sat silently, looking down at the hands folded in her lap. She waited for the storm to break over her head, for already she knew Choate well enough to understand that when he was most amiable, a swift change for the worse in his mood could be expected.

"I did not think it mattered," she said, with an appearance of innocence, "whether I went one day or another. There was nothing in Dorset that needed me, after all."

"Whereas I suppose the Pump Room here did?" he said with a rising inflection. "But let me tell you this—I do not like what I have been hearing about you. A fast life is not proper when you are in mourning. Even someone more hen-witted than you would know that."

"But, sir, I have not been feeling well. And anyone can take the waters for one's health, mourning or not."

"So"—he glared at her—"that is your excuse. Very well, gossip may be wrong in what it spreads all over En-

137

gland. But I fail to see what contribution meeting with known rakes has to do with restoring your health."

Harry Rowse's meeting had indeed provided the spur that brought Benedict here to Bath. She was hard put to hide her satisfaction. But now that Benedict was here—what then? She had no plan for the next step.

"Known rakes," she said. "How can gossip have exaggerated so much? Unless, of course, they mean Sir Alexander Ferguson? I did not know he had such a reputation, sir, or I should not have walked with him."

"You know I don't mean Ferguson." He took a turn around the tiny room, seeming surprised at coming abruptly to a table before he knew it. Then he said in an altered tone, "I am glad to see that the waters have been of assistance. You appear to me to be quite recovered."

"Bath," she said demurely, "has done me a world of good."

He watched her uncertainly for a moment. He had come to Bath in a high flight of anger, overborne Lady Thane's objections to traveling this far, and posted down to Bath to scoop up his ward and put her in her place. He had dark suspicions about her motives, and found that he was not quite sure how to deal with her.

Blast the Penryck lawyer who had gotten him into such a fix! And he could wish that Primula had not been quite so *married*, so that she could have taken the girl off his hands.

His eyes glinted under the black bars of brows as he said, "You will be pleased to learn that the parlor ceiling at Penryck Abbey has been replastered, and new carpets have been installed on the upper floor."

"Thank you." She raised her head then and opened her eyes at him. "But you did not take Mr. Austin's word . . ."

"Not precisely. As I said, I went to Penryck Abbey myself to inspect the repairs and see whether all was suitable for your return."

"You did?" She faltered.

"I do take my duties seriously," he said. He pulled out a chair and set it down facing her. "Now, then, if I could just persuade you that my intentions are better than you think, I should consider myself a success."

"I had no thought that you were not a responsible guardian," she said, once more in charity with him. "To think that you would have taken the trouble! But you expected to find me there? How I wish I had been!"

"No doubt," he said wryly. "But you may rely upon my careful attention to your welfare. Whether I am here in Bath or in London."

"But . . . you will escort me back to Penryck Abbey, will you not?"

"Certainly not."

"But . . . anything can happen, sir. We might be beset by footpads—"

"Not on the highway," he said quellingly. "Footpads are in London. Along with child thieves, purse snatchers, and other manner of criminals. On the highway, on your way back to Dorset, you might meet only highwaymen."

"And you would not protect me from them?" It was a small little cry.

"My child," he said, "I would have the strongest sympathy for the highwayman. Lest you think me captious, I must tell you that while I was at Penryck Abbey, I made a discovery."

"What was that, sir?"

"I discovered that I was right, all the time. I cannot trust you. I do not understand what you hope to gain, but certainly I must keep a much stronger guard upon you than I had at first expected to do."

Her heart sinking, she managed to moisten her lips and say, "I do not understand."

"If you are determined upon a wayward life, I must recommend that you take better care in dealing with your accomplices. For you must know that you have been sadly mistaken if you think that Tom Swann would not talk."

Truly bewildered, she shook her head. "You speak in riddles, Lord Choate."

"Tom confessed all. I found the pole, you know. The pole with which you loosened the ceiling plaster. Ah, I am gratified to see that you do understand me now. But you should have removed the traces of plaster before you turned the disposal of the . . . the weapon, I should say, I suppose, over to your stablehand. He utterly broke down when I asked him how the plaster came to be loosened so far from the source of the water."

"But it was darker there!" she protested hotly.

"Ah, but it was an older stain, and not fresh." He grinned with satisfaction. She was dismayed. She had given herself away with her protest, instead of denying the entire episode. She had wondered whether anyone had seen her. Now she had the answer. Tom must have been watching through the window all the while she worked at the ceiling, once where it was truly wet, and the other mistakenly.

"I should fire Tom if I were you," he said conversationally, "for if he is faithless in little, he will be faithless in much."

"That is an odious platitude," she said with returning spirit. "He was not an accomplice. You must know that I should never put such a burden on a servant. I confess that I did the loosening of the plaster. But I did it alone."

"I am glad to hear it. It is always injudicious to put yourself in the hands of another. Especially a servant. He did say that he had watched you, and you did not know he was there."

"You tricked me!"

"Indeed I did," he said evenly. "You must learn to be wary of traps, if we are to deal together."

"You admit that you will set traps for me in the future?"

"It will not be necessary," he said calmly. "I am sure you have gained your goal, to stay here in Bath, and while I do not like it, I am not prepared to learn to what lengths you would go to thwart my instructions." He gazed at her thoughtfully. "I confess you have managed to surprise me."

She pounced upon one word he had said. "Stay here in Bath? What do you mean, sir? Am I not to go back to Penryck Abbey?"

"I fear that if you did, I might find the entire place burned down, and since I am responsible for keeping your assets intact, I should not like to be criticized for allowing you sufficient rein. So I have decided to let you stay here in Bath."

"Do you mean it? Oh, you are so good, sir!" she said, jumping up and reaching for his hand.

"Not at all," he said. "I simply want to be reasonably sure that you will get into no more mischief."

"But Miss Peek will see that I'm all right."

"That reminds me," he said gravely. "I fear that I have reposed too much confidence in Miss Peek's influence over you. So I shall remove you from her charge."

Her eyes, fixed upon him, filled with tears. She could not see the hesitation that flitted over his face, but it lasted only a moment. He moved as though to say something to her, his hand outstretched to her, but he changed his mind and reverted abruptly to the chilly note that she knew well but which had so far been absent from this conversation. "I have made arrangements for you to lodge elsewhere in town." He glanced around him with scarcely veiled distaste at the small shabby rooms. "With Lady Thane," he said. "She has come down at my request and taken a house in Laura Place. So you will find yourself much more comfortable with her, I know."

She could not stop the tears that slipped rapidly down her cheeks.

"If you turn into a watering pot," he said repressively, "I shall regret my leniency."

"No, no," she said over the lump in her throat. "I shall not cry." The tears slipping down her cheeks were signs of helpless anger, and not of gratitude, as he seemed to think. "So I am to be placed with Lady Thane? And what does my godmother say to that? Or did you give her any choice?"

He surveyed her critically. "I do not know where your misunderstanding arises, but I assure you that I have no influence over what Lady Thane does."

"Whereas you have every power over me," said Clare.

"As you say."

"But what then of your plans?" Clare resumed after a small brimming silence. "Are you staying in Bath?"

"I am not. I . . . have things to do in Kent."

"Oh, yes," said Clare, nodding her head wisely. "For your marriage. I thought it must have already taken place, from the expectations I understood you to have?"

"As you see, it has not. But Miss Morton is planning a great fete at her mother's home in Essex, and I am expected to be in attendance."

"But you do not wish to?"

He grimaced slightly. Then, recollecting himself, he once more donned the impassive mask that was almost a part of him. "It is my duty, so I am told, to assist."

It was not what she expected to say, but Clare's next words surprised her. "You're full of duty," she flung at him. "That's the only word I've ever heard of substance from you. Duty!"

"You are quite right," he said, adding outrageously, "I must commend it to you. Duty, properly carried out, is most satisfying. I am sure, if you thought well upon the matter, you would discover certain duties that come to your hand. Such as obedience!"

Thoroughly angry now, she flared, "And it is your duty, I collect, to watch my every move?"

"No," he said with a smile she could only consider gothic, "I must deprive myself of that duty." Bowing, he took his leave, and she heard him passing down the steps. But she herself buried her face in her hands and let the tears flow as they would.

20.

Clare was not sorry to see the last of the cramped quarters of the Misses Peek's lodging. At first she railed against the fate that had decisively removed Uncle Horsham and substituted a wicked, selfish, arrogant, *unfeeling* man like Lord Choate.

But stepping inside the foyer of Lady Thane's rented house on the Crescent, Clare insensibly began to think that life had not treated her quite so badly, after all.

"And I don't know what you thought Choate should do," said Lady Thane, passing a cup of tea to Clare in the narrow drawing room upon her arrival. It was papered in maroon, and not at all to Lady Thane's taste, which ran more to gilt and ivory, but the owner of the house was a gentleman advanced in years, and he had no wish to change the furnishings merely to suit a tenant. The heavy hangings at the windows succeeded in shutting out a view of the street below, and swallowed up the candlelight from the candlesticks on the mantel and on the long table, leaving the room in wavery dimness.

"I don't know," said Clare in a small voice. The entire drawing room, she reflected, was as large as the apartment over the milliner's, and she realized with a pang how thoughtless she had been to quarter herself and Budge upon the Misses Peek.

"Surely you are better off with me," said Lady Thane comfortingly, "and I must confess it will be good to visit with many of my old friends. I have heard that Lady Courtenay is here, and the Duchess of Argyle, and Margaret Strawn. And even some eligible gentlemen, and while it would not do to encourage their addresses quite yet, I always say that it never hurts to enlarge one's acquaintance." She seemed struck with thought, and then decided she might be misunderstood. "Among quite proper people, of course," she added.

The reference to Harry Rowse was clear to Clare, but she did not respond. She had used Harry Rowse to bring Benedict to Bath, and it had worked as she had planned. But then what? Nothing more except that she would now

143

be housed in luxury, a prisoner just the same. She was restless in her mind, her thoughts in turmoil. She did not know what she expected of Benedict, but she knew that she disliked him excessively, and her rebellious spirit chafed under the yoke she considered too heavy.

Lady Thane prosed along, and Clare murmured responses she hoped were appropriate. When Clare at length was taken upstairs by Mrs. Bishop, the housekeeper, she entered a room that lifted her spirits more than anything. It was yellow, with gold brocade at the windows, and a sunny carpet; the mantel was painted yellow to match; and the chair before the hearth was deep and comfortable. If she were to be a prisoner, she thought, she might as well enjoy it.

"The master's daughter had this room, miss," said Mrs. Bishop, "and her maid next door. I put Budge there. I thought it would suit you, having heard that a young lady was to come. Lord Choate was particularly concerned that you be made comfortable, miss, so if this room does not suit, I shall try to ready another."

Mrs. Bishop looked anxiously at Clare. Clare turned to her with a sunny smile and said, "Thank you so much, Mrs. Bishop. I shall be very comfortable here, thank you. You have made a very good choice for me."

Mrs. Bishop, gratified, took her courteous leave, and Clare sank into the deep yellow chair and stared mournfully at the black grate, contemplating her future.

Her future, as it went along the next weeks, was not what she had expected. Lady Thane, mindful of Clare's mourning, turned down the cards that came her way as soon as it was learned that she was staying in Bath—that information having been current from the time that her traveling coach lumbered in on the Bath Road.

But she managed to visit the Pump Room on a regular basis, and daily took tea in the Assembly Rooms, and required Clare's constant attendance. Lord Choate had been more exercised than Lady Thane had ever seen him the day he came to call on her in her house in Grosvenor Square.

Fortunately he had caught her as she was about to close up her house and retire to the country. Her daughter, Harriet, had been most importunate that she come to visit her, and since Lady Thane knew from past unpleasant experience that a visit to Harriet entailed endless conversation about her son and heir, about her servants, and the great damage done to woolen blankets by the moth, Lady Thane had resisted as long as she was able.

Lord Choate's request—really an intimidating request, given in strong terms by an agitated man—that she come down to Bath and take Clare under her wing was most welcome, and Lady Thane had agreed with alacrity.

She saw now that Clare was dressed demurely, and behaved with meek propriety. And above all, she saw to it that Harry Rowse kept his distance.

To tell the truth, she did not remark any particular glance from Clare to Rowse, and she detected no undue attention to Clare on his part. But she too knew the danger that Choate spoke of, and while she had not been made privy to that disastrous event in the gardens of Carlton House, yet she was wise in the ways of the world, and what she did not know, she could shrewdly guess.

And Harry Rowse was not allowed within speaking distance of her goddaughter.

It was a different matter with Sir Alexander Ferguson. Impeccable of manner and most unexceptionable of reputation, Sir Alex provided escort from time to time. And Lady Thane eyed Clare watchfully, trying to detect a spark of regard for him, in vain.

Clare, dutiful at first, soon found the rigid routine chafing, and longed for the company of Evalina Courtenay. At length, seeing Clare far from the rebellious miss that Choate had described, Lady Thane allowed her to go with Evalina and a maid to visit certain shops.

"The lending library," said Evalina. "I know that Mama is so much better now that she has taken the waters, and it is felt that in another two weeks she will be well enough to travel home. But in the meantime, I am sadly at loose ends."

"I wish I had brought with me Lady Melvin's basket," said Clare. Seeing the blank look on her friend's face, she hastened to explain. "Lady Melvin brought over a great number of library books that she had finished with. I had Wisby send them back when we came to Bath, but I regret the ones I had not read."

"Then," said Evalina promptly, "let us get some more."

The lending library was on a side street just off the promenade, and it was not long before both girls were engrossed in the latest shipment from London. Even Lowry, Evalina's maid, peeped over their shoulders when she thought she was not observed, for she knew that sooner or later she would get her hands on the selections, and read the night away by a flickering working candle.

There were such agonizing choices to be made. Whether to take *Leonora* or to indulge in *The Inheritance*. A reprint of *Camilla*, an old favorite due to be read again, or Charles Robert Maturin's new tale called *The Fatal Revenge*. At length, flushed with anticipation of long, pleasant afternoons ahead, they emerged from the shop. Lowry was bowed down with a basket full of books, and the two girls were laughing as they stepped onto the sidewalk, directly in front of two well-dressed gentlemen.

"What a happy accident!" said the older of the two, lifting his hat in salute. "Miss Penryck, Miss Courtenay, may I be permitted to present to you my good friend Fanhope? Come, Fanhope, make your bow."

Harry Rowse turned to his companion, an inarticulate young man with high points and a masterfully tied cravat. With acute embarrassment Fanhope bowed and with an effort managed a few strangled syllables by way of acknowledgment of the introductions.

"We should like to escort you back to Lady Thane," said Rowse. "It seems meant that we should do so, does it not? Meeting you by accident?"

Clare did not know precisely how it happened, but she was soon walking with Harry Rowse at her side and a head full of chaotic thoughts. Evalina, behind her, was doing her best to set Fanhope at ease, without notable success.

Clare hurried along the street, anxious to regain what she knew was the haven of Lady Thane's presence. She should not have left it, even with Evalina, and Lady Thane's permission.

"Must you hurry so?" complained Rowse. "One would get the opinion that you did not want to be seen with me."

"How right you are!" agreed Clare cordially. "I wonder at you, really, Mr. Rowse. Surely you must know that I have no wish to talk to you."

"It wasn't always like that, was it, Miss Penryck? But I see the thought of the past distresses you. Believe me, I am on my good behavior, and you have nothing to fear from me. But I truly cannot believe you prefer Sir Alex to me?"

He dropped his voice, and entered into a remarkably apt imitation of his rival. "And on the left there, you see the Roman baths. One must wonder how great the Romans would have been had they not succumbed to the indolence engendered by the warm water, although, on the other hand, surely the taste of the waters must result in an eschewing of frivolity and a return to a world filled with mayhem as an agreeable alternative. But on the other hand . . ."

Clare giggled. He was Sir Alexander to the life! But she was fast becoming aware that were someone to see her on such easy terms with Rake Rowse, she would be hard put to erase the stain on her reputation.

The carriage moving across the end of the street caught her eye, and her heart sank. Of all people to see her, even though properly in company with a maid! She wished Lady Melvin had not passed by just then. In moments Clare and Evalina were restored to Lady Thane's protection, but Clare was still anxious over the accidental encounter with Harry Rowse.

While Harry Rowse had been on his good behavior, which was in fact very agreeable to her in her world, which seemed predominantly leaden, yet she realized that she was well out of the encounter. And she was not worried about her own person anymore, for Harry had been most correct in his behavior. But she was worried about her reputation. And although Benedict did not care about her—and since if he did hear that Rowse was paying her marked attention, he would simply put her into a closer confinement than he had already done—she did not wish to put his reaction to the test.

She had not believed she could feel so low in her mind. Even Lady Thane, not a noticing person in general, spoke bracingly to her a few days later. "I must say I had not believed you would fall into such a decline. Whatever will Choate say?"

"Nothing, Lady Thane, I am persuaded."

"You have not eaten above half your dinner, and I know that you had only a mouthful of soup at luncheon, and Mrs. Bishop makes the most delectable cream soup. I think she puts sherry in it," said Lady Thane ruminatively. "Or perhaps a port? No, even a teaspoonful of port would make it quite a different color. I am sure it was sherry.

But then, child, you did not like it? Perhaps I had best send for Mr. Potsworth."

Since Mr. Potsworth, Lady Thane's man of medicine, had only one cure for anything at all, and that was a course of the nastiest waters on the face of the globe, Clare shuddered and assured Lady Thane that she was fine—just a little tired, that's all.

"Well," said Lady Thane at last, "I shall hope to see an improvement, or I shall indeed see that Mr. Potsworth has a look at you."

The air of gentle melancholy that descended upon Clare pervaded even her solitary hours, of which there were few indeed. Lady Thane, whether warned by Lady Melvin or not, now vowed she could not do without Clare at her side every moment. And Clare was glad enough to abide by the rules. Nothing suited her. She even lost interest in the perils of Julia and the uncommon wickedness of the Demon of Sicily. It reminded her too much of her complaints against Choate.

A part of her insisted upon being fair to her guardian. What else was he to do with her? She was in great comfort, with a lady to give her countenance and who cared about her, and she had all the freedom that could be used by a young lady in mourning.

But, said her impish other self, he trapped her on the matter of the ceiling. How had he known that Tom was watching her? She knew that Tom talked to anyone who would listen, and Benedict was eminently underhanded when he took advantage of her servants.

Her thoughts revolved more than she liked around Benedict. But they always returned to the point where they began—what was she to do?

She missed her grandmother; there was no question about that. Even the abbey was not the same, and she had no wish to return to the home she had known when the hub of it was no longer there. But of course she could not wish Lady Penryck back, now that she was out of her pain.

She would be seventeen soon. And that meant, according to Mr. Austin, eight more years during which she must obey the whims of Lord Choate. Not until she was twenty-five would she be mistress of her own money, of her own life. She would not live that long, she was sure, for melancholy thoughts could prove fatal—at least, they often were within the boards of Mrs. Radcliffe's novels.

There was of course one other way open to her. She had not given it as much thought as it deserved, regarding her own marriage as simply a vague arrangement that would have pleased her grandmother.

She had been sent to London to effect such an arrangement, but it did not truly have reality to her. Now she began to devote considerable thought to the subject.

And almost as though to help her along on her conjectures, a caller was announced. "Lady Thane begs you will come down at once," said Budge. "Sir Alexander Ferguson has come to call."

It was not such an outstanding event as all that, Clare reflected. Sir Alex had called before, to take them for a drive, to escort them to tea at the Assembly Rooms, but it was certainly fortuitous that he arrived just at the time when Clare was at such loose ends.

Checking her ringlets, bound back by a broad ribbon, and approving her sober appearance in the dark gray round gown she wore, she hurried down the steep, carpeted stairs to the drawing room.

She found Lady Thane and Sir Alexander chatting comfortably over teacups, and Lady Thane welcomed her with one hand outstretched. "I brought you down to meet Sir Alexander," she said, "because he has brought some fruit, hearing that you were not feeling quite the thing. I wanted him to see that you were truly in good health, although perhaps not quite as vivacious as I should like to see you. But of course," she added belatedly, remembering Lady Penryck, "it is not right that you should be precisely *vivacious*. But . . ."

She grew so involved in her remarks that, recognizing that she would never make her way out of them, she dropped them entirely and took up another subject. "When do you think your cousin Miss Warfield will marry her Scot? You are acquainted with him, I know. Does he not wax impatient?"

Sir Alexander Ferguson answered, after due consideration. "I should imagine that he does wish to have his future settled, and have Miss Warfield—then, of course, Lady MacCrae, as she will be—installed in his home. I do not know which castle he will set up as his main seat. Perhaps it will be Kelso, or on the other hand, it might

well be Tolquhon, for he has added a wing to that building within the past few years. Yet, then too, there is much
to be said for Cruden, for it is a very pleasant seat in the
summer, with the refreshing breezes from the sea. But
of course, one wouldn't take a delicately nurtured female
to such an isolated spot in the winter. . . ."

He sounded so like Harry Rowse's imitation that Clare
was hard put not to giggle outrageously. But her thoughts,
deliberately summoned up to provide a diversion from
amusement, fell upon Sir Alexander Ferguson as a lifelong
companion. She knew she could marry him if she wished.
He had been most devoted and constant in his attentions.

However, a lifetime of "On the other hands" had less
than no appeal at all. But perhaps she could manage
something. She fell silent and listened to the seductive
hum of her scheming brain.

21.

Not until it was over did Clare realize that the Bath interlude was more of an idyll than she knew. The long lazy days, the stifling rigidity of each day's schedule, the lack of excitement, had, in retrospect, a certain charm, and she was grateful, later, for the interval of quiet.

She gave serious consideration to her future, and while she did not think she could manage to live a life with Sir Alex, yet marriage was the one way she could escape from the yoke of her wicked guardian. She had no very clearcut plan. more like a vague desire that something would turn up to show her what next to do.

But when it came, she did not at first recognize it. The catalyst came in the form of a letter to Lady Thane from her daughter.

"Listen to this," said Lady Thane at breakfast. "Clare, here's a letter from Harriet—I suppose it will be full of humdrum. . . ."

Her voice died away as she began to peruse it. When she was halfway through she began to voice little wordless sounds, and by the time she had reached the end of the letter, Clare sat stiffly with her coffeecup arrested in midair, her attention riveted.

"What is it?"

"It's infection! That's what it is. Harriet says little Braintree is deathly ill, the nurse is down with it, she herself is faltering with the fever, and she begs me to come to her!"

"But of course you must go!" cried Clare with instant sympathy. She knew that in spite of what Lady Thane said, her world revolved around Harriet, and while she might like her better at a distance, still, when the clarion call sounded, Lady Thane was at once ready to respond.

"I shall pack," she assured Lady Thane, "and we will be on our way at once."

Lady Thane, who had risen to relieve her feelings by a few brisk steps, sank down again in the chair. "It won't do. I must not take you, Clare, into a house of infection. For whatever ailment they have, Harriet feels that she has

151

contracted it, and certainly I could not expose you to such peril."

"But you must go . . ."

"And so I shall. But what shall I do with you? Choate expressly charged me with your care. I really should not desert you."

"But you know that you are needed there by Harriet much more than I need you. Do let me give Hobbs instructions to pack for you. I shall stay here, and be all right."

In the end Clare prevailed, for it was clearly Lady Thane's first duty to travel to Harriet at once. Fortunately, Clare's recollection that Lady Melvin was in town brought Lady Thane to send an urgent request that that lady come to see her.

"For I vow, Lady Melvin," she said when her visitor was announced, "I do not know which way to turn. I cannot leave, and yet I cannot stay."

It was the kind of situation that Lady Melvin relished. She was able to solve the entire problem, set all to rights, and bask in the reflected credit without in the least inconvenience to herself.

"Of course you must go. If I had a daughter I should not hesitate in the least. In fact, I judge I should already be on my way, with orders to send on my baggage as soon as it was ready. But I have just the solution for Clare."

"Then you will take her," said Lady Thane.

"No. I dare not, you know, for Sir Ewald is cross as a bear with his gout already, and another person introduced into the household would certainly send him flying. But suppose Clare were to stay here, in this house, and Miss Peek come to stay? Lord Choate thought she was eligible enough to lend Clare countenance in Dorset. I myself did not quite agree, and as it turns out I was right," she added obscurely, "but if I keep my own eye on the establishment, then I think Clare will take no harm. Do you not agree?"

Lady Thane, beset by anxieties and a haste to be gone, agreed hurriedly, and Lady Melvin sent her on her way soothingly.

But Lady Thane was not so lost to her duty as to forget what she owed Lord Choate. She scrawled off a hasty letter, sending it posthaste to Lord Choate at Marianna Morton's home in Essex, where it was said Choate was helping his beauty to prepare a fete for her mother's tenants.

"Please be assured that under no other circumstances could I be persuaded to desert my post," she wrote. "But you must agree, and I am sure if you do not that Mrs. Morton could tell you what a mother's fears—of course, it is a grandmother's, I mean—can be, and I must fly to dear Harriet. But Clare has promised me faithfully that she will not peep out-of-doors unless Lady Melvin herself accompanies her. It is the best I could do, although I do not quite like to leave Clare so cloistered, for she has an impatient temperament and once she is resolved upon something, she does not like to wait upon events. Not that I expect any *events*. But I am so overset that I hardly know what I write, except that I am doing the best I can. Yours faithfully, Helen Thane."

So urgent were Lady Thane's instructions to her messenger that, upon being told at Morton Chase that Lord Choate was in London, he scarcely stopped for refreshment in the servants' hall at the Chase before taking again to the road.

The letter reached Benedict at a peculiarly inopportune moment. He had drunk deeply the night before. He remembered that he had gambled heavily, but he would not have known whether he had won or lost except for the scattering of green bank notes over the floor of his bedroom, like leaves on the forest floor. He had flung himself the night before on his bed without undressing, although Grinstead did manage to remove his boots before being cursed out of the room, and now, holding his head as he sat on the edge of the bed, a half-empty cup of excessively strong coffee on the night table, he stared at the letter in his hand.

"What the devil does the woman mean!" he muttered. His valet, rightly judging that he was not expected to comment, opened the curtains another six inches, allowing the daylight to reach his lordship's eyeballs in minute stages.

Choate set himself to read the letter once again, puzzling out, this time, the words he had found illegible the first reading, and cursing the system of education that did not require females to write so one could read them.

The upshot was, he decided, that that abominable brat was once again alone in Bath, of all places in England where he did not wish to see her adrift. Notwithstanding the assurances of Lady Melvin, as transmitted by Lady Thane, he held no conviction that Clare would stay meekly in the house on the Crescent. He had little experience of her common sense, but more than enough of her rebellion and her defiance, and her—

"Good God, Choate!" said Ned Fenton from the doorway. "I knew you won last night, but surely you didn't intend to throw all the green around like that? Looks like a lawn in here!"

Struck, Benedict looked up and noticed the bank notes for the first time. "I had no idea! Did I win all that?"

"Luck was phenomenal," confirmed Ned. "Never saw anything like it."

"Lucky at cards, they say." Benedict spoke wryly, and Ned glanced quickly at him.

"I know the rest of it, Benedict, and if we hadn't been friends from our cradles, I shouldn't dare to say what I think."

"Then don't, Ned," groaned Benedict. "I venture to say we are agreed. But you see there's no way out." A gesture from Ned reminded him that Grinstead was still in the room, and Benedict roused himself. "Sweep up this mess," he commanded. "I shall require breakfast in a quarter of an hour. Ned, join me?"

Hardly waiting for Ned's nod, Benedict handed him the letter. "Read it, and see if it says what I think it says. My head's like a gas bag this morning, and I fear I may float up to the ceiling in a moment."

While Benedict plunged his head into a basin of cold water, Ned pored over the letter. "She writes ill—"

"And ill news too," spluttered Benedict, reaching for a towel blindly. "I don't know what I shall do."

"By the looks of it," said Ned at last, in a judicial manner, "your ward is alone in Bath. I can't think that Lady Thane would be so careless as to leave her thus."

"She isn't," said Benedict. "If you will read the last page, you will see that Miss Peek, who has as much character and backbone as a wet sponge, will be with her. And Miss Peek—so Lady Thane says—will prevent that brat from stepping outside. I wish I may see the day that that happens!"

Ned watched his good friend dress. He had much to think over, and it was a strong desire in him to make a suggestion or two to Benedict. But long experience had taught Ned that Choate did not relish being told of his faults—and in fact Ned could see only one. But that was a major fault, and over breakfast his tongue could no longer obey his better instincts.

"You were certainly over the eight last night. The drunker you got, the better your luck was. I believe you left young Acton without a feather to fly with."

"Too much the worse for him," gritted Choate. "He had no business to wager so deep. I rather imagine he would not have plunged had he not thought that he would get the better of me with the help of liquor. You cannot expect me to turn back my winnings?"

"I am not such a sapskull as to think that," said Ned with vigor. "Nor do I quarrel with your idea that Acton would pay back anything he had won if you were at a disadvantage. That family always runs a bit close to the wind."

Choate dismissed the entire Acton family with a wave of his hand. "What am I to do, Ned? Bedeviled by two women, and I don't quite see my way clear ahead. Bassing, take away this food and bring me some more strong coffee."

Ned said thoughtfully, after he had watched Choate down a steaming cup of coffee, "It seems noticeable to me that you are drinking far too much for a man who is to be married to a raving beauty this fall. Wasn't there some kind of affair she was having at her country place? You missed that, I think?"

"I wasn't there, if that's what you mean. I can't say that I felt the want of it."

"I know you're going to take offense at what I'm going to say . . ." began Ned.

"Then don't say it," recommended Choate.

"But," Ned continued doggedly, "I think you don't want to be married."

Benedict regarded the bottom of his coffeecup. Looking around, he saw that Bassing had left the room, and he roused himself to pour another cup. "Whether it is better to drown in port or drown in coffee, that is the question," he paraphrased. "You are quite right. I could wish my parents had not been so anxious to settle my future for me. But then, Miss Morton has expected to marry me since she was in leading-strings, and I know not how many she has turned off, waiting for me."

Not many, thought Ned, but this time he was wise enough to remain silent. For if Benedict did not know that Miss Morton's sharp tongue and domineering ways had turned away more than one suitor, leaving only the most desperate of fortune hunters to linger, then Ned was not going to tell him. Faithful to Choate she might be, but temptations galore she did not have.

"What am I to do, Ned?" repeated Benedict. "The brat will not stay where I put her, and I am in honor bound to take charge of her. And I cannot think it would be wise to place her in the charge of Marianna, after our marriage."

"I quite agree," said Ned earnestly. "But, can you not explain to your ward—"

"Explain nothing!" exploded Choate. "She has wit enough to know what she should do, yet she persists in putting me in the wrong. I thought her safely at Penryck Abbey, in the charge of her own governess—against my better judgment, for I had wished to bring Mrs. Duff to her."

Ned, remembering well Primula's formidable companion-governess, shuddered.

"Through some device she managed to convince Miss Peek to take her to Bath, where she promptly fell in with that rake Rowse."

Ned nodded sagely. "That's why Lady Thane went down."

"Exactly," said Benedict. "And now the brat has fobbed off Lady Thane—"

"Come now," protested Ned. "You can't blame your ward for the plague, or whatever, in Cromford's nursery."

Benedict, still fuming, ignored him. "That brat has been nothing but trouble!" he said, bringing down his fist upon the table, so that the cups jumped, and one overturned, spilling coffee across the white napery. Benedict hardly noticed, and Ned reached for the bell pull.

"You said 'bedeviled by two women,' " said Ned, after the mess had been cleared up and they were alone again. "You mean Lady Thane? It seems to me that she has been more than amiable."

"No, no, of course I don't mean her. I mean Marianna,

who's after me now to take her to Italy on our honeymoon. And that ward of mine."

"I wonder why you take on so about her."

With an obvious effort Benedict pulled himself together. "You are right," he said at last. "I am far too irritable lately, and you are a true friend to put up with me when I am so disagreeable." He smiled then, the rare one-sided smile that transformed his usually stern face.

Encouraged, Ned resumed, "I wonder why? You were never so testy—until now."

Sensing an underlying meaning in his friend's words, Benedict regarded him suspiciously. "What do you mean by that?"

"You know my mother? A very clever woman, at times, and I remember one thing she said. I don't remember just now what it was with regard to, but what she said was that it takes a bright fire to generate so much heat."

Benedict looked at him as though his friend had taken leave of his senses. But he had much respect for Ned's mother, and uneasily believed that there was a kernel of truth in everything she said. He dared not, quite, dismiss Lady Fenton out of hand.

"What does that have to do," said Benedict carefully, "with me?"

"Wish she was here," said Ned uncomfortably. He had said more than he intended, and he could not go further without running the risk of insult.

"So do I," said Benedict promptly. "Do you think she'd take Clare Penryck in if I brought her up to Derbyshire?"

"No," said Ned promptly. "My mother is ailing."

"I had not known that," said Benedict. "My sympathy to her. But I collect that she is planning her usual trip to Florence for the winter?"

Ned, caught in his own trap, nodded. "But she already has her arrangements made."

Relenting, Benedict said in an altered tone, "I wouldn't for the world repay Lady Fenton's kindness to me in the past by saddling her with that imp!"

Ned nodded. "It really wouldn't do, you know. I should hate to think what mischief the child could do in Florence . . ." He thought a moment, then added, "Or in Bath, for that matter."

A queer light gleamed in Benedict's eyes. "I am going to take care of that chit of a girl. I will set out tomorrow morning for Bath, and I will set that child straight, once and for all!"

Ned laughed. "I think I have a pressing need to arrive in Bath tomorrow myself. I wouldn't want to miss this for the world!"

22

Although Benedict had left London with his anger still burning well, by the time he arrived in Bath he was able to meet the host of the Christopher, whom he knew, with affability, and a sure knowledge that no pains would be spared to house his cattle well, that the bed would be warmed and dry, and there would be plenty of wood for the fire in his grate, were the weather to turn cool.

Ned Fenton, who had driven down in his own curricle, was lodged in the next room, and watched Benedict set off toward Laura Place with some misgivings. He was well aware that the more affable Benedict seemed, the more iron had entered into his will.

But when Benedict was announced in the drawing room of Lady Thane's rented house in Laura Place, Clare Penryck and her companion were unaware of the formidable mood of the man who came in and made his bow.

Clare was normally quick-witted, but her attention was still taken up by the disagreeable discussion that she and Miss Peek had carried on ever since breakfast, resulting in an uneaten lunch and an anxiety that fretted her nerve ends.

Miss Peek, remembering belatedly that Lord Choate had expressly directed her to remain with her charge at Penryck Abbey, now wished to make amends for her dereliction by returning to Dorset at once, but Clare, equally set upon her own scheme of bringing her existence to Lord Choate's attention, remained adamant in her determination to stay in Lady Thane's house, even unchaperoned.

Clare was nettled because she had not heard a word from Lord Choate in the three days since Lady Thane had left, but her heart leaped when she heard his voice in the hall and, a moment later, he entered the room. With creditable poise she rose and extended her hand civilly to Lord Choate, and he took it.

Now that her guardian was actually in the room, he seemed larger than she remembered. She began to suspect that she had committed a great folly.

She was not comforted when she saw a spark, which she

mistook to be anger, flaring in his eyes, before he bowed over her fingers. By the time he turned to Miss Peek he had himself well in hand again.

"I am gratified that you came so quickly to bear my ward company," he said. "It was most kind of you."

"N-not at all," stammered Miss Peek, wishing desperately that she had not acceded to Clare's wishes and come to Bath in the first place.

"Perhaps you would be kind enough," said Benedict smoothly, "to bring Miss Penryck a cup of tea?"

"But I do not in the least feel the need of a cup of tea," objected Clare promptly, clutching at the safety of Miss Peek's presence.

With the utmost affability Benedict said, "You will." The smile with which he accompanied his words could only be described, Clare thought with a sinking feeling, as wolfish.

"Pray, Miss Peek," she began, her hand outstretched in a pitiful appeal, "don't go."

But Lord Choate looked levelly at the governess, and Miss Peek, her head in a whirl, scuttled out of the room. Choate watched the door close behind her, and then turned to his ward, who had taken up a defensive position before the gold-and-white mantel.

"Now, Miss Penryck," he said evenly, "perhaps you will provide me with an explanation?"

"Of . . . of what?"

"Of why I am forced to post down from London to find you here, when I did not expect to."

"Then where, sir, should I be?"

"In Penryck Abbey," he said repressively. "Or, if you persist in staying in Laura Place, then with Lady Thane. Instead of that, I perceive that you are here without your godmother, with only Miss Peek to keep you company."

Clare had expected him to post down from London. After all, this was what above all else she wanted. The reality was not quite the same as the interview she had constructed in her dreams.

"My poor memory has served me badly," he said mendaciously, "but I thought I distinctly told you that Miss Peek was not able to lend you sufficient countenance in Bath."

He lifted one black bar of eyebrow, inviting her comment. She could not keep silence.

"You did, Lord Choate. But it was surely not my fault that Lady Thane had to leave Bath. I did not know what else to do."

"I don't suppose it would have been eligible for you to go with Lady Thane when she left?" His voice was heavy with sarcasm.

"Oh, no, sir, you cannot think that." Clare widened her eyes.

"This establishment," he said with a stifling air, "was set up, since you wished strongly to stay in Bath, on the understanding that Lady Thane would be here. You cannot accuse me of thwarting your *every* wish, you know."

"Not quite that," said Clare with reviving spirit. She was quick to sense an advantage with her guardian, and while she had expected that he would roar down upon her breathing fire and smelling of brimstone, so far he had been reasonable. "But I did not think, either, that you would wish me to die."

"Good God," he said, startled. "What kind of Cheltenham tragedy are you enacting for me? Who said anything about dying!"

"You did," she said unfairly. "You wished me to go with Lady Thane . . . and no doubt catch the plague."

Mystified, Lord Choate watched her. "Plague? Surely not?"

"She clasped me to her bosom," improvised Clare, "as though we would not meet again. In this life. For you must know that Harriet's son has taken the infection and the doctors fear the worst."

Lord Choate took out a blue enameled snuffbox and studied its contents. Then, without taking any, he closed it and put it away again. His anger fled, routed by the liveliest amusement. How artless the child was, and how unexpectedly she displayed flashes of wisdom! He became aware that his interest had been fairly caught, a fact that must be firmly set aside.

But he could not refrain from asking, in a conversational tone, "How much of that is fustian?"

"You guessed!" Clare exclaimed. "Not really much—except the part about not meeting again. But the boy seems really dreadfully ill, so Harriet wrote, and Lady Thane could not stay while there was such an urgent need of her."

"I should like to see Lady Thane in a sickroom being of

any use," he said critically. "But then again, perhaps I misjudged her in that way, too."

Miss Peek opened the door, but neither of the two inside the room noticed her. She took one look at the antagonists and withdrew as silently as she had come. Quite properly recognizing that the request for tea was a subterfuge, she told a footman to remove the tray to the kitchen, and herself went across the entry to the book room to wait out whatever scheme was being laid out by Lord Choate.

While she would not have yielded to anyone in her affection for Clare, yet she was uneasily aware that the little girl with the mischievous disposition had outgrown her control. She hoped, truly, that Lord Choate would find some other female to cope with the child. What Clare needed was either a thorough thrashing, a strange thought from a governess who had long inveighed against corporal punishment—but there were some cases! she thought obscurely—or a husband who would tame her. Miss Peek, knowing the prospects, had little hope of the latter.

If only Lord Choate weren't betrothed! He possessed sufficient strength of character to tame a wife. Miss Peek sighed and gave herself over to speculation about what was really happening on the other side of the salon door.

Lord Choate, Miss Peek guessed correctly, was glaring at Clare. "I fully understood the urgent reasons for Lady Thane's departure," he said, in a close approximation of an apology. "But her letter was ill-writ. At any rate, this changes nothing."

Clare sank into a small bergère chair that was uncomfortable at best. Now she scarcely heeded it.

"Lady Thane's presence is the only possible condition that would allow you to stay here in Bath. You are in mourning, you are a very young female, and only your godmother's company would make your presence in Bath eligible. And you do not now have such protection."

"But what will I do then?" It was not quite a wail.

"You will return to Penryck Abbey."

Clare clasped her hands tightly in her lap. It was all going wrong. She had longed to see Choate rushing to her, and he had done so. But he had still the air of regarding her as a dreary nuisance, no more. And while Clare had no very clear idea of what she wanted, she denied with every fiber the notion that she would once again be put on the shelf.

"And what will I do at Penryck Abbey?"

"Stay there," he said, with a blast of fierceness. "And stay out of mischief until you grow up!"

His sudden attack put to rout the last of Clare's self-possession. She had bungled all, and since her confidence was built on shifting sands—a maturity beyond her years in some ways, but a dreadful lack of experience in other phases—it crumpled all at once.

She could not look up at him. All the memories of London came back to her—the accident in Oxford Street, the prince regent's ball, Harry Rowse in the dark garden.

Harry Rowse trying to scrape up her acquaintance here in Bath, and her snubbing of him—knowing that she was at heart afraid of him.

And underlying all of this, the exacerbating presence of her wicked guardian glaring down at her and treating her as though she were a left parcel. It was more than shabby.

At a moment when what she needed more than all else in the world was understanding, a bit of reassurance, and someone to tell her all was well, she looked up to see Benedict's hard gray eyes and tight lips, looking like a man holding tight rein on his rage lest it burst its bounds and bring him to disaster.

The words were wrung out of her. "Did I do so badly?"

Benedict, watching his ward with mixed emotions, felt the stir of an emotion he had not heretofore experienced. Call it compassion, he told himself. He was moved to say, "Not at all. For someone with so little experience, and so young in addition, you did quite well. I think Lady Thane was too sanguine when she expected that Ferguson would make an offer. And of course you would not have accepted it."

"I wouldn't?" said Clare, startled.

"But that is all past. I would suggest that you put it out of your mind. There is no need for you to think of marriage, at least until your mourning is out."

"And then?"

"Then . . . we will see," Benedict temporized.

"I see," said Clare, looking down at her hands folded in her lap. "It will depend, of course, upon what Miss Morton wishes."

Aghast, Benedict stared at her. "What has Miss Morton to do with it?"

"You remember that you have in the past discussed my

affairs in great detail with her. I am well aware of her low opinion of me. I wonder that you did not send her to see me, to transmit your wishes."

Benedict eyed her levelly. "I may have spoken rashly in the past. But we are now on a different footing, you and I, and you misunderstand me if you think that I have so little sense as to discuss my business affairs with Miss Morton." In fact, he added to himself, I shall refrain from discussing much of anything with her. The years stretched ahead, surprisingly barren and dismal. He had not quite seen them so before.

Clare went on as though he had not spoken. "Strange—I had never thought that I was not competent. I managed Penryck Abbey on my own for much of the time. Of course," she continued, striving to be fair, "I would not have ordered the ceiling repaired, or new carpets to be fitted without Grandmama's permission, but never did I need Miss Morton's approval to guide me in how I should go on."

Benedict stiffened. But Clare paid no heed. It was as though she were seized by a powerful emotion. "I shall, in the future, make it my affair, Lord Choate, to avoid bringing myself to your notice. For your regard, you know, is tantamount to Miss Morton's attention. And I do not think I could abide being under her discipline."

She glanced up at him, and was surprised to notice that he seemed strongly moved. But she could not refrain from prodding once more. "It is all very well for you to be directed by her wishes. But my grandmother did not have Miss Morton in mind when she made her last arrangements." She eyed him with speculation. "Nor, I think, did she fully consider the consequences of the arrangements she did make. It is too bad that I did not have an opportunity to enlighten her in time."

Benedict had now had time enough to consider his remarks. Ordinarily he would have given Clare, or any other person of whom he had charge, crisp instructions or directions, and that would be the end of it. But something in Clare's vulnerability reached him, and he softened his intended remarks. Unfortunately, his words still came out more unfeeling than he knew.

"I agree," he said repressively. "I too should have liked to talk with your grandmother. But, unfortunately, I had no idea she intended to fob . . ." He brought himself up short, not quite in time.

"Fob me off onto you?" said Clare. "I feel, somehow, that Miss Morton's words, not yours, are coming to me. Is this true?"

"Leave Miss Morton out of it," gritted Benedict out of his own guilty conscience.

"I shall be glad to," said Clare tartly. "Especially since she is not yet your wife. And I do not understand why she has so far refused to wed you. Can it be that she had knowledge of your evil temper?"

Stung into unwise retort, Benedict said, "She has set the date, twice."

Warned by the leaping light in her eyes, he said, "Never mind. My evil temper has nothing to do with it."

Clare tucked in the corners of her lips in a secret smile.

Benedict felt a sudden surge of panic. A vision assailed him, of a man tottering on the edge of a stretch of deadly quicksand, and then the impression was gone. But it was enough to warn him away from the spell his ward was unconsciously weaving. He was a man of wide experience, and he knew only too well what havoc this slip of a girl might wreak, were he to give in to his overwhelming impulse.

Because he dared not allow full rein to his compassion, he spoke harshly. "I shall send at once for Mrs. Duff. Miss Peek is clearly ineligible. My sister's companion will escort you back to Penryck Abbey, and I do not wish to hear any more about your not allowing her to stay. Believe me, Mrs. Duff is the least of the restraints that I can use."

Tears brimmed and spilled down Clare's cheeks. "You could not be so *wicked*!"

"Mrs. Duff will be here to take up her new position at the end of the week. So steel yourself to say farewell to this sojourn in Bath. The end of the week, not one day longer!"

23.

Mrs. Duff! The threat that Benedict had held over her head for weeks had now descended and would become reality by the end of the week. She had no more than three days left of freedom, of being Clare Penryck of Penryck Abbey, instead of schoolgirl Clare, to be guarded and tutored by a termagant of a governess.

While Clare had never met the famed Mrs. Duff, yet she knew instinctively that if Benedict thought that lady could be the answer to what he considered his ward's waywardness, then she was a lady that Clare wanted nothing to do with.

Miss Peek returned after Benedict had left, her light blue eyes round with apprehension. "My dear," she began, "what has he said that has put you into such a dreadful pucker?" She eyed askance the ominous signs of mutiny in her charge, and thought with a sinking heart that she was no longer able to sustain such constant alarms. I'm just too old, she thought with more rebellion than she had ever experienced. I must just tell her I will not stay with her.

Almost as though reading her mind, Clare said, "Peeky, you will not believe this. But that wicked man is bringing a horrible woman to take care of me!" She was so intent upon her own injustice that she failed to discern the momentary relief that leaped in her dear governess's eye. "As though I needed a dragon to watch me!"

Miss Peek, galvanized by the realization that she was not going to have to live with Clare for the next year, took her courage in her hands and said mildly, "But my dear, you know that he has his duty to perform, and I must say he is doing just right. It is really walking on the brink to stay here in Bath. While dear Lady Thane sponsored you, of course there could be no question of propriety, but now, you must admit that it is ineligible for you to be here alone."

There was time enough during Miss Peek's representations for Clare to lose the peak of her anger. She was still rebellious, but reason came in to lay its cold hand in hers. "I do know," she said at last with a hugh sigh. "Between you and Grandmama I have been brought up to know what is proper. But why is it, Peeky, that everything I want to do is ineligible, and everything that is proper is so utterly repressive!"

"My dear, you would not wish to be disrespectful to your grandmother's memory," suggested Miss Peek.

"Of course, I wouldn't. And I do not chafe against the year of mourning, even though it must seem so to you. No, what I cannot like is that odious man telling me what to do in that very contemptuous way!"

"My dear, I hadn't noticed anything other than his very polished manners."

"So, you have fallen under his spell!" railed Clare, but Miss Peek's acute ear could detect that soon Clare would be more amenable, and she could then tell her a few things that, while unpalatable, could be most helpful to her.

"I wish that he would go off and marry his Marianna," scolded Clare, "and both of them leave me alone!"

Miss Peek was startled. There seemed more heat in the complaint than was justified. But oddly, Miss Peek was abruptly reminded of an episode in her own youth—one that she had not thought of for years. There had been a young curate whose attentions had become marked, and her father disliked him intensely. Just so had Miss Peek railed against her fate. The memory cast a brilliant light upon her dear Clare, an enlightenment which did nothing to cheer her. Clare was destined to have a very bad year, she feared.

In a hasty attempt to apply oil to troubled waters, Miss Peek blundered. "Perhaps Lord Choate will arrange for you to come out in London again next year. Probably the Little Season would be most appropriate. You will have the summer to prepare your wardrobe, and then what a fine swath you will cut!"

"And come out," said Clare, dangerously gentle, "under the wing of Marianna Morton? I shall not do it!"

"But that would not serve!" cried Miss Peek. Then, reflecting, she understood Clare's remark. "You mean, Miss Morton will be Lady Choate by that time. But, my dear . . ." She thought better of her remarks and concluded lamely, "Time enough for that next summer. But whatever happens, my dear, you must remember that Lord Choate is a man of great honor and integrity, and he will do nothing to damage your prospects."

"My prospects!" repeated Clare darkly. "I wish I may know what they are."

Miss Peek, realizing that she could say nothing that Clare would heed, turned the conversation into other channels, where it limped along, prodded by Miss Peek, ignored for the most part by Clare.

That night Clare turned over every word that Benedict had spoken to her, much as an intent scientist turns over a stone, marveling at the revelations beneath.

Benedict had, she determined, two main streams of thought that he followed. One was to immure her at Penryck Abbey, like a gothic heroine, with a dragon of a chaperon whose repressive ways would kill her own spirit. And the second was to get her off his hands as quickly as possible. The second was, of course, responsible for the first. But there had been hints dropped by Lady Melvin, by Miss Peek, and even by Lady Thane, to the effect that Benedict would take the earliest opportunity to marry her off. True, they had not said so in so many words, but they certainly expected that he would arrange a marriage for her, and then all would be solved!

Not likely! thought Clare.

But until she was married, or until she reached the age of twenty-five, she would be a millstone around Choate's neck.

There was quite simply no place to turn. She had escaped from Penryck Abbey with the muddled idea of forcing Choate to take notice of her. He had, and she was learning just how formidable an opponent he was. All the advantage was his. There was nothing she could do, no one to turn to, no place to go. Benedict Choate had, very cleverly, stopped all the bolting-holes.

To top it all, he was importing a perfect stranger to watch his prey to see that she did not escape.

She would, quite simply, give anything in the world to escape the position that Benedict had placed her in. However, she was devoid of helpful ideas.

The sleepless night she spent added nothing to her acuteness of mind. She woke up lethargic after the doze she fell into toward dawn, and her head throbbed. Perhaps I am falling ill, she thought hopefully, regarding her tongue in the mirror. She could see no sign of illness, and she took her continued good health as another sign of doom.

That afternoon—Thursday, one more day on the way to the dreaded Saturday—callers were announced by the housekeeper, Mrs. Bishop. When Clare entered the maroon salon, she stopped inside the door in amazement. The two women standing in the center of the room were known to her, but she had certainly not expected Miss Marianna Morton and Mrs. Morton to call on her.

"G-good afternoon," said Clare, suddenly overcome by shyness. She felt unusually dowdy, in the face of Miss Morton's fawn pelisse, buttoned from throat to hem, and topped by lavish furs. "I am sorry that Lady Thane is away, for I know you wish to see her."

"No," said Miss Morton crisply. "I—that is, we—came to see you. But I wonder whether we might not sit down? Or perhaps you do not trust the furniture? I am quite aware that sometimes rented rooms are not as we should hope them to be."

"Marianna, my dear," said her mother, "I am sure Lady Thane's arrangements are not to be questioned. My dear child," she added, advancing upon Clare with outstretched hand, "how glad I am to see you. And how sorry I was to hear of your grandmother's death. But then, she was quite ill, I believe?"

"Oh yes, she was, for many years," said Clare. "But pray be seated. I shall ring for tea, or perhaps you would prefer coffee?"

"Nothing," said Mrs. Morton, "thank you. We are engaged at the Assembly Rooms in a half-hour, so we must deny ourselves the pleasure."

Miss Morton had been fidgeting with her gloves, an unusual gesture for a lady who was considered the first stare of elegance. Her mother glanced speculatively at her. She had not wanted to come, first to Bath in the wake of Lord Choate, and then, more especially, to the house that Lady Thane had taken. But Marianna was as determined in her own way as her father had been, and Mrs. Morton had long given over any hope of abating her daughter's headstrong ways.

She longed for Marianna's marriage quite as much as her daughter did, for it represented to her an unaccustomed access of freedom from a nagging supervision, but she recognized her duty, and accompanied Marianna this far.

But now Marianna was exhibiting a frenetic nervousness that her mother did not like. Mrs. Morton sat silently in the satin-striped chair where she could watch the two young ladies.

"Well," began Marianna, "I half-expected to find you not receiving company."

"Oh, not at all," said Clare doggedly. "I must always be at home to you, Miss Morton. And Mrs. Morton, of course. I am sure my guardian would wish it."

"The story is current in London that a certain man of low reputation—I am sure you will know to whom I refer—has been taking up much of your time."

A dull flush crept slowly upward from Clare's throat into her cheeks. Miss Morton said, "I see that you understand my reference."

"I assure you," said Clare stoutly, "that Lady Thane was always present whenever I received anyone." Clare knew very well that Harry Rowse was the subject of Miss Morton's conversation, but she was conscious of a growing detestation of Benedict's fiancée, and since Benedict had already brought her to the lowest point of her existence, she was not quite willing to submit equally to Miss Morton. She was too young, they said? Very well, she would *be* too young!

"I must tell you," she added innocently, "that my guardian has given permission for me to receive in Lady Thane's absence. For you must know that she has been called away. A sad occasion, I fear."

"Her daughter?" suggested Mrs. Morton.

"Oh, yes, ma'am. The grandson too, I believe. Dear Harriet was sadly upset when she wrote, and Lady Thane left at once. I have not heard how the patients are faring."

Marianna fumed, "I cannot believe that Benedict was so lost to his duty!"

"You doubt my word?" said Clare with just the right touch of submission. "But I am sure Lord Choate will confirm it, if you really need to be assured of his care of me."

"Now, Marianna," interrupted Mrs. Morton. "I am sure, my dear, that Marianna means no reflection upon your honesty."

Clare said nothing. She was beginning to understand

that Marianna loathed her quite as much as Clare disliked her.

"I cannot believe," said Marianna, reluctant to cease worrying the subject, "that Benedict would admit Harry Rowse to your company! Especially after what happened at Carlton House!"

"I wonder," said Clare, "how it is that you are informed as to what happened at Carlton House?"

Marianna looked startled, and then had the grace to bite her lip in chagrin. "Of course Benedict told me. He also told me why he had to come down to Bath. To take care of his ward, he said. But I understand that he feared Rowse's advances to you."

Mrs. Morton took a hand. "Marianna, I am sure Choate did not say anything like that."

Marianna turned on her mother. "But you do not know what transpired when Choate and I were alone."

Mrs. Morton said bluntly, "You were not alone. You received a note from him saying he must hasten out of town."

Clare's perception was quick. So Marianna and her mother were at odds! Also, she understood that Marianna's curiosity was overweening, urging her to follow Benedict to Bath to check up on his activity. And, too, she knew that Marianna would simply die rather than confess it.

"But then, are you to take the baths?" said Clare innocently. "For you must know that Lord Choate does not plan to stay in Bath above a few days."

"Benedict told me," said Marianna repressively, "in his *note*, that he wished me to come to Bath. After all, I am his fiancée, you know, and he has the utmost confidence in my discretion."

"Betrothed, but not wed," said Clare, suddenly allowing her resentment full sway. "And since he can count upon your discretion, how is it that I overheard you spreading his remarks far and wide? And that, too, at Carlton House."

"Marianna, you didn't!"

Marianna looked discomfited, but recovered rapidly. "An eavesdropper! Now I have heard everything. No wonder that Choate is so anxious to get you off his hands!"

Mrs. Morton sat in a state of shock. Her daughter was exhibiting some unpleasant traits that reminded her forcefully of the late Mr. Morton, and doubts began to stir in her as to the wisdom of allowing Choate to hear any of this. If word got to him of Marianna's excessive ill temper and manifest indiscretion, he might cry off.

And then, she began to remember, Marianna had already set the date twice, and Choate had deferred what he called, without obvious emotion, "the happy occasion." And while Mrs. Morton would not advocate a marriage solely for material benefit, yet forty thousand a year was not lightly to be cast aside. By the time Mrs. Morton had decided to make some strong representations to her daughter, in private, on the subject of curbing her tongue and her temper, the conversation had advanced a step. Clare was now appearing beleaguered, and Mrs. Morton decided to put an end to this futile exercise.

"It is your fault," pursued Marianna, "that Choate has postponed our wedding."

"My fault!" A strange light leaped in Clare's eyes.

"He must deal with your paltry affairs," seethed Marianna, "and put aside our affairs until you are settled. And I warn you, Miss Penryck, that I shall not abide the outcome of this. I intend to marry Lord Choate, and I intend to set a date before Christmas, and, believe me, he will not postpone the marriage again."

Clare looked down at her hands, folded in her lap. There seemed to be nothing to say. She held her breath, letting the words flood over her.

"I shall see to that," Marianna continued. "I have a cousin who would be most eligible for you. We scarcely see him. In fact, I have not seen him for a twelvemonth, so you see he would be just the thing. For I shall not allow Benedict to be belabored by you, harassed until he doesn't know what is best for him."

"Marianna, don't meddle," warned her mother.

It was then that Marianna, full of her own resentments, left the truth to fend for itself. Mendaciously she informed Clare, "I hadn't wanted to tell you, for I thought you might resent my knowing so much of Benedict's plans for you, but I have already broached the subject to him, and he agrees. The arrangements are already in train, you know, and Benedict assures me that the moment your year of mourning is over, your betrothal will be announced. And we'll not have you on our hands anymore."

She glared at Clare in triumph. Mrs. Morton was ap-

palled, but not so much so that she did not see the spark
of emotion that welled up in Clare's eyes as she looked up
at Marianna. She was struck, at that moment, by a most
unexpected idea. She was stirred to protest, believing
rightly that Marianna was lying, but the look in Clare's
eyes—the look of complete abject misery—was too strong
for Mrs. Morton to do aught but gasp inwardly in
compassion.

Her own breeding, unlike her daughter's, was impeccable though, and now was the time to put an end to this
impossible situation. She rose to her feet and shepherded
her daughter to the door, brooking no delay, and saying
quite proper and meaningless things to Clare.

Her last look, as she closed the door to the maroon
salon behind them, was of Clare sitting where she had
been, her face buried in her hands, and her shoulders
shaking as though racked with sobs.

"Well, Marianna," said Mrs. Morton astringently, "now
you've outdone yourself."

24.

Clare believed she had touched the very bottom of existence—Mrs. Duff on her way, jingling jailer's keys, so to speak, heralding ten months of close confinement at Penryck Abbey.

Clare was full of self-incrimination. Why hadn't she let well enough alone? Her thoughts boiled as they accused her of all her sins. Why had she decided to loosen the ceiling plaster? If she had not, Benedict would not have thought she was incorrigible. Besides, Clare had mischievously pretended to encourage Harry Rowse. And that had brought disaster upon her. Not only was she to return to the abbey, but she also now had a marriage to look forward to.

Her own marriage was even now being arranged, without even consulting her, to a cousin of Marianna Morton's! She could not have expected much else, she decided, remembering how Benedict had always overridden her wishes, even if he had done her the courtesy of asking what they were.

But to hear it from Marianna! That was debasing! Why hadn't Benedict told her himself? Surely she would have taken it better from his own lips. But perhaps he did not dare to face her with it?

That was wrong. Benedict would face anything, and even take pleasure in inflicting hurt upon her. She was now past reasoning, and let instinct take over. But instinct played her false, because no slightest doubt crossed her mind that Miss Morton had lied, for reasons of her own.

The only reason Benedict had not told her about his plans to arrange a marriage for her was that her wishes, her thoughts, her likes were of no possible concern to him.

She was a duty, an onerous, troublesome millstone around his neck, and, being a direct man, he was taking the earliest possible steps to rid himself of her care.

He could not even wait for a seemly time to elapse after her mourning. There were eight years yet to go before she would be free of her wicked guardian. For seven of them, if he had his way, she would be wed to a man she did not know, and Benedict's guardianship would be early terminated.

Her sobs at length subsided. She sat a long time, devoid of thought, not moving. She had not yet turned the corner to look into the future. There would be nothing there, she knew, and what was the use!

But at the bottom, there was no place to go, and one cannot live in the limbo of desperation forever. When Mrs. Bishop came in to light the candles, she roused from her lethargy.

"Come, now, miss, sitting here in the dark like this! I don't know what Dawson was thinking of to let the curtains go like this, with the fog drawing in, and the mist so dark and all!"

Clare roused herself and was forced to look outside following Mrs. Bishop's bustling figure as she pulled all the draperies closed. "It's only three o'clock!" she marveled, thinking that at least the time must have gone on into the next week. "And already dark?"

"It's the mist rising from the river, miss," explained Mrs. Bishop. "The rain will set in by nightfall, you mark my words."

It was just the weather for Clare's mood, she decided. She longed to go for a walk, but of course she could not without Lady Melvin with her. She moved to the window and drew the curtains apart, to gaze out upon Laura Place.

The traffic was almost nonexistent. Probably the weather had reduced all the ailing to huddling by the fireside. The cobbles glistened in the fine mist. But there was one pedestrian along the street, a woman, and as she drew near, looking up at the buildings to mark her way, Clare recognized her. With a gasp, she breathed, "Mrs. Morton! Whatever can she want now?"

She hoped that Mrs. Morton had thought of a call to make elsewhere in the street, and she dropped the curtains so as not to be recognized. But in a moment, Marianna's mother was ushered into the maroon salon.

Mrs. Morton crossed the room, holding out both hands to Clare. "My dear," she said kindly, "I could not reconcile my conscience at leaving you so downcast an hour ago. I have come to talk to you, my dear, knowing that you have no mother to comfort you and Lady Thane, alas, is out of the city."

Clare regarded her with sturdy defiance. She considered Mrs. Morton as bad as her daughter, since she had stood by and let Marianna say such wounding things. But in this she was mistaken.

"My daughter is sometimes very thoughtless," said Mrs. Morton, sitting on the sofa next to Clare. "And I doubt not that some of the things she said wounded you deeply."

The Penryck pride stirred. "Miss Morton overstepped her authority, that is true," said Clare. "She has nothing to say to the purpose when she tries to instruct me in my duty."

"I know this," said Mrs. Morton. "But I came to tell you that Marianna is not so harsh as she seems. She has been, in most cases, exceedingly thoughtful of me, and while I cannot approve of every action she takes, yet I am persuaded that she means well. But that is not to the purpose. I should like to hear, my dear, of your plans for the future."

"Do you not know them?" said Clare. "I am to return to Penryck Abbey at the end of the week. I am still in mourning, of course, and my guardian felt it wise for me to live a more retired life."

Until, she thought, he can marry me off to Marianna's cousin! Her bitter thoughts were reflected in her face for all to read, and it was not Mrs. Morton's fault that she did not read them aright.

"You must agree that this is wise."

"Of course, ma'am. But I am not quite used to having my wishes so ignored, and I do not think I shall be able to accustom myself to such a life."

Mrs. Morton was startled. She had thought to come to console Clare for her unhappiness. Mrs. Morton was quite sure she knew the source of Clare's misery—the girl had developed a schoolgirl passion for her guardian. This was most understandable, for Lord Benedict Choate was an exceedingly personable man, with exquisite manners, when he chose, a great deal of address in dealing with females, and an air of intriguing aloofness. In fact, Mrs. Morton thought, he was just the kind of man to appeal to a mere child with her head full of romantic notions. Or, to tell the truth, he was the kind of man to appeal to many a settled matron, such as Mrs. Morton herself!

"It is too bad," she soothed Clare, "to have one's hopes so dashed! But I must tell you this, my dear. It is not everyone who can have all she desires, you know. There are arrangements already made, don't you know, that cannot with honor be changed."

And it would be best, thought Mrs. Morton, if Benedict could marry Marianna at once, instead of these unsettling postponements. If Clare could see that Benedict was beyond her reach, being already wed to the dashing Miss Morton, then she might the more readily recover from her mistaken hopes.

"No arrangement should be allowed," said Clare resentfully, "that cannot be altered. I mean, ma'am, that there is enough unhappiness without deliberately asking for more."

Clare was still in her dark mood, thinking of Benedict's arrangement of a marriage for her with Marianna's cousin. It was kind of Mrs. Morton to try to soften the blow, but Clare was, at times, a realist, and if the arrangements were already made, as she hinted, then nothing either Mrs. Morton or Clare could do would change them.

Unfortunately, her thoughts were running along a different road from Mrs. Morton's. Since Mrs. Morton was aware that Marianna's threat of a marriage to her cousin was empty, since there was in actuality no cousin at all, she overlooked the possibility that Clare believed every word that Marianna spoke. There was no way for Clare to know that Marianna lied, but Mrs. Morton, bent on telling Clare how hopeless it would be to dangle after Benedict, was unaware of Clare's real fear.

After Mrs. Morton had taken her leave, Clare began to reflect. Mrs. Morton had been kindness itself, but still, she had come only to reconcile Clare to a marriage in the next few months with a man whose existence had not been known to her until this afternoon.

Clare had rarely felt so alone. She had been encouraged to think for herself, during the years at the abbey when her grandmama had left things to her, but never had she had such strong wishes that she could lay the entire problem of her life in someone else's hands.

The only possibility—to turn her life over to Benedict—had, in spite of Grandmama's best intentions, gone awry. And all that was left was Clare herself. It was her life, after all, and if it went wrong for her, at least it would be her own fault.

There were two things she could do: one was to go along with her guardian's wishes, and marry someone she had never heard of. Before even seeing him, she had taken an intense dislike to him, for anyone of Marianna's kin could not be eligible for Clare.

The second thing was to refuse the marriage. And then, when Marianna became Lady Choate, to live under her rule. And that was even more ineligible.

But eventually a third prospect presented itself. It was not what she would have liked, but her likes were no longer of any moment.

Clare pounded with her clenched fist upon her knee. By this time, she had retired for the night. A maid had lighted a fire in the grate to chase away the damp of the rainy night, and she huddled in a wing chair before the fire.

"If Choate wants me wed," she said aloud, "and off his hands, I can oblige him. He need not be put to any straits over it, and I am not bound by any arrangements he may have made with *her* cousin." The fire at length burned low. "If he wants me wed," she continued eventually, "I shall arrange it myself. Why not? It's my life!"

So by Thursday night, with Saturday and Mrs. Duff looming threateningly on her horizon, Clare, her mind made up, slept like a baby.

Friday morning, she awoke and, lying in bed waiting for Budge to bring her tea, she went over every detail of her scheme. Seeing no fault with it, she tossed back the coverlet and rang vigorously for her maid.

"Land sakes, miss," said Budge. "I was coming all the time, but—"

"Never mind that, Budge. I must go out this morning. Pray set out my dove-gray walking suit, and be ready to accompany me by ten o'clock."

Budge demurred. "But, miss, was you expecting to go out before Lady Melvin comes? I don't think—"

"That's all right, Budge. Take this tea away, and bring me some toast. I'm starved!"

"But—"

"No buts, Budge. Do as I tell you. And not a word to Mrs. Bishop, mind!"

Budge, balked of giving vent to her feelings in the servants' hall, turned mutinous. "Now, I have my orders, miss," she said unwisely.

"And I've given you some new ones, Budge. Come, now, don't let's quarrel. I can't do without you, that's the truth."

Somewhat mollified, Budge hastened to follow her instructions, and thinking darkly, "I wonder what young miss is up to now, and I don't think I'm going to like it at all!" she made ready to accompany Miss Penryck at ten in the morning, as Miss Penryck deliberately left the house in defiance of all instructions to the contrary.

Putting off the somber tones of her thoughts of the night before, and donning, like a new frock, an expression of anxiety, she tripped along the Crescent and onto the Parade.

She strolled slowly, with an air of preoccupation, searching the crowd out of the corner of her eye. At ten in the morning, only the gouty, those in wheelchairs, and those attending them were to be seen. One or two exceptions were known to her, and soon she espied the one face she was looking for.

"Sir Alexander!" she cried, prettily putting out her hand to greet him. "Just the one man who can help me out of this great fix I find myself in!"

Sir Alexander bowed over her hand. "My dear, you must tell me how I can be of service to you."

"N-no," she said abruptly, "it is too bad of me to worry you with my troubles."

Beguiled by the sidelong glance bestowed upon him, he insisted, "Believe me, Miss Penryck, nothing would please me more than to be of whatever help I can. You must learn to trust me, for I hope you know I am always at your service."

Allowing herself to be coaxed, she burst out in a confiding way. "You know that Lady Thane has left Bath?"

His jaw dropped in surprise. Clare rushed on. "She was called away—to London. I simply must get to her. Her protection is vital to me."

"But your guardian?" objected Sir Alexander.

"Oh, he is no help, you know. He is engrossed with Miss Morton, and I have not been able to talk to him at all. But I must go to Lady Thane, and I thought you would be able to tell me just how to go on. Shall I hire a post chaise? Or, if I took my maid, could I go on the stage? I am persuaded that I shall be safe, even though uncomfortable, but I shall be much more miserable if I stay in Bath alone, I promise you."

He said heavily, "It is surely not what I would expect

from Lady Thane to leave you alone in a rented house. Why did she not take you back to London with her?"

She had no answer ready. She looked into the distance and bit her lower lip. "Please, Sir Alexander, don't press me for reasons. I simply wish your advice. How shall I go about hiring a post chaise?"

"It is completely ineligible for you to travel to London in such a fashion. I should take a very strong position against it, I must tell you."

Tears sprang to her eyes. "Oh, how I wish I were wed!" she cried. "I would not feel so unprotected, so . . . so very much alone!"

"Wed!" cried Sir Alexander, startled. "I should hope that you would not wish to be wed for a few months yet. At that time, the proper time after your bereavement, I should like to speak to your guardian for your hand. I did not wish to speak of it to you until I had spoken to him. Even though it would be most improper in me to speak too soon, yet I confess that it much alarms me to see you in such distress, when I do not have the right to take your burdens upon my shoulders. On the other hand, since in a few months I shall be possessed of that right, then I do not see any real harm in helping you out of your fix at this time."

She put her hand on his arm. "Nor do I, Sir Alexander." She smiled up at him. "Then you will help me?"

"Be assured that I will do whatever I can do for you," he said handsomely. "But first I think I should talk to Choate on your behalf."

"Oh, no!" she cried out in alarm. "You must not! Promise me that you will not trouble him!"

"Why, what is this now? Surely you must see that he is the proper person—"

"Oh, no, he is the last person!" she interrupted. "He is so stern, you know." Seeing Sir Alexander still doubtful, she improvised hastily, "Besides, I have asked his permission."

Sir Alexander was assailed by real and valid doubts. But he was in a fair way of losing his heart to the minx before him, a sensation new to him. He strongly suspected that were he to marry her, his life would be changed from the orderly routine he cherished to an existence of strong currents and uncomfortable riptides. But no man could resist such an anxious look, could he? Sir Alexander, for one, could not.

"I don't think," he said, "that I can assist you in making your arrangements."

"You can't!" she cried. "Then I'll go alone!"

"On the other hand, I see that neither can I allow you to go alone to London. So I shall accompany you. I shall get my traveling chaise ready, and by Monday, I think—"

"Monday!" she cried out in anguish. "I must go today."

She had succeeded in startling her rescuer. She could read mutiny in his features, but before she could be sure of that, his face softened and he said, "Well, well. Now, don't cry, not here in public! I shall take you today."

"Oh, wonderful, Sir Alexander!" she cried out sunnily. "Now, at once?"

He temporized. "Let us say directly after luncheon. We shall soon be on the way to London!"

He doffed his hat and went on his way to make the necessary arrangements. Budge came up to her mistress after his departure.

"Be it he is going to take us to London?" she demanded, her ruddy complexion paler than usual. "Today?"

"Yes, he thinks so," said Clare, too elated by her success with Sir Alexander to be cautious. "But on the way, I'll see about diverting him. My real aim, dear Budge, is Gretna Green, and I cannot go without you."

"Oh, then that's all right," said Budge, vastly relieved. "I feared it was going to be Lunnon, and I couldn't abide with that."

25.

Sir Alexander Ferguson knew, humbly, that he was in general considered a dull dog. The blood of his Scottish forebears ran sluggishly in his veins, and much as he longed to emulate the feats of derring-do of others of his name—a Ferguson fought at Fontenoy, and a Ferguson's name appeared on the rolls of the Black Watch—he had become resigned to the idea that never would such opportunities come his way.

But now, he realized he was pleasantly titillated at the thought of a hasty departure from Bath, traveling with the young lady he already thought of as the future Lady Ferguson, for all the world as though they were eloping to Gretna Green! His proper soul cringed at the lengths his romantic heart contemplated. Never mind, he consoled himself—never in the world would I suggest to that delicately nurtured girl that I even thought of Gretna Green!

However, he moved with unaccustomed haste as he returned to his lodgings and gave instructions to Angus, his groom, for his traveling chaise to be ready in an hour, and for Mackie to pack sufficient clothing for three days in London. There was an hour before he must leave to meet Clare. The time weighed heavily on his mind, and at last his conscience told him the right thing to do.

He could not break his word to Clare. But now the entire scheme, no longer supported by the evanescent romance in his iron-bound spirit, looked havy-cavey to him. He wished he had not lost his head in the aura that surrounded that winsome miss. But it was too late to back out now. There was a small part of his mind that suggested that he did not exactly wish to support a lifetime of alarums and excursions—it would not suit him at all. But he had given his word to Clare, and he must keep it.

But caution, plus a very real respect for Lord Choate's powerful temper, led him to shore up his defenses in advance. He found that he had not exactly believed Miss Penryck when she said she had obtained Lord Choate's permission for this trip. He now doubted it completely, for

Choate was too much of a stickler to countenance such a hasty trip to London.

He sat down at his desk and penned a missive to Lord Choate. Surely he could do no less. It took some hard thinking to word the note properly. In fact, the more he reduced the journey to writing, the more he realized that it was a distinctly rum tale. But at last he was satisfied with his note, and gave it to the page in his lodging house to take to Lord Choate. And with a clear conscience, if not a light heart, he ascended into his chaise, totally unaware of a pair of eyes bright with curiosity and a certain amount of speculation watching him from across the street.

Harry Rowse, possessed of a jaunty, devil-may-care attitude as part of his considerable social assets, was just now at a low point in his fortunes. He had almost come to agreement with a baroness in her own right, possessed of wealth and little else, but she had at the last moment cried off. The hag, so Harry thought of her, had shied away at some untoward rumor that had come her way.

The gossip, Harry learned, was spread by Miss Morton, that paragon of young ladies, who had spread far and wide the tale of Harry's attempt on the Penryck child's virtue the night of the regent's ball. Miss Morton could have possessed herself of the details of the episode only from her betrothed.

Harry nursed his burning resentment. Not only had he been balked of the culmination of his advances toward Clare, but also of the more lasting, if less delectable, benefits of marriage to the wealthy baroness. The blame for Harry's misfortunes—so Harry believed—was to be laid directly at the feet of Lord Benedict Choate.

Harry had not before felt such a scalding rage, an unholy desire for a toppling revenge on anyone as he now felt it for Lord Choate.

It was not by chance, as Clare had thought, that Harry Rowse was in Bath. He, too, had heard rumors that Choate was having difficulties with his ward, and where there are difficulties, Harry had often found there were often ways to reap advantages. So Harry, partly to escape his creditors, and partly as a questing adventurer, came to Bath.

The diligence of his inquiries and personal surveillance at last, so it seemed, was to bear fruit. Ferguson and Miss Penryck, thought Harry with a gleam of hope. They had seemed mighty serious as he had watched them converse. And now clearly something was astir. For Ferguson's men were readying the coach, and his groom was giving agitated orders. Harry was not close enough to hear Angus' words, but the air was full of hurry and urgency.

If Ferguson were to leave town, directly after talking so long with Choate's ward, then Harry would take the road in his wake. He dared not try to remove his own curricle, for he had a strong suspicion that the stableman would insist first upon payment for stabling and board for his pair. Harry slipped away on his errands—first to find a livery where he was not known, and then to pick up Ferguson's trail. It should not be difficult!

The Ferguson coach lumbered out of Bath at a speed that boded ill for the stated desire of Sir Alexander to reach London by the evening. Since Clare's intentions were not to reach London at all, her only fear was that they would be observed in their departure and overtaken before she could divert Sir Alexander to the north.

Clare had now, in the coach, time to consider the consequences of her impulsive venture. She had only one goal in mind at first, to show Benedict that she did not need him to arrange her own marriage. She was not *precisely* pleased with Sir Alexander, but she believed her own choice was better for her than Choate's candidate, especially if the bridegroom were in any degree related to Marianna Morton.

It was no use to speculate on a future that might include a London season, with all the gaiety that accompanied the search for a marriage mate.

"That wouldn't be so bad," she said aloud to Budge. "I could stand going back to Penryck Abbey if it were only until next fall."

"But we ain't going to the abbey!" Budge reminded her with some satisfaction. Budge was seeing more of the world than she had ever dreamed of, and while Lunnon was still the den of the evil Old Nick, and the dregs of the world, all waiting for Budge to set one foot awry to pounce upon her, yet she was becoming inured to this junketing around the countryside with Miss Clare.

Miss had said Gretna Green, and Budge, while she may have guessed that the coachman, with whom she had a word or two as they left the Crescent, had no intention of leaving the Bath Road to London, she nursed an inner superiority at her privy knowledge. If miss said Gretna Green, then Gretna Green it was! Wherever that might be!

Sir Alexander, riding his hack ahead of the coach, ignored an ill-favored inn at a village whose name he did not know. He was intent on traveling as far along the road from Bath as he could. He, too, had time to think as he rode through the brilliant fall sunshine. He had greeted the adventure with expectations and a feeling that he was up to snuff, rescuing a maiden in distress, and ready, armed to the teeth, to do battle with all comers.

But the long ride gave second thoughts a chance to work powerfully in him, and as the day wore on, the force of logic pointed out his errors. There could be no real reason, he believed, for Miss Penryck to fly to Lady Thane's arms in London. If he had refused to take her, as reflection told him he should have done, he now thought she would not have gone alone, regardless of her threat.

He covered a few more miles, thinking slowly, but to the purpose, and a good bit beyond Woolhampton he came to a decision. He turned back to the coach. At a sign from him, coachman drew the carriage to the side of the road and waited.

Clare thrust her head out of the window. "Oh, what is the matter? Why have we stopped?"

"I do not wish to speak in front of your maid," said Sir Alexander in a manner she could only consider as ominous. "But I think it would be advisable were we to return to Bath."

"Return!" shrieked Clare. "Oh, no, you could not be so cruel as to think that. You would not turn around, would you? To take me back to . . ." She stopped short. She had not informed Sir Alexander of the nature of Benedict's threat. She bit her lip. She was positive that Sir Alexander would make no bones about taking her back if he knew that she was fleeing from Choate.

"Well, I do not think it a good idea to continue on to London. There is no chance that we will be able to arrive before nightfall, and what Choate will say when he finds out we have had to stop at an inn overnight, even with your maid, I dare not think of."

"Choate will not know of it," she said with vigor.

He had developed a mutinous streak of which she had previously been unaware. She was sorely in a cleft stick.

She was determined not to go back. Nor did she truly want to go to Gretna Green. Her head ached, and she had a lurking suspicion that she was behaving in such a ramshackle way that her grandmother, could she see her, would have been horrified.

She could not quarrel with Sir Alexander. She had not thought clearly ahead, and if she needed more proof that she was too inexperienced to face the world alone, she now had it. If only Benedict were not already arranging for her marriage with a stranger!

She did not give up. "Perhaps we could stop for a bit and talk about this?"

"It's no use," said Sir Alexander. "But I confess I would be glad of a bit of mutton. Always think better when I've got a full stomach."

They moved on at a slower pace toward the next town, where there would be a respectable inn, so Sir Alexander said. He had been on the verge of telling his charge that her guardian by now was apprised of her flight. Perhaps he would do so at the inn. He had been beguiled, he saw now, by the appealing look in her wide eyes, and he had been led astray by his wish to appear in the light of a knight-errant in her regard. Folly! All folly! he thought, and did not quite see his way out of it all.

In truth, Sir Alexander would have been far more worried had he been able to look with far-seeing vision down the road from Bath, on which they had traveled.

A good way back, delayed by the need to argue forcefully with a reluctant Bath liveryman, who at length was overborne in the matter of hiring out a gig and a single horse to a man whose cut he did not at all like, drove Harry Rowse. He was putting the horse to it, fearing that he would come upon the Ferguson coach too late for his purposes.

If Clare was eloping with Sir Alexander, thought Harry, by this time she would be heartily sick of him, and would welcome a bit of gallantry. He had no clear idea of what he was about—it would depend upon what he found when he came upon them.

If Clare was tired of Sir Alexander, it would take little to turn her in his direction, willingly. Or if she had already given in to Sir Alexander's importunities, then there was no reason why Harry Rowse should not also enjoy Clare's wantonness. So he thought. He was much of an opportunist, and he would wait upon events to instruct him. But in any case, he drove in great satisfaction at his own enterprise. For whatever happened, he would be able to serve the high-and-mighty Choate a bad turn. He began to whistle as he laid the whip upon his horse.

In the meantime, Benedict, having the night to think over his interview with his young ward, was, this Friday morning, having second thoughts. He recalled unpleasantly her stricken face when he told her that he had sent for Mrs. Duff. It was not his intention to be cruel, and the realization that she considered him wicked and unfeeling moved him more than he liked.

His entire intention was simply to see her settled. His own life was in pawn to a woman he had little feeling for, but he was determined that his ward would not be doomed to such a life as his own.

Unfortunately, he was expected to lunch with Marianna and her mother. He had been unpleasantly surprised when he learned that they had come to Bath in his wake. He had more than a suspicion that his betrothed was pursuing him out of curiosity and a possessiveness that he did not like. But there was no way out of it, and he sighed, dressing with his usual meticulous care for a luncheon that he looked forward to as one does to a visit to a tooth-drawer.

He formed the intention of cutting short his luncheon with the Mortons and making his way to Laura Place to see Clare Penryck, to reassure her about Mrs. Duff, to whom he would privately give instructions to treat the girl with kindness.

So he hardly listened as Marianna set herself to beguile his interest, thinking ahead with surprising pleasure to the afternoon meeting with Clare.

"You must know that although we have been here only since yesterday, already there is more going on in Bath than in a week in London!" cried Marianna gaily. "Lady Courtenay is here, and can hardly walk, so they say. But the baths are doing her such good. And the Duchess of Argyle. I haven't seen her since I can't remember when. Do you remember, Mama?"

Mrs. Morton, thus appealed to, said she didn't remember either. She had been watching Benedict with a speculative eye since his arrival. Her visit to Clare yesterday had given her much to think on, and she was struck by Benedict's attitude. It did not seem more than usually aloof, but, instructed by Clare's emotional reaction, she could see that he must appear nearly godlike to a girl of Clare's limited experience. She was quite sure of Clare's feelings, but she could not detect how Benedict felt.

If Benedict had a *tendre* for Clare, it was not visible even to Mrs. Morton. But she made a resolve to speak firmly to Marianna about curbing her great propensity for gossip, lest it turn Benedict away from her in disgust, for she thought she detected an absentmindedness in him that must not be allowed to continue.

When she attended once more to the conversation—or rather to Marianna's monologue, for Benedict responded only in monosyllables—Marianna had reached Harry Rowse. "Under the hatches, you know, since Lady Lancer turned him down. I fancy that was quite a blow. At any rate he is here in Bath. I confess I should worry about your Miss Penryck, except that she is totally out of society now. I did hear that they had been seen together."

"Miss Penryck will be returning to Dorset shortly," said Benedict. "I am convinced that the rumor you speak of was no more than that. She has been with Lady Courtenay, or Lady Thane, most of the time she has been here."

"Of course," said Marianna, withdrawing to a safer position. "When we are married, you will have no further worries about her. I can say with all sincerity that I will be most happy to take her charge upon myself. I fancy I shall be able to instruct her, and surely when she returns to London . . ." She stopped short. Benedict had quite clearly forgotten her, for he stared across the table at a figurine on the side table with great concentration.

His mind's eye filled his thoughts, however, with a clear picture of a girl with coin-gold ringlets and clear blue eyes brimming with tears that she was gallantly determined not to shed.

"I'm sorry," said Benedict. "I have quite forgotten an engagement that I made before I knew you were in Bath. I must beg to be excused."

He stood up and bowed to Mrs. Morton. "Do not trouble to see me out. I fear I am almost too late, as it is. Do forgive me."

He left without apparent haste, but Marianna, looking

from the window, remarked, "He's almost out of sight already. Where do you think he is going?"

"I don't know," said Mrs. Morton astringently. "But you will be well-advised not to ask when you see him next. In the meantime, my dear, I should like to speak to you about what I fear may become a grave fault in you."

Mrs. Morton drew her chair close to her daughter's and began to speak in great earnestness.

If she had known where Benedict was heading, she would have been even more dismayed. For Benedict was hurrying on his way to apologize to his ward.

26.

Benedict arrived at Lady Thane's rented house, and was admitted by Mrs. Bishop. He inquired for his ward, and received a shock.

"Miss isn't here, my lord," said Mrs. Bishop in a stern, disapproving voice. She knew what was proper and what wasn't, and the way affairs were managed around here did not measure up to her rigid standards.

Benedict was conscious of a letdown. He had made up his mind to apologize, and the delay was offsetting. "Then I shall wait," he said, unbuttoning his coat.

"Not much use, I think," Mrs. Bishop informed him. "For miss and her maid will be long-delayed."

"What do you mean by that?"

"I mean that miss went out, with her maid, and her bandbox, and I surely know a gentleman's traveling coach when I see it."

"And you did see it?" said Benedict smoothly.

"No thanks to miss, I can tell you," said Mrs. Bishop darkly. She was not responsible to anyone but the owner of the house, and miss could go or stay and it would make no never-mind to Mrs. Bishop. But right was right. "She slipped out of the front door as quiet as you please, and if I hadn't just happened to be looking out of the upstairs window, I wouldn't have seen the coach stop right down at the corner and miss get in."

Benedict, seething, put a few more questions to the housekeeper, received a description of the coach, and left the house. There was no doubt in his mind that the vehicle belonged to Sir Alexander Ferguson. And while Choate could not at once decide what had driven Ferguson mad enough to take off with a schoolgirl in a traveling coach, he could wait for an explanation until he caught up with them. And catch up with them he would.

The first stop was at Ferguson's lodgings. Here his fears were confirmed. Sir Alexander had left Bath. According to the page, "His lordship's gone and taken all with him. Left in such a hurry," said the page, "that he didn't have time to give me the sovereign he promised me to deliver a note to some swell over on the Parade."

Benedict regarded the ill-favored urchin with such severity as to make him cringe. "A note? Could it have been addressed to me, by any chance? Lord Choate?"

"I dunno. Can't read. But he didn't give me the sovereign." The boy was cowed but not conquered. If he could succeed in getting his sovereign, he would be possessed of the largess that dreams are made of.

"Let me see the note, if you will," said Benedict, tossing a small coin in the air. The lad saw that it was clearly not a sovereign, and philosophically lowered his sights.

"He said," said the urchin without conviction, "that he would give me a sovereign, sir."

"I wish I may see the day that Sir Alexander Ferguson hands out sovereigns as tips," said Benedict pleasantly. "But I warn you that my patience is not inexhaustible." He pocketed the coin.

In moments, the elusive note had been produced and the coin had changed hands. The page scuttled away. Even a shilling was better than nuffin, he thought, rightly.

The note from Sir Alexander did nothing to allay Choate's fears. "The little wretch!" he said, clenching his fists. "Wait till I get hold of her, suborning Ferguson like this. She knows full well Lady Thane is not in London! I wonder what her game is this time?"

He did not stand still. Even as he promised himself the utmost of revenge on the girl to whom he had been longing to apologize less than an hour before, he returned to his own rooms, ordered his curricle and the grays, and took time only to tell Grinstead that he did not know when he would be back.

He curbed his pair sufficiently until he reached the eastern outskirts of the city, and then he put them right along. The fine-bred horses ate up the miles, and Benedict began to entertain hopes of catching up with the runaways within the hour. Ferguson's coach couldn't begin to make the speed that the light curricle could, and Benedict turned his mind to formulating well-turned phrases that would serve to dissuade his ward from ever trying anything like this again.

By the time another hour had passed, and there was still no sight of his quarry, Benedict was in a towering rage. Of all the ramshackle, idiotic things to do—to cajole Sir

Alexander Ferguson into such folly as taking her to London. For the first time he began to wonder whether Sir Alexander was quite the stuffy gentleman he had thought him. Surely it was not the act of an innocent man to lend himself to such an escapade!

Benedict was too well aware of the havoc his ward left in her wake to blame Ferguson for the runaway, but his rage did not diminish as far as Clare was concerned.

Unbidden, Lady Fenton's remark, as passed along by her son Ned, occurred to him. "Too much fire for the cause. There's more to it than on the surface."

Benedict refused to consider anything other than his need to get the girl back. There was a revelation for him just beyond the brink of his thoughts, but he did not want to explore it. He had a dark feeling hat he did not want to know more than he already did.

His mood was thus dangerous when he became aware of an obstacle in the road ahead. A closer view told him that it was a gig drawn by a horse that appeared to be lame on the off hind foot. It could not be Ferguson, and Benedict had no interest in anyone else. He drew to the right, ready to pass, but the gig did not give him room. Instead, incredibly, the driver turned his vehicle into the center of the road and dropped to the ground to face Benedict.

For a moment Benedict wished he had taken time to allow Vilas to accompany him. Two armed men would not always be enough to assure safety on the road. But Benedict had not wanted to admit a groom to his confidence, and indeed he had every reason to believe that he could manage one armed man.

For he saw, with some disbelief, that the driver of the disabled rig stood now with a pistol in each hand. Benedict, a notable shot, reined in with prudence. If the fellow lost his poise because of unnecessary defiance, he might by accident hit his mark.

The desperate character in the road took a step toward Benedict's slowing curricle, and Benedict recognized him. "Rowse! I had heard that you were in desperate straits, but I had not expected to see you turning highwayman."

"Nor have I," retorted Rowse. "This job horse has played me false, and I was about to inspect the damage." He put a pistol away, and made as though to holster the other, but with a casual air that did not deceive Benedict, he still held it. "Looks too lame to me to go on."

Watching Rowse bend over his horse's front leg, Benedict toyed with the idea of offering assistance, but the purpose of his journey did not allow for any delay. He could catch up with the Ferguson coach before Reading, if he were not delayed. At that point, roads led to Gretna Green, to London, toward Andover—though what Clare and Ferguson might be doing in Andover escaped him.

After a few moments, while Rowse dealt with his horse, had grown into a lengthier time, Benedict suggested mildly, "Could you not draw your gig over to the side, Rowse?"

Rowse straightened and came to stand only a few feet from the curricle. "I could, Choate. But I don't think I will. I should imagine that you too are in pursuit of your ward."

"Too?"

"And it does not suit me to allow you to interfere again. For you know, don't you, that Miss Penryck has taken to the road? In all likelihood, she is on her way to Gretna Green. I should imagine you would not like that above half, would you?"

Gretna Green! Choate had read Ferguson's note carefully, and there was no mention of Gretna Green, or of an elopement. In fact, that ponderous Scot had said, in surprisingly few words, for him, that they were on their way to London, to Lady Thane's.

But Benedict also knew that Lady Thane was not in London. Had that wily minx cozened Ferguson into an elopement? Choate would not put it past her. He reflected on these points in a moment, but Rowse grew impatient.

"That beguiling child got away from me once before," said Rowse, somewhat irritated, "but she will not do so again. I promise you that. She won't end up at Gretna Green, I can tell you."

"What makes you think she intends to go to Gretna Green?" asked Benedict. The situation was murkier than he had expected to begin with. At first it was a simple pursuit, but now, with this idiot Rowse in the way, with a loaded gun in his hand, Benedict trod warily.

"Well," said Rowse with an air of reason, "where else would she go? Ferguson ain't one to play false. And I would already be talking to him, instead of you, if this horse hadn't gone lame."

"Tell me, Rowse," said Benedict conversationally, "what your intentions are toward the lady?"

Rowse laughed aloud, a harsh sound that startled Choate's grays. Benedict brought them under control again with his left hand, his right one holding the whip.

"What do you want to know for?" demanded Rowse. "There's nothing you can do, anyway. I'll just trouble you to step down, and I'll take your cattle. Prime goers, ain't they? The great Lord Choate wouldn't drive any job horses, the way I have to," he finished viciously. He waved the pistol at Choate.

"It seems to me," said Benedict thoughtfully, ignoring the loaded pistol, "that you are not so much interested in the lady as you are in Ferguson. Am I right?"

The pistol wavered. Rowse asked in an altered tone, "What if you are? Ferguson's the kind who will pay well to keep scandal away from his door. Once I point out to him the way things look, or will look when I get through dropping a few hints in the right ears in London, he will make it worth my while to keep silent."

Benedict regarded the man on the ground with scorn. "There is no limit to what you will do, is there?"

"No," Rowse said, considering, "I don't think there is. But Ferguson won't see the jest, I fear. How delicious it will be for a man of such ponderous respectability and the most conventional of motives to be barred from Almack's, lest he run off with the young ladies!"

"I fail to see the jest myself," said Benedict. "Your dealings with Ferguson are your own affair. But I warn you, the safety and good name of my ward is entirely my business, and you will be well-advised to keep clear of Miss Penryck."

The pistol came up again, and Rowse said in a deadly tone, "I think there is no reason for me not to indulge my fancy both for money and for a bit of dalliance with a pretty maid."

"You can't be so lost to decency," said Benedict, his voice dripping the scorn he could no longer conceal, "as to pursue a well-bred young lady just out of the school-room!"

"So well-bred," countered Rowse, "that this schoolgirl starts off cross-country with a man who is not related to her? In a closed coach, besides, and beyond all that, I should be greatly surprised if Ferguson knows the plans of that schoolroom miss!"

Benedict lost patience. He was increasingly anxious about what might be happening on the road ahead, and desperate to overtake the runaways before they reached Reading. It would be much more difficult to track them down, when a choice of roads was open to them. Besides, it would take tedious inquiries and more curiosity on the part of those he asked than he wished to sustain.

"Get out of my way, Rowse!" he said viciously. "You're hopelessly out of it to think you can come up with them and seduce my ward. Lay one finger on her," he added with menace, "and you will wish you had never lived."

Momentarily intimidated, Rowse stepped backward in the road. Then, with a laugh, he chortled, "A great deal of fire, Lord Choate! Only a guardian? You make me laugh. You've got a fancy for the girl yourself! This too will cause a stir in London, in the right ears!"

"Why nobody has killed you before this," hissed Benedict, "I couldn't say. But I know that after this I shall indulge myself in dealing with you. *After* I rejoin my ward."

His fury was out of bounds. He could see the effect his rage had on Harry Rowse, and he regretted it. Rowse clearly thought that Benedict had a *tendre* for the girl, and nothing Benedict could say would change his mind. His very anger only reinforced the conviction that he could read in Rowse's face.

Lurking under the surface of his thoughts stirred the conviction that there was more truth than falsehood in Rowse's accusation. Lady Fenton's dictum came back to him again. He bit his lip on the words that sprang to his tongue.

Rowse seemed to be in a deep study. He stood too close to the grays' heads for Choate to drive around him, and the hired horse and rig of Rowse's moved erratically across the road.

"How much?" said Rowse at last.

"For the grays?" demanded Choate unbelievingly. "Out of the question. You'll just have to get to town the best way you can."

"For my silence," retorted Rowse. "It won't do you any good with Miss Morton, to hear how you scorched out of

Bath to keep your schoolgirl from running off with another man. I wonder—"

"That is positively the last straw!" seethed Benedict. "Out of my way or I'll run you down. I warn you, Rowse, if I see your face again in Reading, in London, or anywhere on earth, you are a dead man!"

He began to turn the grays around Rowse, not too carefully, for at that moment he had not the slightest aversion to sending the splendid horses directly over Rowse's body. Rowse, reading rightly the ferocious expression on his enemy's face, lifted his pistol and cocked the hammer.

With a reflex motion, Choate, incensed at Rowse's dastardly demands, raised his whip and flicked it. The same touch of the whip that would, in the park, take a fly from his horse's ear, this time unerringly cracked around Rowse's right wrist, and caused Rowse to cry out in pain.

Everything happened at once. Rowse could not remember firing the pistol, but the report deafened him. Even though the whip had deflected his aim, and the ball did not reach its mark, yet the results were disastrous as he could have wished.

The grays, unused to loud noises in their ears, reared out of control. Rowse, seeing the great forefeet above his head, dodged desperately. He did not, saving his own skin, see Benedict thrown from the curricle as the horses, maddened, bolted.

But when the smoke cleared, and Rowse, to his surprise, found that he was uninjured, he saw, on the hard surface of the road, his enemy, stretched full length and unconscious.

Harry approached and knelt beside him. Never a man to lose his head, first he made sure that Choate was unaware of his surroundings. Then, with fingers made swift by practice and by the need for haste, he transferred the contents of Choate's note case to his own.

For a moment he looked down at his enemy. A momentary pang of pity crossed his mind, and he nearly decided to look about him for help for Lord Choate.

The pang lasted hardly as long as a breath, and Harry Rowse, noting that his own gig and the curricle and the grays were totally out of sight, turned his back on Choate.

Patting his full note case with satisfaction, he set off on foot down the road in the direction he had been heading before Choate had caught up with him. At first that had seemed like a disaster, he reflected, but he was well out of it, with enough money to hire a curricle and pair at the next town, and before nightfall he would be much surprised if he had not come upon the runaway couple.

He began to whistle an air that sounded much like a triumphal march, and his steps quickened to keep pace with the rhythm.

He never looked back at the body lying spread-eagled on the road behind him.

27.

The little settlement that Rowse soon spied as he stumbled along the pavement was no more than a wide place in the road. But Harry Rowse's memory stirred, and he recalled a worn building, roofed with unhealthily aged thatch, where the ale was unsafe, but, upon application of certain funds, a glass of French brandy could be obtained

Thanks to Benedict Choate, Rowse had brandy money. He did not quite like the idea of leaving Benedict unconscious on the highway, but his thoughts ran more along the line of his victim's recovering and talking. The way his affairs had been going recently gave him every encouragement to think the worst.

Balked by Benedict Choate of a simple little flirtation in the grounds of Carlton House, Harry had developed a sizable desire for revenge. Riding out of Bath in a hired rig, he had seen the chance both for Clare and for revenge on her guardian. But Benedict had again overtaken him.

He stopped along the road and looked behind him. No one followed. Not even a sign of the job-rig he had rented could he see. But he forgot that at once. He had the dibs to do better than a horse who went lame at the first opportunity.

With the prudence engendered by years' experience of necessary shifts to make do, he counted the money again, selected a small note, and tucked the rest away in an inner pocket. It was a fool who revealed money in any public place, especially one so ill-visaged as the ramshackle inn just ahead.

The small note was large enough to obtain a glass of the brandy, and he took his drink to a table before the dead hearth. He was the only occupant of the taproom, besides the surly owner, and uneasily he shifted his position to a place nearer a window. At worst, he could smash the grimy pane and be away.

"Thee came a-walkin'," said the owner, "and ask for my brandy? You look like a London toff, not one of those hereabouts."

Rowse did not rise to the bait. "I don't suppose you've got a horse I can buy?"

"Buy, is it?" The host rubbed his unshaven chin. "Aye, I've got one. But it'll cost you!"

He had made an error, thought Rowse. He would have concealed his new wealth better had he suggested renting. He made amends now. "Of course it'll cost me!" he countered. "I didn't think to steal it. But you'll want twice the value for half of the beast, and I think I won't buy a horse that'll go lame just out of sight down the road."

At length, the innkeeper having sworn that the horse the ostler led out would be a prize at Tattershall's—"except that I like to keep a good bit of horseflesh meself, don't you know"—Harry cantered down the road in pursuit of the Ferguson coach. He had toyed, while feeling the brandy that he owed to Benedict warming his throat and heartening his mood, with the idea of sending help back to his unwitting benefactor. But he feared the innkeeper would, quite rightly, suspect him of having a hand in the affair, and even set the sheriff on him.

He thought he had already given rise to sufficient suspicion to give the innkeeper quite enough to think about. With the ease of long practice, he put all unpleasant things out of his mind, and Benedict Choate was forgotten.

Harry, finding the horse a better goer than he expected, gave his thoughts over to what he would do when he overtook Clare.

Miss Penryck was a puzzle to Rowse. She had seemed to be glad to see Choate in the garden, but shortly after that she had run out on him. Then she defied him—rumor was exact enough on this point—and ran off to Bath. Rowse had not overlooked the forbidding frown of the black Penryck eyebrows when Choate spoke to Clare on the street in Bath.

But she had fled, and Benedict had come in hot pursuit, and there must be a reason. Summoning up all he had heard in Bath, Rowse came to a conclusion that satisfied him. She hated her guardian and feared him as well. She was taking any means to flee from her guardian, and Harry began to smile. She surely could not be eloping with Ferguson. No girl in her right mind could take Ferguson for even as long as the coach ride from Bath to London, let alone Gretna Green. If he were not wrong, Clare would be heartily sick of Ferguson long before they reached Reading, where they could take the road to the north.

Harry had decided, by the time the spire of Newbury Church appeared above the horizon, on his approach to Clare. He had now the infallible key to winning Clare's gratitude, if not affection, and he was a poor man if he could not work all to his advantage.

Harry, while not of formidable intellect, yet was shrewd in his assessment of people. As he had predicted, the inn at Newbury housed two people at great odds. Sir Alexander, always careful of his cattle, had stopped to bait, and Clare, remembering that she had been too excited to eat breakfast, was ravenous.

In a private parlor, she was served strong coffee and a fine pink slice of ham, and Alex and Benedict alike were forgotten until she had demolished her meal.

Then she set herself to cajoling her escort into a better humor. All would be lost—even more than lost—if she did not now escape Benedict, and Sir Alexander was her last hope.

She smiled sunnily upon her protector and said, "We turn north here, Sir Alex, or in Reading? I do not quite know my way in this region, except that I once heard that the Lindsays live not far away. Near Hungerford, I collect. That is not far, I think. I inquired most carefully at Bath about Shenton, you know, Choate's sister's place."

"Why do you not go there," inquired Ferguson heavily, "instead of this madcap trip to town? If you are tired of Bath, as you say."

"Oh, but I couldn't!" said Clare. "Lady Lindsay is in her brother's pocket, you know, and besides, I have never met her." Looking sideways at her escort, she perceived, as she should have before, that Sir Alexander was looking more sober than usual. In fact, one might have called him glum with some accuracy.

Her fears were realized as he said, "I do not like this journey. It is against all regular behavior, and I do not like to think what will be said of me for consenting to it."

"But we will not need to hear what people say of us," she said winningly, picking up her bandbox. "Are your horses rested now? I vow I feel much better myself."

Sir Alexander was not quick-witted, but he was dogged. He did not like the journey, that was true, and even if its purpose were to transport Miss Penryck to her godmother in London, an unexceptionable goal, yet he now remembered her question about turning north here or at Reading.

London, as even Miss Penryck would know, was not to the north. "North?" he said ponderously. "Why should we turn north?"

"To get to the Great North Road," said Clare, eyes wide. Behind her look of innocence, she was swiftly revising her scheme. She had not meant to explain to Sir Alexander that they were eloping to Gretna Green until after they were well on the way. She had expected to talk privately with coachman, but Sir Alexander was about to foil that hope.

Sir Alexander did not even look startled, she noted. It was as though some deep lurking suspicion, hidden away until now, were surfacing, and his worst fears emerged into the light.

"I should have known," he said heavily. "The Great North Road. I do not like to appear stupid, Miss Penryck, but can it be that you believe we are eloping?" His voice rose almost to a squeal.

With calmness that covered her thudding heart, she said, "I thought you wished to marry me. You did say you were going to ask Choate for my hand. That was only this morning! But I see I have been sadly mistaken."

"Good God, no! At least, I mean, yes . . . I mean . . . I suppose I want to marry you."

Eyes blazing, she glared at him. "Well, if that isn't outside of enough! Such a lukewarm proposal, if that is what it was, which I very much doubt. Lady Thane certainly mistook your intentions, and what she will have to say to you doesn't bear thinking about!"

Goaded, Sir Alex burst out, "But we're not going to Lady Thane's—not if we turn north!" Then, aghast at his own words, he turned a fierce eye on her. "But we're not going north. I promise you that!"

"You don't want to marry me?" she said in a wee voice.

"No, I didn't say that. Don't cry! I can't stand to see a lady cry! I'm willing to marry you, don't worry! I think you would want to wait till you're out of mourning!"

"I . . . I can't!" Her voice was muffled in her handkerchief.

Alex might have taken her up on that, but his thoughts were solely turned toward himself, in a state of trance over the impending change in his status. "Married. Well, I suppose it would come to that. After all, a man's got to marry *some*body. . . ."

As a reassuring remark, it lacked a good deal. Clare's temper flared like a torch in the night, but she swallowed hard and hung on to it. She could not afford to alienate Sir Alex, and in all fairness she had to admit he had gone along with her plans against his better judgment, and she must make allowances for him.

But more than anything else the realization came to her that she was heartily sick of Sir Alexander. In fact, she was weary of the whole escapade, and longed to be back in the maroon salon of Lady Thane's establishment in Bath. Even to hear Benedict ringing a peal over her would be better than this!

But she was not one to refuse her fences. She had started this, and she would see it through.

"Well, then"—she smiled at Alex—"it's all settled. I'll try to be a good wife to you, believe me."

"Well, well," said Sir Alex, restored to a semblance of good temper, "it's not so bad after all. We'll be married, but we'll do it in the right way, and not this havey-cavey elopement." He crossed to her and chucked her under her chin. "Come, now, smile at me. That's better."

She managed a watery smile. Perhaps it would all turn out all right after all. Benedict scorned her, Lady Thane abandoned her, but Alexander Ferguson wouldn't. She could do worse. . . .

"But why can't we be married at once!" she cried.

"Why should we?" Ferguson said bluntly. "You'll want clothes, I suppose, and . . . and all those things that are customary."

"Because! Because Benedict wants me to marry somebody else!"

Sir Alexander was startled. "You mean . . .? You don't mean—?"

"Oh, for goodness, sake! Say one thing or another!" she cried out, losing her temper in one magnificent burst. "Yes, I mean—Benedict wants to betroth me to some idiot relative of Miss Morton's, and I won't do it! I'll die first!"

The courage of his Scottish forebears at last came to his rescue. He said bluntly, "But you don't intend to die. You intend to elope in a way I cannot imagine anyone who still wants to hold her head up in society could do. I am glad I found this out before it was too late."

She had done it now. Woefully she raised a tearful face to him. "You're going to cry off?"

"Certainly not," said Ferguson. "We Fergusons always do what we say we will do. But I meant before Choate gets here. I must think how I should explain to him that I knew nothing of this." He lapsed into reverie.

"Choate? Benedict? He's coming?" She took a few running steps toward the door. She turned back then and fixed her tormentor with a steely gaze. "You have betrayed me, Sir Alexander."

Cheeks reddening, he exploded. "I have done nothing of the sort! Do you know what you are saying? I suppose you'll put the entire blame on me! I'm seeing a side of you, Miss Penryck, that I am not happy about."

"Nor am I with your sniffling, canting ways! You were glad enough to leave Bath with me *in a closed carriage*, and now you're crying off! I should have known better than to trust such a . . . such a *reed*! A spineless, good-for-naught reed!"

She was growing up, she thought later. Even in the height of her anger she did not reach for something to throw. She turned her back on him and glared, unseeing, out of the window. Her thoughts milled in confusion. She must do something, but she did not have the slightest idea what would be best. It was not left to her to decide.

"Well, we're both out of temper," said Sir Alexander in a mollified voice, "and we'll see what can best be done when we get to Grosvenor Square. I think we should go on to London, and let Choate catch us up." And I will be relieved, he thought, to have you off my hands until I can think straight, and another few hours to think what to say to Choate. More and more he was of the opinion that contemplating marriage to this spitfire was a great folly.

To his surprise, Miss Penryck burst into a laugh. "Lady Thane is not in London," she informed him. "She has gone to visit her daughter, Harriet, who is dreadfully sick with the plague!"

The scales falling from his eyes, Sir Alexander said merely, "I suppose that's another of your inventions, Miss Penryck. On the other hand, I dare not take a chance. I must go and make arrangements to return to Bath at once. I do not envy Lord Choate," he added with feeling, and left Clare alone in the parlor.

She sank into a chair, fiddling with the handle of her bandbox. Endlessly tracing the braid, she thought only of the mull she had made of it all. She had been so headset on following her own desires that she had alienated all in her life, first Choate, then Lady Thane, and now Sir Alexander. But it was Choate who stayed in the center of her darkling reflections. Strangely, it was not what he might say, but how he might say it that bothered her most. She could—after today—nearly welcome the stern Mrs. Duff.

The door opened, and closed again.

Thinking it was Sir Alexander, she did not look up. In a resigned voice she said, "Are you ready?"

"That is quite an invitation, Miss Penryck," said Harry Rowse. "If I thought you meant it for me, you wouldn't be sorry, believe me."

"What are you doing here!" she cried out, rising to her feet in some trepidation. "How did you know—?"

"Now, that is not quite the welcome I had imagined. But I daresay that when you have heard my news, you will think better of me. Perhaps not welcome me with open arms, as yet . . ."

He left the sentence tantalizingly in the air, but she did not rise to his bait. He was rushing too fast, he knew, but somehow he couldn't help it. Seeing her again roused some feeling that had long been a stranger to him. It was a feeling such as one might have for a frightened kitten, inexplicably mixed up with a very masculine wish to have her for his own.

"News?" Clare faltered. "But there is nothing you can tell me, I am sure. We have this morning come from Bath, and nothing could have happened since then. Unless . . . Is it Benedict?"

Things were going very well, thought Rowse, with a half-smile creeping over his face. "You will be grateful to me of all men," he pronounced, moving toward her with his hands stretched toward her.

"I wish you will not behave . . . in such an unsettling way," she said, backing toward the window. "I wish you will tell me your news, if you indeed have any, and then leave me."

He nodded. "Very well, I will play your little game with you. Just now you are the apprehensive maiden. It becomes you very well. I should compliment you upon your performance."

"Performance?"

"Oh, quite. I imagine it should beguile any man—of lesser intelligence then I. Sir Alexander Ferguson, perhaps."

"I d-don't know what you mean."

"I mean this girlish, innocent role you assume. Of all people, don't try to cozen me. After all, I know you are on the romp with Ferguson. Of all things, your lack of delicacy is astounding. What do you think people will say?"

"No one knows about it," she said, her lip trembling. It was bad enough that she had just told herself the same things, without hearing them from Harry Rowse as well.

If only Benedict were here, she thought longingly. She would rejoice if he just now came in the door, drawling in his languid fashion, stripping off his gloves before inviting Rowse outside to plant him a leveler . . .

"I know about it," Rowse assured her. "It is a shame that I cannot indulge my desire to rescue you and restore you to your guardian, unharmed. But you see, I am not so well in the pocket as your other friends."

"You are no friend of mine!"

"How true! And yet, I think you could learn to like me a little better." He started toward her. "I remember you did not object to me in the regent's garden."

"Don't come near me!" she cried out. She was aware now that her foolishness seemed to have no end. To be at the mercy of a man like Harry Rowse—no one could sink lower!

"Why not? Surely Ferguson is not man enough to appreciate such a delicate piece as you are? You will find me much more to your fancy, don't you know? And yet, on the other hand . . ." His voice dropped into his mimicry of Sir Alexander's laborious periods. She smiled reluctantly.

"But Lord Choate will take care of you," she warned him. "If you touch me, I swear he will call you out. He never loses his duels, you know."

"I know of one that he lost," said Rowse, coming to a stop and lazily regarding her.

"Oh?" she said, startled.

"The one that has left your wicked guardian *hors de*

combat. Somewhere on the road between here and Bath."
The lazy look left his eyes, and he started toward her, this time with strong purpose. "Now," he said as he grabbed her wrists and pulled her hands up, to rest, clenching helplessly into fists, on his chest, "don't I deserve some thanks for that?"

28

"Thanks!" she echoed, stiff with indignation.

"Of course," Rowse said smoothly. "How many times have you said you did not need a guardian? How many times, I repeat, did you bridle against Choate's tight rein?"

She backed away from him as he took a step toward her. He stopped now and held out his hand in appeal. "Let us have done with such fribbles as thanks between us. I had hoped at first to encounter Ferguson, for I have some dealings with him, as you might guess."

"I know of none," she said sturdily. "But I should like to know what you meant by Choate's being *hors de combat?*"

"My dear, I thought you were better educated than that. *Hors de combat* means 'out of battle.' "

"I *know* what it means," retorted Clare furiously. "Where is Benedict?"

"All in good time." He hesitated. In an altered tone he queried, "Where is your escort? Or has Ferguson gotten tired of you already?"

"Wretch!"

"I had thought that such a little spitfire might intrigue the dogged Scot for more than a day. Not quite a day," he amended with a judicial air. "I wonder . . ."

"He is *not* tired of me!" cried Clare.

The gleam in Rowse's eyes told her she had spoken foolishly. "Not tired yet?" said Rowse silkily. "Then . . . But I must inquire into what is, after all, a very private matter between you and Ferguson." His voice changed abruptly. "Where is he?"

She gestured vaguely. Rowse's evasiveness was giving rise in her to a deep suspicion. She had no reason, based on experience, to believe him, either when he said Choate was incapacitated or when he said Choate would not come after her.

"Out there somewhere," she said. "But I wish I knew——"

"I shall tell you all you need to know," said Rowse, resuming his stalking advance toward her. "You are safe from Choate for now, perhaps forever. I should imagine

Ferguson is not quite the companion for your tender years. You were much misguided—"

"Stay away from me!"

"—to run away from Bath, don't you know. Everyone there will soon know that you are in such disgrace that you will never recover your credit. Now, it seems to me—"

"I don't care what seems to you," raged Clare, more afraid now than she had ever been. "You touch me and I'll kill you!"

"Strange," said Rowse, stopping as though caught by the novelty, "that's just what Choate said to me. Just before the mishap, of course."

"Mishap! I wish you will tell me, where is my guardian?"

"You forgot something, my dear. It is your *wicked* guardian. I have heard, not from your own lips of course, but from the lips of others, that you have often called him that."

"Oh, how I wish I had never been so foolish!"

Rowse, for all his vaunted experience with the frailer sex, misread her meaning. "I agree that not every young lady would consider such a very improper escapade. But—if Ferguson can indulge his fancy with you, then I see no reason not to enjoy myself, too."

He made an unexpected rush toward her. She stumbled backward, but she felt the hard wall of the cupboard behind her back. She was trapped. "Don't touch me!" she breathed desperately.

"Or you'll kill me? How brave of you." Rowse was clearly enjoying the pursuit, she saw, much as a cat delays the kill of a kitchen mouse. Perhaps she could distract him. . . .

Over his shoulder she could see the door. It was opening slowly, and she widened her eyes. Here was her chance!

"Help me!" she cried out, but her voice was too small to carry. "Oh, help me, please!"

Rowse's eyes darkened. The smile lurking on his thin lips turned cruel. "Don't try that," he advised her. He jerked her to him, and sought her lips. She twisted, in vain. Her blood thrummed deafeningly in her ears, and she writhed in torment under his brutal kisses.

"I've just got them to hitch up the team again," said the voice of Alexander Ferguson beyond the door. "Coachman gave me no trouble. I think he fancies you, Clare . . . Clare?"

He now stood in the doorway of the small parlor, and Clare, hidden behind the large figure of Harry Rowse, was not at first visible to him.

At the sound of Alex's voice, Rowse abruptly released Clare and let her fall sharply against the cupboard latch. A sharp pang went through her, but she scarcely noticed in her unbounded relief.

"Oh, Alexander!" she cried out in a strangled voice. "Oh, how glad I am!"

Sir Alexander said hopefully, "Then you are ready to return to Bath! I do think it best."

Then the situation before him began to penetrate to his slow wits. There was Clare, panting as though she had run a race, wiping her lips savagely with the back of her hand. And there was Rowse, a contemptible person he had thought—if he had thought of him at all—was still in Bath.

Clearly something was amiss. Sir Alexander manfully began to deal with the trouble. "What are you doing here, Rowse? I can't believe you came to force your attentions on the lady traveling under my protection, as it appears."

"Oh, stuff it!" said Rowse with great rudeness. He strove to put some order back into his ruffled shirt and his wrinkled waistcoat—the gold brocade vest to which he was partial was in pawn in Bath—and realized that nothing he could say could soften the impression that Ferguson clearly had.

"Remember Miss Penryck!" exclaimed Ferguson, appalled.

"Oh, I do, I do," said Rowse, recovering his aplomb. "In fact, she has been in my thoughts since I left Bath. Having noticed, you might say, that something untoward was going on . . . I must say, Ferguson, that to see you eloping with a well-bred young girl—lass, I suppose you Scots say?—shocked me to the core. And I could not rest until I saw that I was mistaken in your intentions. But, you will see . . ." He gestured toward Clare, cowering in the corner, still panting for breath. She was regaining her self-control, now that Ferguson had returned, and with the immediate danger past, she turned over the information that Rowse had let drop, or had given out as truth.

She watched with only half her attention as Ferguson

and Rowse faced each other. Rowse was increasingly
bland, and the little smile lurking at the corner of his
mouth boded no good. He was truly a very bad person,
she realized, and while she had known enough not to allow him any liberties, yet she had not yet plumbed his
depths.

Ferguson—on the other hand—gave every appearance
of standing as strong as the Grampian Hills. And she realized, too, that his wavering grasp on events was due in
part to her own waywardness. But Rowse was now coming
to the point.

"I came to see for myself what dastardly plot you had
hatched," he said, "and I confess, Ferguson, you surprise
me with the devious malice of your scheme."

Ferguson, already badly rattled by the unexpected turn
of events, and Clare's deceit, sputtered, "It's not my fault!
Although I must not put the blame on Miss Penryck. I
knew better. But she seemed so—"

"Delectable?" inserted Rowse, purring.

"No, no! Desperate! I vow I did not know . . . I must
see Miss Penryck back to Bath, to her guardian."

"Ah, yes, the wicked guardian," said Rowse. "I do not
know just where you will find him."

"He's in Bath!" asserted Ferguson stoutly.

"Not . . . quite," said Rowse. "But then—"

"Ask Mr. Rowse where Choate is," interrupted Clare.
"He won't tell me. All he says is . . ." To her great dismay, her voice choked with a sob, and she could not go
on.

Rowse lifted an eyebrow. "I can't believe my eyes. The
poor persecuted ward doesn't want to be free? Like a bird
in a cage, when the door is left open, fearing the world.
Like that, Miss Penryck?"

"Oh, never *mind!*"

But Rowse had already forgotten her. His eyes nar-
rowed, and he frowned at Ferguson. "Now, let me ask,
how much?"

Ferguson gazed blankly at him. "How much what?"

"How foolish you are! Let me draw you a picture of the
future, Ferguson. You move to London for the Little
Season, and all goes well, or nearly so. But by Christmas,
when all the *ton* retreat to their country houses, and hold
great gatherings of all their friends for the holidays—then
is when Dame Rumor is a welcome guest, scurrying from

one great house to another, with the latest *on-dit*. Your name, I promise you, will figure largely in such tea-table chatter. And when you come back to London after Easter, you will find every door of quality closed to you."

"But . . . why?" asked Ferguson, totally bewildered.

"You ask why?" Rowse placed both hands on the table between them and leaned forward. Clare was completely forgotten now, and she took advantage of the respite to sort out her thoughts.

"You can't imagine, Ferguson, that ladies with marriageable daughters would spurn you? A man with a very respectable fortune and of well-enough family?"

Sir Alexander was slow-witted, true, but his conscience, clear as spring water, armored him against the unwelcome truth that Rowse was explaining. "Why should they?"

"Because, my friend, you have run away with a child, a miss just out of the schoolroom, against the expressed wishes of her guardian, compromising her beyond repair. And you ask why?"

"But Choate surely couldn't object to my escorting her to her godmother . . ." Then the truth began to dawn. Clare had misled him into thinking that her godmother was in London. And only an hour ago she had revealed the depth of her scheming mind. Lady Thane was not in London, and Clare herself planned to elope to Gretna Green to escape Choate.

"I see you understand," said Rowse, studying Ferguson's features, for once losing their impassiveness. "Now, I say—"

"Where is Choate?" demanded Ferguson. "I must make amends. I must explain—"

"Don't worry about Choate," said Rowse contemptuously. "He . . . had an accident."

"Where?" demanded Clare shrilly, her worst fears realized.

"Back on the Bath Road," said Rowse. "No matter. He's likely dead now. Now, Ferguson, I repeat my original question. It has taken us a long time, has it not, to get back to it?" His voice became savage. "Now, Ferguson, *how much for my silence?*"

"This is blackmail . . ." began Sir Alexander Ferguson, glaring impotently at his tormentor. Neither of them noticed Clare leave the room.

She hurried through the hall, to the stableyard. There, in

its lumbering majesty, stood the old-fashioned coach with the Ferguson arms on the panel.

The coachman, lounging against the wheel, straightened when he saw her and smiled. He was indeed partial to Clare, and took a dark view of the activities of his employer. He had been gratified at his instructions to make ready to return to Bath that very day, although, if truth were told, he was not as happy as all that about finishing up the journey in the dark. But it was better than stopping overnight along the way, where who knew what might happen to the horses, and besides that, there was young Miss Clare . . .

"Coachman," said Clare, "let us go at once. Can you not take me back along the Bath Road? I dare not wait a moment longer. Please hurry!"

"Now, then, miss, Sir Alexander is not the ogre . . ." coachman began, but she looked at him with such appeal in her eyes, that, despite his better judgment, his loyalty to his employer faded.

"I cannot wait. Don't you see, Lord Choate is behind us, and he may be in trouble, and I dare not wait for Sir Alexander. Besides . . ."

"Right and tight, Miss Clare," said coachman, beckoning vigorously to a groom. "Let down the steps, stupid. I will help the lady in. Hold the horses there, we're off in a moment!" The name of Lord Benedict Choate worked powerfully in coachman. A lavish man with a tip, was Lord Choate, and the contrast between him and the thrifty Ferguson could not have been stronger.

The coach, swift enough even to suit Clare's impatience, turned in the innyard, threaded the high gate successfully, and trundled west on the road to Bath.

29.

While these affairs were in train, other events were occurring along the Bath Road. A carter, coming up from Stanley on his way to Bradenstick, was forced off the road by a pair of magnificent grays, rolling their eyes and trailing ribbons.

"Runaways," pronounced the carter astutely, and began to watch for further signs of trouble. The grays had lost their curricle some way back, where the carter in due course came upon it, racked up against a beech trunk just off the road.

The carter pulled his lone nag to a halt, wrapped the reins around the post, and dismounted. With his usual thoroughness the carter considered the wreck, and began to search the environs. No sign, he decided, of ary person.

At length he resumed his journey. Around the bend, only a few rods from the curricle, he came upon Benedict, no longer sprawled upon the road, but rolled to one side, doubled up as though in unbearable pain. The carter nodded wisely, halted his cart and horse, and knelt beside the injured man.

"Arm broke," he informed his horse, since there was no use in talking to Choate, "and worse, if I'm any judge. Now, then, stand still, and we'll see what can be done."

The carter's assistance was of such effectiveness that before long Benedict's inert form was bundled into the cart and conveyed to the closest inn in the direction of Bath. The carter knew well the inn ahead, where Harry Rowse had found refreshment, and he judged that the likes of this gentleman would be fair game for a bunch of cutthroats.

"And I'm not about to hand him over to such as they," he said stoutly, in explanation to the reluctant innkeeper. "Now, then, Pruitt, let's get him out of the cart so's I can be on my way. Late enough as it is."

"I don't want him here," said the innkeeper. "Suppose he dies? No end of trouble. I won't have it."

Said the carter shrewdly, "I doubt not that those grays I saw beyond stableyard on road have something to do with this. They chew grass nice as you please, now their fright

213

is over. But I'll be bound they belong along of this man. I wouldn't want anyone to know, was I you, that I had turned down a gentleman what owned cattle like them."

The carter's cogent arguments proved effective, and soon Benedict Choate was carried gingerly up the stairs and put into the best bed directly at the top of the stairs. The inn was not pretentious, but the landlady was kind, and experienced.

"Mark my words, Pruitt," she said in a lowered voice after she rejoined her husband behind the taproom counter, "there's going to be some questions asked about that man." She nodded her head toward the stairs she had just descended. "That's *quality*. Never saw such fine shirt as he has. All blood, a-course. I took his clothes off. Best send for doctor."

"You think I'm stupid?" countered her spouse. "First thing I did. Can't get here fast enough to suit me. Mind you, it's too much to have a man dying upstairs, and us not even know who he is."

She nodded. "There's robbery in it, to my mind. No money, and nothing else to show who he is, but his ring. I can't read the sign on it. There's bound to be someone along asking questions. Let's hope," she finished gloomily, "that we don't have just a corpse to show."

While this conversation was taking place, the Ferguson coach lumbered heavily along the highway, its passenger peering fearfully from the window, first on one side and then the other.

What can have happened to Benedict? she wondered. Rowse had been so very vague about the circumstances in which he had left Choate that she was sure he told the truth. Had he been lying, she thought, he would have been quick with imaginary details. But *hors de combat* could mean almost anything. . . .

She was torn between the urge to tell coachman to hurry, hurry, and the more reasonable reflection that if they traveled faster she might overlook something of prime importance. She was ready to go all the way to Bath, and inquire at Choate's lodgings, if she needed to, to ascertain that he was in health. But she darkly doubted that he was safe. Rowse had been too sure of himself.

She remembered that Ferguson had told her that he had left a note for Choate. Knowing her guardian as she did, Clare was positive that he would let little time pass before he was on the road after her. He might not care about her, but he surely cared about his legal responsibility. A cold comfort, she thought, but still, better than nothing, for it did mean that he would rescue her.

But Rowse had seemed unconcerned about the possibility of Choate coming to her in time to escape his own advances. There was only one reason why he could feel so genuinely safe. He must know precisely Benedict's condition.

Full of foreboding, she almost missed the one clue that lay along the road for her. "Oh, stop, coachman!" she cried. The coach labored to a halt, and coachman descended from the box with difficulty.

"Now, what is it, miss?" he puffed, but she was already down from the coach and hurrying back along the road. He followed, along with a footman, after giving strict orders for the curious groom to hold the horses, or he would *give him one*. Clare found the racked-up curricle.

"Do you think it could have been Lord Choate's?" she queried, and cried, seeing coachman's solemn nod, "Whatever can have happened?"

"Best go on and ask, first place we find," suggested coachman. "Looks to me like curricle headed west, so we'll just go west. Don't worry, miss. Like as not we'll find him, all right and tight."

Find him they did, at the inn. But he was not "all right and tight."

Pale but resolute, she marched into the inn, prepared to ask searching questions. She found she would not be put to any trouble about it.

Taking a deep breath, she began, "I saw a wrecked curricle," and was promptly interrupted. The landlady, a kindly smile upon her face, broke in, "Ah, I told my man there would be someone come to ask. The man himself is upstairs, and the doctor coming, but I don't know . . . Is he a relation, miss?"

"My guardian," said Clare. "But you said doctor? Is he ill?"

Solemnly the innkeeper spoke over his wife's ample shoulder, "Nigh dead."

When at last she stood by the bedside of her guardian, she realized that the inkeeper spoke only the truth. In fact, he seemed already passing from life. Her heart sank to her toes, and she knew the color drained from her cheeks, for the landlady reached out to support her.

"No, no," she exclaimed impatiently, "I'm all right. Do ... do you know the nature of his ... injuries?"

"Not all," said the landlady, Mrs. Pruitt, honestly. "Arm broken, but that's little enough, when all's said. But the doctor—"

"Where is he?" Suddenly Clare felt a surge of energy and spirit. If Benedict was about to die, at least he had not done so yet, and there were things to be done.

"Pray send to hurry the doctor," she begged. "He must come at once. I would send my own footman, but I need him for another errand."

"I'll send my own boy this time," promised Mrs. Pruitt, struck by the slim girl's stamina under the staggering blow that had nearly felled her. From that moment on, the landlady was a stout cohort of the "pretty miss, in such a taking about her guardian that I feared we'd have two down."

Furnished with pen and paper, Clare sat down to consider the exact wording of the note she would send to Benedict's sister. She had no clear idea of how far away Shenton was, but she knew it was her first duty to inform Lady Lindsay of her brother's terrible straits. At length, not quite satisfied but believing that speed was more essential than delicacy of wording, she folded the note and sent the footman on his way with urgent words about the need for haste.

She went back upstairs, removed her bonnet and pelisse in the room set aside for her, and hurried back to sit with Benedict until the doctor arrived.

The light was failing when at last he puffed his way up the stairs. "Sorry," he said, upon seeing Clare, "baby case, you know. Thought he'd never come. Couldn't leave."

His examination of Benedict, with Clare holding the light as he directed, was not so brief as his speech. At length, puffing his lips in and out as he worked, he set Benedict's arm, with the rugged help of the ostler, who had the impression that a bone was a bone, whether human or equine. Clare all but called out in protest once, but she glanced at Benedict, whose gray face was wet with perspiration, and kept silent. He had enough to suffer without knowing she was there.

At length the doctor was satisfied. He sent the ostler away, and wiped his brow. "A hard one," he said.

"W-will he be all right?"

The doctor looked back at the patient, bandaged, reclining on clean sheets. "He's still alive. That's all I can say. Depends. I'll send a nurse to watch the night."

"Never mind," said Clare. "I shall not leave him."

It was a long night. He roused once, and groaned. Clare hurried to him, taking his hand. "Dear Benedict. I'll get the medicine the doctor left."

Helping him to raise his head, she managed to coax the few drops of laudanum in water down his throat. His brow was feverish, and she was wild with worry. He was surely dying!

"You," said Benedict with startling clarity. "You here."

"Yes, Benedict. You must not try to talk."

"Where's . . .?" The effort was too much, combined with the laudanum, which took quick effect, and Benedict lapsed back on the pillow and slept.

Clare sat in the chair nearby. The night wore on. She dozed, in spite of her determination to stay awake, and woke with a start each time. Listening for Benedict's breathing, she moved silently to the bedside and waited until she was reassured by the rise and fall of his bandaged chest. Two ribs broken, said the doctor, and we'll have to hope that one of them didn't puncture his lungs.

Seeing him breathe quietly, she crept back to her chair and pondered. It was her fault that Benedict had come to this state. If she had not been so headstrong, she wouldn't have gone off with Alexander, and Benedict would not have come after her and run into Rowse.

It was a tangled web, the farther she looked back upon her own sins. There seemed to be no end to them, from the moment she had arrived in London to the dreadful scene at Carlton House, where she had fled in tears. No wonder Benedict was furious. She thought darkly that whatever decorum she might gain with the daunting Mrs. Duff would be of no avail.

If Benedict died, it would be her fault.

She was wakeful now. The dawn at last lightened the sky toward Newbury, where Sir Alexander sat without his coach and his servants. She dismissed him with a mental wave of the hand. He was as nothing to her now. She had considered marrying him, since Benedict . . .

The truth came upon her like a physical blow. Since Benedict was out of her reach, then she would settle for anyone. Even Sir Alexander Ferguson!

It was a devastating blow. She could not sit still, but rose and tiptoed to the bed. She looked down upon the still face, carved as though from ivory, and reflected. Was it true that these features would be ever in her heart, that she could never be happy without Benedict's steady presence, without his calm assumption that he knew best for her, without the lowering knowledge that he was, indeed, always right?

It was true.

She stifled a half-sob in her throat. Even so, the tiny sound reached Benedict in his stuporous sleep, and he stirred, his eyes opening to narrow slits. He reached his sound hand toward her. "You came," he muttered thickly. "My very dear—"

"No, no, Benedict," she breathed, wincing a little as she realized that she had not once thought of sending word to Marianna in Bath about Benedict. Now, with her new knowledge, she knew why. Her lapse must be attended to. The morning would be time enough, she thought, kneeling by the side of the bed. Benedict's grip on her wrist was reassuringly strong. Surely a dying man had no such strength!

Comforted, letting her hand lie comfortably under his, she laid her head on the coverlet and slept.

30.

Clare sat in her private parlor at a late breakfast of ham, scones, and fresh butter. Two cups of strong coffee routed the impression that her head was filled with lumps of cotton. It would take more than coffee to wear away the stiffness from kneeling on the floor for hours while Benedict clung to her hand.

The landlady was kindly keeping an eye on him while Clare ate. Mrs. Pruitt expressed gratification at the appearance of Lord Choate this morning. "See, his face is paler, that's a good sign. Shows less fever. He's cooler than yesterday, you'll notice. He might just do."

Thus reassured, Clare enjoyed her breakfast and began to think what was best to do. Sir Alexander's footman had not returned from his errand to Lady Lindsay. Clare hoped that it meant good news, that he had stayed to serve as guide to the inn, rather than the dreadful possibility that he might still be wandering around the byroads of Wiltshire looking for his destination.

The need for informing Benedict's betrothed of his desperate condition nagged at her. Still she did not stir. She was too shaken by the great revelation that had come to her with the day's dawning to form phrases that would not betray her.

In her troubled state, her sense of humor strove to aid her. She could write to Marianna and say, "Thanks to your meddling in my affairs, I was forced into headlong flight, and Choate followed, with the result that he lies now near death!"

There was the matter of her own guilt, and she wished to confess it to her guardian herself before the tale had been filtered through Marianna's malicious mind. Her guardian—she heard the words echoing through the empty places in her mind. Had she really always called him her *wicked* guardian, as Rowse had claimed? If she had, then she was thrice guilty—for leading Rowse to false conclusions, for putting Benedict to the trouble of pursuing her, and in addition blackening his name among all she knew.

For Benedict was no wicked guardian; she knew that now.

More than this—she could not now face Benedict or his fiancée until she had regained a measure of control over her runaway, traitorous emotions. If she were to live her long, barren life without Benedict, she must curb this wayward and totally irresponsible desire to fling herself on him and sob her heart out.

She was in love with Benedict, true enough. But he was in love with Marianna, and not with his foolish, *green* ward. He had said distinctly, "You came." Who else but Marianna?

Her hand shook as she set her empty cup down. She sank lower in her mood, and hardly heard the tumult that erupted suddenly in the innyard. When at last the noise rose to a level that penetrated her small parlor, she hurried to the window.

It was a sight worth looking at. From the wide yard gate back to the stable, there was motion. The center of attention was an enormous traveling coach, beautifully hung on swan's-neck springs in the latest degree of comfort. The coach was drawn by a team of four glossy chestnuts, the coachman on the box hard put to hold them until the two grooms sprang down from the box and ran to their heads.

The equipage was certainly the property of someone of great importance, judging from the scurrying ostlers, the prancing outriders, each one heavily armed—Clare counted four, besides the two footmen on the boot. Mine host stood at the door in welcome. Clare could hear the impatient footsteps of the landlady in Benedict's room overhead as she hurried to the window just above.

The footmen sprang to open the coach door and set the steps. Clare watched spellbound as the occupants descended. First were two maids, followed by a man carrying a black bag, clearly a surgeon. Then, with the maids and the doctor together assisting, with exaggerated care for the person of their mistress, down stepped a slender woman of great elegance. She darted quick, birdlike glances around her, but even from Clare's window it was clear that the lady wore a frown of anxiousness, and at once her identity was plain.

Lady Lindsay, Benedict's sister, had arrived, with sufficient staff to run a country house, so it seemed to Clare. She hurried to greet the newcomer.

"So," said Primula Lindsay, "you are Clare." Her smile, as she held out her hands to take Clare's, was dazzling, and Clare at once felt all her burdens lifted from her shoulders.

"I was right," said Lady Lindsay obscurely. "How is my brother? I see you have been sitting up with him all night." At Clare's baffled look, Lady Lindsay continued, "You are very tired, you know. Such a harrowing experience! You must tell me exactly how it happened, but first, let me make my physician known to you. Mr. Otten, Miss Penryck. Now, perhaps landlord could take him to Benedict?"

"I will take him. Mrs. Pruitt, the landlady, you know, is with him now."

But Lady Lindsay drew Clare's hand through her arm and said, "No, we shall let Pruitt—is that your name?—take Mr. Otten up. He will take Shute"—she motioned to a footman, who sprang to obey—"and let us know. Lindsay was most reluctant to let me come. But I told him, Choate is my brother and I have known him much longer than I have known you, you see."

Still talking gently, she drew Clare into the parlor with her, and made her sit in the chair she had just now vacated.

"I think you said that it was your fault?" Primula said, testing the coffeepot with her hand. "Cold coffee is one thing I cannot abide." She turned to her hovering maid. "Here you are, Megg. I suppose Yarrow is upstairs? Just so. Get us some hot coffee, and tell the landlord we must not be disturbed except by Mr. Otten. Then do you run upstairs to help Yarrow with the bedrooms." She turned to Clare and said, "You must know that I have brought my own bedding, enough for your room as well. I am persuaded that you have been too anxious to rest at all. I am prattling, don't you know, because I am so very distressed, and I shall not make sense, I fear, until I hear from Mr. Otten that Benedict will do."

They drank the hot coffee in silence that, to Clare's surprise, was companionable. Primula's friendly eyes seemed to look right through her, and, to Clare's heartfelt pleasure, appeared to like what they saw. They both sprang to their feet when Mr. Otten came in.

"Tell me!" commanded Primula. "Fear not for my condition, for it is much harder not to know the truth, you know."

Thus adjured, Mr. Otten said, "He'll do, he'll do. But it was a near thing. Doctor was competent, far as I know. I think, with your permission, your ladyship, I should stay on here a bit, just to make sure."

"I'll have them make your room available," she said at once, "right next to Benedict's. Can I see him?"

Mr. Otten went up with her to Benedict's room. They stayed there for what seemed to be a long time, to Clare, and when Lady Lindsay came down, she was alone.

"He will do," said Primula, greatly relieved. "But he is so weak." She came to sit beside Clare. "I can rest easily on his account now," she announced. "But it seems to me you are equally in dire straits. Can you tell me about it?"

It was the first kindly word that Clare had heard recently, the first truly sympathetic interest that touched her, and her eyes filled. "I . . . I'd like to," she said gratefully, and began.

She omitted nothing, from the time that her grandmother had told her she was to go to Lady Thane in London, until this morning when Lady Lindsay's coach swept into the yard in such overpowering grandeur. "You can't guess how relieved I was to see you!" Clare finished. She had forgotten nothing in her narrative, but she had seen no reason to burden Primula with the revelation that had come to her when she saw Benedict helpless and dying. That feeling was a secret she would always keep to herself—it was the least penance she could perform to atone for her headstrong rebellion that had brought her guardian to such low ebb.

Primula looked searchingly at her brother's ward. Did the poor child think that her regard for Benedict could pass unnoticed? She had long held a guarded antipathy toward Marianna Morton, and looked with favor now on the golden-curled girl who would make, so his sister thought, a much better wife than the domineering Marianna. Something would have to be done, she decided, but there wasn't the faintest hope of rearranging Benedict's life unless he wished it. And even so, she knew Benedict well enough to know that he would not back off from an arrangement made in good faith.

"I suppose," she said delicately, "that your regard for Sir Alexander has waned?"

"Sir Alexander?" echoed Clare blankly. "Oh, yes, yes, of course, I only thought . . ." Her voice died away. She had only wanted to make Benedict jealous, she realized now. And she would not admit that to anyone.

"I wonder whether it might not be well to send Sir Alexander's coach back to him?" suggested Primula.

"Thank you, I had quite forgotten it. I'll do so at once."

"But you will stay?" pursued Primula.

"Of course," said Clare, adding, unconsciously revealing her newfound docility, "I don't know yet what Benedict would wish me to do."

Primula, with a frown, continued to study the question of her brother's marriage after Clare had gone to give orders about the coach. Primula had a shrewd notion of how things stood with Clare. But it was too soon to quiz Benedict about his feelings.

Two days later, Lady Lindsay and Clare were still at the inn. Lady Lindsay's servants provided the party with the utmost comforts the small inn could provide. The patient upon whose well-being the entire inn revolved was making progress after the first day of Primula's visit. Mr. Otten's care was assiduous and effective, but in spite of the medicine, the mulled claret, the changing of dressings, the bathing of the fevered face, he remained restless.

Clare thought he was still overly feverish, but Primula noted with bright-eyed interest that he seemed more quiet when Clare sat with him. At such times, he would search the coverlet until his hand touched hers, and then he seemed content to let his hand rest, covering the small fingers until he fell asleep.

In the late afternoon of the second day, while Lady Lindsay wrote a long and reassuring letter to her anxious husband, Benedict was pronounced well enough to venture, with help, down the stairs to sit in a chair in the small private parlor.

Supported by the two footmen and encouraged by Clare, Primula, Mrs. Pruitt, and Mr. Otten, Benedict collapsed in a chair. He was weak as a kitten, but no longer feverish, he said. But Mr. Otten decided he was well enough so that he himself could return to his duties at Shenton, and he departed in the Lindsay coach, which would shortly return for Lady Lindsay. It was planned that Benedict would return to complete his convalescence at his sister's home.

"And you, Clare? Will you be able to find enough to do at Shenton?" queried Primula.

"I don't think Benedict wants me to go there. I confess I don't know quite how to go on, but I am persuaded that he would wish me to return to Penryck Abbey. Mrs. Duff is to come to me there, I think."

"Do not fret about it yet, Clare. When Benedict is well enough, we will see what he wants. But I wish to tell you that you are always, today or any day, welcome at Shenton. With or without Benedict, you know."

"Thank you!" Clare was reluctant to see these few days come to an end. She had become exceedingly fond of Primula, and of course it was sheer delight to tend Benedict, to watch the black eyebrows lift in amusement, to prepare his meals for him. Mrs. Pruitt meant well, but Clare fancied that Benedict ate better if she sat with him. She knew that ahead lay a great void, which would last her entire life.

"But you know Benedict will soon be married," Clare added wistfully, and the melancholy look in her eyes stirred Primula to thoughtful speculation.

31.

That night, Clare, unaware of Lady Lindsay's train of thought, wrestled with her own. To give up her love for Benedict, just when she had found it, tore at her more than she could bear.

But the Penryck resolution, so often deployed in a losing cause, now came staunchly to her rescue. If I must confess to him, she thought, best I do it while I can, before Marianna comes to stir everything into a worse muddle!

The next morning, before her courage could turn tail, she descended to the parlor where Benedict sat, bundled warmly, to his disgust, in coverlets, his feet up on a stool, looking every bit the invalid he was. His mood, never tranquil, was exacerbated by the necessity of allowing others to do the simplest offices for him. He could not even beguile the devil's own black mood by the ordinary actions of the day.

His descent into the parlor the day before had done him no apparent harm, and he demanded as his right the assistance to get him dressed in a brocade dressing gown, the sleeve folded neatly over his broken arm, and helped downstairs to sit in the parlor.

Clare had not come to help him this day, as she had previously, It would be hard enough to screw her courage to the point, she knew, so she waited until she saw Lady Lindsay leave the private parlor. She stood a moment outside the door while she swallowed the unaccountable lump in her throat, and then slipped inside the door and closed it softly behind her. The man in the armchair sat with his back to the light, so she could not see the expression on his dark countenance. But she could see that the heavy black eyebrows were drawn together, boding ill for the success of her mission.

"Sir?" she quavered.

His head came up immediately, and for the space of a breath there was a queer hungry look in his thin face. Then, as though erased, it was gone.

"What is it?" he demanded. His voice was harsh, as

though he had decided to keep Clare at an unhappy distance. She did not flinch, though she quailed inwardly.

"I . . . trust I see you better?"

"You do," he said. "I believe that my sister plans to carry us to Shenton tomorrow."

"Truly?" cried Clare, her eyes shining. "I am so glad. You cannot believe how dreadfully you looked when I first saw you."

"If it were parallel to the way I felt, I could believe it," he said, less severely. "I know I have you to thank—"

"Well, you see," said Clare carefully, "that is why I came . . . that is, why I waited until Lady Lindsay had left . . . I know there's nothing I can say that will make amends."

Choate had thought he could never be harsh to this child again, knowing how tightly she had wound herself into his heart, but his weakness, coupled with long habit, betrayed him. "Try," he recommended sternly.

Her chin quivered. Must he make it so hard? Trying to think of his coldness as a penance, she moistened her lips with the tip of her tongue. "I'm more sorry than you will ever know," she said in a low voice. "I never truly thought you wicked. I just wanted you to *notice* me!"

She was looking with apparent concentration upon her folded hands held tightly before her. She did not see the wry twist to Choate's sensitive mouth.

"I noticed you," he said. "But you know—"

She scarcely heeded him. "I must not intrude myself upon your affairs any longer. But I just simply could not let you wed me to someone I didn't even know!" Her voice rose with the force of her emotion. While she had decided that she must ever be submissive to Benedict's wishes, it was proving more difficult than she had imagined.

"Wed you to some . . .?" queried Benedict. "What is this? More of your wild imaginings? What could I have possibly said that could have suggested any kind of marriage to your fevered brain?"

"Don't be angry," begged Clare in a forlorn voice that smote Benedict with force. With more experience than Clare, he knew precisely what had happened to his own emotions, and also, he knew that his strongest urges, his most ardent wishes were impossible to fulfill. There was Marianna . . .

To his surprise, his ward, having come to stand directly

before him, echoed his thoughts. "Marianna—that is, Miss Morton—told me about your plans for me. If she shouldn't have betrayed your confidence, I am sorry to tell you she did. But you see it was her cousin and . . . and, all of it, and I just couldn't . . . And even Sir Alexander was better, for you see, I know him . . ."

Her little broken phrases, while not explicit, still had enough of the facts in them so that he could shrewdly guess the rest. Marianna had meddled once again, and the details could wait. He himself felt vastly weary, no longer in control of his thoughts or his speech. He closed his eyes.

Clare said. "Oh, I've tired you! I'm sorry. I'm just as you said I was—a child, not old enough to know *anything!*"

"Did I say that?" said Benedict, a one-sided smile on his face, his voice unexpectedly gentle.

Clare was overcome. Dropping to her knees beside him, she rested her hands on the coverlet and gazed earnestly into his face. "I'll do anything you say, Benedict, even go back to the abbey with Mrs. Duff. Just say you forgive me for all the trouble I've made!"

That lopsided smile still transforming his face, he reached out to touch her hair. "Forgiven," he said softly.

Overcome, Clare buried her face in the coverlet and wept. He stroked her golden curls tenderly, while a dark expression settled on his bold features. When Lady Lindsay opened the door and saw them thus, Clare kneeling and Choate's caressing fingers entangled in her ringlets, she withdrew without a sound. Neither had noticed her, she knew.

But what a coil! Primula Lindsay was conscious of a sudden relief that Lindsay was not at hand to keep her from doing what she thought best. He was a good man, but he would never countenance her meddling in her brother's affairs.

However, Primula, knowing her brother well, and loving him far more than he knew, was determined not to stand by and see two people who meant much to her insist upon a headlong descent into a life of misery.

What could she do? Lindsay would say: Mind your own affairs, my love! But that was one thing above all that she could not do.

The picture of Clare and Benedict troubled his sister

through lunch. Although Clare had bathed her face, and showed little sign of her recent storm of weeping, yet she was unnaturally quiet. Primula glanced at her brother, eating what he called "pap for infants," and thought the haggard look of strain on his features was not all owing to his injuries.

Primula was exercised to such a point that, immediately after the table was cleared, she sent Clare upstairs.

"For you bore the brunt of the nursing before I came, and I am quite sure you have had little sleep even now. But I shall keep the invalid company while you rest."

Clare stood doubtfully, torn between a longing to stretch out and sleep, and a wish to stay with Benedict. But in truth she was exhausted, and the lure of the soft bed upstairs, furnished with Lady Lindsay's sheets and down comforter, was irresistible.

After Clare had left, Primula began to wish she had thought out her approach to her irritable brother. But she saw his eyes linger on the door through which Clare had disappeared, and taking a deep breath, she plunged.

"What are you going to do about her, Benedict?"

"Do, Prim? I suppose she will come to Shenton with us?"

"She says not."

A frown creased Benedict's brow. "She will do so if I . . ." He stopped short. He did not meet his sister's anxious eyes. "That's what led to all this, you know," he resumed with a little laugh. "I was too inexperienced to avoid the blunders I've made all along the line."

"You? Inexperienced?" Primula laughed. "With three sisters, a fiancée, and who knows how many—"

"Never mind how many! You make me sound like the Grand Turk! Which I am not, you know."

"Too much trouble," agreed Primula. "Monogamy is much easier." She was returning to her usual playful manner, seeing that Benedict did not flare up at once. "The only questions is, dear brother—monogamous with which one?"

He was silent so long that she thought he might have slid into unconsciousness. His dreadful condition of only a few days before was still too new in her mind for her to accept silence from him. But he was fully awake.

"With my duty," he said at last, his voice harsher than she had ever heard it. "I cannot do else."

Primula regarded him with affection. "It goes hard for me to see my dearest brother riding breakneck into a most wretched existence. For you know, I cannot like your betrothed. Nor, I think, do you, else why would you have postponed your wedding so many times?"

"I cannot break off, with honor."

Primula talked on, but made no headway. At last, taking pity upon his drawn face, she rose and kissed him on the forehead. "Very well, Benedict. You may be miserable, with honor. I do not myself think honor is that important, but I do know what store you set on it. But I warn you, Benedict, I shall keep Clare with me as long as I can, and my home will be hers."

"And I must stay away?" Benedict quirked one black eyebrow in a quizzical manner. He was indeed recovering, thought his fond sister.

"Your honor will no doubt guide you," said Primula dryly, "and I trust it will be of some comfort."

Suddenly Benedict turned ashen, and so desolate that Primula longed to take back all she had said. But the fact remained that Clare was in love with Benedict, and if she was not mistaken, Benedict had, for the first time she could recall, fallen in love himself.

Benedict spoke then, more to himself than to her, and she leaned forward to hear better. "I was warned. Oh, yes, all took it into their heads to warn me—too much heat in me for the degree of irritation that brat caused. But I had no idea of what they meant. How wrong I was, not to see where I was heading!"

Primula held her breath, not knowing what would come next, but believing that her brother was in such sad straits that talking might provide at least some ease.

"It was jealousy that brought me here," Benedict said at last, a lost look in his eyes that she had never seen before. "Not that she disobeyed me, Prim. I simply could not see her go off with Ferguson."

"I agree."

"Or," added Benedict, as though she had not spoken, "with any other man. Prim, *what am I going to do?*"

Cry off was the cure that sprang to Primula's lips. But she dared not suggest it again. She considered a long time. Finally she said slowly, "Perhaps Clare will get over it. She's young, and surely, next year, I shall be free to divert her into other channels. You are a very personable man,

Benedict, and it is only natural that she should develop a *tendre* for you."

"Do you believe that?"

She did not deign to answer, for the truth would take away the force of her arguments. She did not know how to extricate Benedict from his unhappy betrothal. But she had to try. She needed time now to think of some scheme. Temporize, her common sense instructed her. "I should feel it best that you send her to Penryck Abbey with Mrs. Duff. And I'll take you to Shenton to regain your health. Clare could well be on the way to forgetting you if you are out of sight."

"She might forget," said Benedict in such a low voice that she was not sure she heard aright. "But *what about me?*"

32.

The answer to Benedict's question came sooner than anyone expected. It was only a couple of hours later when there arose a scurrying in the innyard that heralded the arrival of a person of some importance.

"I can't see out of the window," complained Benedict, snatching at straws to beguile his mood. "Come, Prim, tell me what's going on."

"In the innyard, I suppose you mean," said Primula testily. She was still irritated over what she considered her brother's illogical stubbornness, and only his wan face and the tragic look in his dark eyes reconciled her to pity him. "Some merchant, I suppose. There's hardly been any travel to London, you know. There's nothing going on in town."

Obediently she crossed to stare out of the window. Her eyes widened as she beheld the occupants of the chaise descending. The young lady who emerged first was known, without pleasure, to Primula.

"What does she want?" queried Primula, nettled. Benedict made a movement as though to rise from his chair, but she waved him back.

Marianna's eyes flashed anger that Primula could see even from the window. She paid no heed to the stouter woman who descended the chaise steps in her daughter's wake. Benedict, his curiosity awakened by his sister's posture at the window, exerted himself to turn his chair to afford him a better view.

"Good God! Marianna!" he exclaimed.

"Exactly," said Primula. "Now, Benedict, let's get this encounter done with."

"Primula," said Benedict in hollow tones, "I wish you will not let your impulsive temper—"

"Pooh!" said Primula. "Sit down. You're in no state to be marching around the room."

"I wasn't marching!" said Lord Choate indignantly. With a swift alteration in his mood he said, with appeal in his voice, "I can't see that woman! Prim, get rid of her, do! Tell her I'll see her in London. Tell her—"

231

"Anything?" said Primula quizzically.

Too late Benedict saw the opening he had given her. "Now, Primula . . ."

But it was too late for either of them to set their ideas in motion. Marianna Morton had swept into the inn, her mother following slowly, as though reluctant to bear any share of her daughter's actions.

At that precise moment, Clare, having failed to find refreshment in her troubled slumber, was descending the stairs from the upper floor, and came face to face with Marianna.

"So!" cried Marianna Morton in a carrying voice. "Harry Rowse was right! How is it I find you here?"

"Perhaps because for once Rowse told the truth," said Clare, stung to retort. "Although how he knew we were here passes my understanding."

"No thanks to you that I learn that my betrothed is lying at death's door. *You* did not see fit to send word to me. I find that most inexcusable."

Mrs. Morton had come in behind Marianna, and heard the last of this exchange. She had the darkest fears of the probable outcome of her daughter's temper. In spite of the strongest representations she had made only a few days ago to Marianna, her daughter was in no way attempting to bridle her tongue.

"Marianna . . ." said Mrs. Morton, without effect.

Marianna had eyes only for Clare. "You little schemer!" she accused. "To find you here in an inn, with Lord Choate, alone, passes all decency. Let me tell you, my girl, that your devious, deceitful plot will not get you what you want."

"All I want," interrupted Mrs. Morton, realizing that more strenuous measures were necessary, "is for you to lower your voice and not shout your affairs to the world."

Marianna did not respond, but when she spoke again her voice was a degree lower. "A likely tale Rowse told— that you had eloped to Gretna Green with Ferguson! A mere excuse! I warn you that you cannot deceive me as to your true purpose."

Clare was past the point of caring about what she said. She had lived through a strenuous few days and nights, watching at the bedside of her guardian, rocked to the core by the realization that she loved him totally, hopelessly. Now Marianna Morton appeared, bothersome as a buzzing fly, and no more important. Clare even made a small gesture, as of brushing away a gnat, before she said in a quiet voice, "I think you are mistaken, Miss Morton. Once again. I had no plan in coming here, except—"

"Except to bring Benedict to think he had compromised you so that he must marry you. I warn you that he will not change his mind. He loves me, and he has given his word—"

"As to that," said Clare meticulously, "I could not say. Whether he loves you or not must be his affair. But I do venture to wonder whether you are in fact as attached to him as you would wish people to think."

"What!"

"You have come rushing out from Bath, under the impression that he was injured, and yet," pointed out Clare, "you have not yet asked how he is faring."

Marianna said shrewishly, "He was not hurt badly. Rowse said so!"

Clare said reasonably, "Since Rowse was responsible for Benedict's accident, then you must be sure that the truth is not in him. But I think you said 'lying at death's door'?"

Just then the outer door opened and Ned Fenton stepped in from the yard. So Marianna and her mother had brought an escort with them!

"Oh, Miss Penryck!" exclaimed Ned. "Glad to see you're here. How's Benedict?"

Mariana, probably ashamed of her own lapse in the matter, turned on Benedict's friend. "Not very badly injured, after all," she cried. "For this young person was here to beguile his convalescence!"

"Marianna," said Mrs. Morton severely, "that is more than enough."

Clare had been too sorely tried. She burst into tears. "He was nearly d-dead!" she said tearfully.

"I doubt it!" said Marianna stoutly, even though she was beginning to think she had in truth made a mistake. "But no matter what you say, the fact remains that you and Benedict have spent several days together in an inn, unknown to your friends, and without anyone to lend you credit." She eyed Clare carefully, as though deciding where to plant the mortal dart. "I wonder what Lady Lindsay will say to this escapade of yours!"

During this last speech, Lady Lindsay appeared silently

in the doorway from the private parlor. None of the others saw her, nor had they seen the parlor door open just after their arrival. But Ned Fenton, not so bent on watching Clare, now caught sight of Primula. "Then Benedict *was* in danger!" he exclaimed.

Lady Lindsay stepped into the room. "Oh, yes, he was," she said calmly. "And he has dear Clare to thank that he is alive now."

Her remarks worked powerfully on Marianna, reducing her to openmouthed astonishment. Mrs. Morton found her tongue. "Well, miss, you see how right I was. Your tongue has at last got you into trouble that you can't smile your way out of."

Marianna recovered her speech. "How long," she demanded of Lady Lindsay, "have you been here?"

Primula, enjoying herself and taking advantage of the opportunity so neatly handed to her, smiled sweetly and said, "I confess, Marianna, your preoccupation with the seamy side of life gives me cause to wonder. Your upbringing, I know, has been of the best, for I have the greatest respect for your mother. But I cannot help but wonder at you! It is beyond imagining that there could be anything of impropriety in the situation here. Benedict at death's door, his life saved by his ward."

Ned turned to Marianna and said with unaccustomed bluntness, "What an opinion you have of Choate! I wonder you want to marry such a man, if you think him capable of such ramshackle behavior!"

Primula, not relenting at the sight of Marianna's appalled features as she realized the grave mistake she had made, added, "In response to your question, although I do not admit your right to ask it, I have been here with Clare almost from the start. And—I tell you this only for my dear Clare's protection against your malicious tongue—during the hours before I came, the physician will bear witness that Benedict was totally unconscious, incapable of moving a finger." She surveyed Marianna with a calculated look. "I don't look forward to calling you 'sister,' I must tell you."

Marianna tried valiantly to regain her position. "Had I known, Lady Lindsay, that *you* were here—"

Benedict's voice interrupted her. He was leaning against the doorframe, and his pallor spoke eloquently of his trials. But his drawl was strong enough as he said with a trace of amused contempt, "I had never realized until now, Marianna, how very vulgar you are!"

Marianna blanched as though he had struck her in the face. She had whistled him down to the wind, she knew, and a chill descended on her. She searched wildly for words that would mend all, but her mother forestalled her.

"Choate, I cannot say how glad I am to see you so much recovered. We were informed falsely on several counts, but *my* faith in you—little though you may regard it, and I could not blame you—never wavered." She shot a dark glance toward her daughter.

Marianna lifted her chin. "I shall give you no cause in the future, Choate, to question my devotion to you—"

"No!" Mrs. Morton delivered herself of the monosyllable with force. "I shall no longer countenance this marriage. Marianna, I have watched you riding roughshod over everyone who comes within your sphere, and while I am inured to such treatment, I feel that I must make amends to Choate, and to Miss Penryck, for your behavior. I shall not agree to a union with so little prospect of success. Come, Marianna. I am thinking that we might tour Italy this winter. . . ."

Mrs. Morton ushered her stunned daughter out of the inn. She did not look back. Ned Fenton, reading Mrs. Morton's mood correctly, disappeared to order the coach readied for the return journey. Those Mrs. Morton had left in her wake stood in a way dazed, as the waves of the affair subsided slowly. From the outside floated back to them the final word from Mrs. Morton. "It will be *my* decision, Marianna, and you will remember that I shall brook no further impertinence from you. . . ."

Lady Lindsay breathed a huge sigh, composed of satisfaction and relief. But Clare's eyes were on Benedict. "Oh, my dear sir, you must not stand so long. Here, lean on me, let me help you back to your chair. You have recovered so marvelously that you must not jeopardize your health . . ."

Shute sprang quickly to Clare's aid—Lady Lindsay suspected rightly he had been hovering just out of sight, but not at all out of hearing, in the hall—and together they got Benedict to his chair. His bloodless features told the cost of his exertion. Clare dismissed Shute and watched Benedict. She poured a glass of port, and urged him, "Mr.

Otten says you must drink a lot of this to replace the blood you lost."

"He said nothing about the effect on my head," complained Benedict. But the look in his eyes softened.

After a long time, she ventured, "Are you heartbroken, sir? Your betrothal . . ."

"Not so much that I can't be cured." His smile was sweet and tender, and she read a light in his eyes that, this time, she interpreted aright.

"Will you, my dear ward, provide my cure?" His gaze was quizzical, and oddly uncertain. He was rewarded by the sight of tears slipping down her cheeks. "Now, my dear watering pot, if you do not wish it . . ."

"Oh, no, Benedict, I wish it above all things! I just c-can't stop crying, that's all!"

Lady Lindsay, lingering with purpose in the hall, heard what she had longed to hear. She closed the parlor door and left them alone. Remembering the *glowing* look on her brother's face, an expression she had never expected to see, she smiled to herself. This wedding would not be postponed, she would wager.

Clare's year of mourning would be over next June . . .

Lady Lindsay chuckled. It was going to be a long, long year!